BEFORE

FINN ÓG

Also by Finn Og

Charlie

The Sea and the Sand

Too Close to Home

Before

Vinci Books

vinci-books.com

Published by Vinci Books Ltd in 2026

1

A CIP catalogue record for this book is available from the British Library.
Paperback ISBN: 9781036700034
The EU GPSR authorised representative is Logos Europe, 9 rue Nicolas
Poussion, 17000 La Rochelle, France
contact@logoseurope.eu

For my curly crew. You're deadly.

Chapter One

"I WILL NEVER UNDERSTAND why you did it."

Áine was tiring of the lockdown. Three weeks in and there had been no lift in mood. "You should get yourself listed as critical," she said.

"Is that a joke?" It was the first time Sinead had spoken all morning.

"No."

"Don't be so stupid. I'm sad, not critically ill."

"What? Get a grip. I mean, you need to be working. Get yourself a pass as a critical worker – a frontliner. I'm sure plenty of women out there need your help, even more so with this craziness. Domestic abuse must be through the roof – people cooped up all the time."

"Maybe."

"You might not be a nurse, but sure the Pope in Rome knows that what you do is important."

Such backhanded compliments were as much as her twin could generally manage, and were frequently followed by …

"And, sure, if you don't get out of my face soon, you'll have me as depressed as you." Áine attempted a cheeky grin, hoping for an involuntary chuckle, but such suppressed smiles had vanished, along with the two people Sinead pined for, into the Irish Sea.

"Don't, Áine," Sinead said, guilty at taking her sadness out on her sister but unable to shake the hurt.

"Look," Áine said sighing, "there's no point living in a place as tricked out as this if we don't put it to good use. If you're really not going to get over that gobshite, maybe the best thing I can do is try and help you find him."

"He's not a gobshite." Sinead stirred and looked up. "You do know that, don't you?"

Áine relented a little, but it was not in her nature to allow concessions without a jag. "I know he's got a hell of a body count," she said, "but, yeah, I know you think he's a good man."

Sinead stared at her sister. "I need to know that you really do see that, Áine. I really think I need that right now. And don't lie, and don't bloody joke. Tell me, am I insane?"

Áine walked barefoot over the deep-pile carpet to the enormous window. She surveyed the Liffey, considering what to say. No boats stirred on the river; there were no cars on the normally gridlocked quay. The conference centre to her left had been shut down – the financial quarter from which she had finally started drawing a handsome wage once more, was like a ghost town.

"You're not insane," Áine said softly. "And he's a mad, bad influence on you, but he is a good guy – despite it all."

"For real?"

"Sure, you only need to see him with that child." She paused, placing her hands against the glass. "With you," she almost whispered.

Sinead managed a sad smile for the first time since her world, and everyone else's, had ground to a halt.

———

"ARE YOU SURE, NOW?" Áine said, not looking at her sister but staring up into the bank of screens.

"What do you think?" Sinead replied.

"I think this is going to take time because he's no dope. And time is money. I'm one of the few people making cash during this crisis, so if you're still doubting yourself …"

"Áine, I didn't doubt myself," Sinead said, confused.

"Then, what did you do?"

"I just couldn't go right then."

"What? Why?"

"Loads of reasons," she said, knowing that she sounded like a child.

"Like what?"

"Like work." Sinead shook her head, baffled that she should have to explain.

"The work you haven't done for the two months since they left?"

"We couldn't have predicted the pandemic."

"You were off work long before lockdown."

"Will you stop."

"So that's it – you didn't go with them cos of your job. The thing you've been wanting more than anything else these past few years, and you stayed because of work."

"What do you mean, *wanting more than anything else these past few years*?"

"Ah, sis, anyone could see it. Even when you couldn't."

Sinead tried not to let her eyes well.

"Don't go soft on me now," Áine continued. "I need you on the ball."

"I didn't realise it was so obvious."

"You know who knew?"

"The Pope in Rome." Sinead sighed. "Well, I'm transparent, so."

"That's not a bad thing," Áine softened. "People know where they are with you, which is more than you ever knew when you were with him."

"I did know, eventually."

"I kind of gathered that, but you never explained."

"We talked. Finally, we talked."

"Did he say it?"

"What?"

"Did. He. Say. It?"

Sinead just stared at the screens.

"Shit, Sinead. Are you sure you're sure about this?"

"I don't know if he's able to."

"What?"

"Say. It."

"Why?"

"Because of before."

"What *before*?"

"His wife. Her death. His work – well, he'd already told me a bit about his work."

"What did he say?"

"I can't tell you." Sinead frowned apologetically.

Áine exhaled her frustration in a long breath. "Murky, so."

"Difficult," Sinead said.

"And before that? What about his, I dunno, his childhood?"

Sinead's eyebrows raised a little, her lips pursed. Her head shook gently, involuntarily.

"Nothing?" Áine tried to suppress her incredulity.

"It never came up! I know him *now*. That's what's important."

"Well, where did he grow up?"

"In the north."

"Northern Ireland?"

"Yeah – well, hardly northern England?"

"You never know with these army types."

"He's not army. He's not from a military family, I don't think."

"You don't think? Do you even know what county he lived in?"

Sinead said nothing.

"Where did he go to school? Did he go to college?"

Sinead stared hard ahead, avoiding her sister's eye contact.

"What did he do before he joined the military? Does he have—"

"Áine, I don't know," Sinead snapped, frustrated at herself as much as her sister. "You never know when to just let up, do you? Can you never just read the signs to take it bloody easy?"

Sinead was standing now, but Áine was bristling at the uncharacteristic outburst.

"This is where you tell me I have no emotional intelligence, is it?"

Sinead resisted the urge to nod.

"Well," Áine filled the awkward silence, "I'd say it's not me is lacking in emotional intelligence. When a man you love – and have loved for years, finally gets round to asking you to

5

run away with him, you say yes, Sinead. You say *yes*. If you love him, you get on the feckin' boat and you throw all else to the bloody wind. *That's* emotional intelligence. But it seems to me you know less than you needed to about him, so that's what held you back. Not work, and not leaving me on my own – even though you never said it I know you were thinking it, even though it is the stupidest of reasons. So, as the established emotionally intelligent one, I suggest you find out more about him – all that background stuff you're pretending isn't important, before you take the leap. Because something held you back, Sinead, and it wasn't work, and it wasn't me."

Sinead sat heavily into one of the swivel chairs. The tears that came felt as big as rocks as they thundered down her cheeks and splashed onto one of the keyboards. "How am I supposed to find stuff out now? They're gone, dear knows where to."

"Well, then, aren't you lucky you're in Mission Control?" Áine said, guilty at her rant and desperate to insert some cheer into the fractious conversation. "And aren't you doubly lucky that the other person who cares for you is a genius with such technology?" She swept her hand around the bank of servers and screens as an estate agent might show a reception room.

"Do you really think you can find him?" Sinead's puffy face turned up to her sister, eyes red yet hopeful.

"I dunno, to be honest. He can be devious when he wants to be, and he's been living under the radar for a long time. The problem is he thinks he's on the run, doesn't he? He'll be watching his back."

"Well, at least we'd be able to tell him he has nothing to worry about."

"*If* he doesn't," Áine said wryly.

"I thought you said?"

"That was four weeks ago. Investigations progress – at least they're supposed to."

"Well, can you hack in again and see?"

"I can, but that's dangerous craic, Sinead."

Her twin looked at her pleadingly.

"Let's see if we can find them first – try to make some sort of contact, then we can see. You seem to have forgotten what happened last time I cracked into a government system for that man."

"I haven't forgotten. But this isn't for him, it's for me," Sinead said.

"Low," Áine muttered, with the beginnings of a smile.

"Well, it was you who said I need to know more about him. If you find him, I can ask."

"Just seems weird that you don't know shit, yet he knows everything about you."

Sinead froze, staring at her sister. "You didn't tell him, did ye?" she said, eyes like frisbees.

"What?" Áine said, equally incredulous. "No! Course not. But surely you—"

"No." Sinead shook her head vigorously.

"Go way." Áine shook her head. They sat in silence for a few seconds. "So *before* is a place neither of you have been to." Her eyebrows took a long time to fall.

Chapter Two

THEY LOOKED at the screens for a full minute, Áine's fingers hovering above one of the three keyboards until Sinead said, "So how do you do this?"

"Normally I have some place to start," Áine conceded. "Throw me a bone here."

Sinead looked blank, slumping for a moment before her back straightened. "He left Dún Laoghaire Pier eight weeks ago – to the day," she said brightly, suddenly hopeful.

"Right," said Áine, hammering on the keyboard and hunting some code directory that had scrolled up on one of the screens. "Let's have a look, then."

The tapping and clicking continued for a few minutes and Sinead worked hard at keeping herself from asking questions. Instead she tried to guess which monitor she should be gazing at, and managed to remain silent until they all turned a greyish-white.

"What's that?"

"Exactly," said Áine.

"Have you been detected? Is this some sort of shutdown?"

"Not unless their security is incredible. This is the CCTV from Dún Laoghaire on that day."

"What?"

"It's weird – the system seems a good spec, so the images shouldn't be poor at all."

"Ah, no," Sinead said, the answer dawning on her.

"What?"

"It's fog."

"It was foggy?"

"It was unbelievable. Seriously, I've never seen fog like it."

Áine's fingers danced over the keys again as she peered up at data and specifications. "The cameras in the harbour are pretty good – they've got Smart IR and Defog."

"What does that mean in the human world?" Sinead said. "And how are you even able to see them?"

"Anything on a wireless system is vulnerable – even high-end systems like this. And what it means is that we should be able to access improved images. So long as they kept a file of the defogged version. No point in them having it if they don't use it. I'm just working out how ..."

"You know the time frame to look at?"

"Yeah, I remember you leaving with Isla to meet him, and I remember you coming back without her."

Sinead's brow tightened at the thought.

"Here, look." Áine swirled a stylus on a trackpad, as if reeling in a fish. Sinead stared hard as the greyness of the pier loomed out of the white static.

"That's too close to the end of the harbour. You need to move right."

"This is cool. It's a layered file, like photoshop. Right is what direction – north, south, which?"

Sinead closed her eyes. "East, I think. Kind of south-east." Áine moved the pen again. "There's the ice cream kiosk!" Sinead shouted.

"Alright, alright."

"That's where Isla got down onto the boat, and some local fella was there."

"Who?"

"Doesn't matter. But that's the right place."

Áine swirled a little more until a pole emerged against the grey.

"That's a mast," Sinead said excitedly.

"Get you, Sailor Sue."

"Go down a bit, to the water."

The image tilted to reveal a bold white structure with a flash of orange at the back.

"That's it! That's *Sian*."

"Who's Sian?"

"*Sian*'s the boat."

"Right. You're thinking of living on that boat?" Áine said, baffled.

"It's lovely inside, actually. Loads of room."

"It's the size of a caravan."

Sinead ignored the quip. "There, she's moving." Sinead watched, her throat suddenly swelling to a throb as the boat turned from the harbour wall and left the shot.

"He didn't hang about."

"No," Sinead said, remembering the exchange.

"Can't have said much, so."

Sinead ignored the implication. "Can you follow it?"

"I need to find another camera." Áine pummelled the keyboard until eventually another grainy image was offered and she began to swirl again. *Sian* was leaving the harbour and turned right. Sinead could just make out the large figure of Sam at the helm, and Isla tucked under his arm, hugging his hip. The tears came again.

"So that's like south-east, isn't it?"

"Yeah." Sinead's tone had fallen.

"Well, it's a start, isn't it? He has navigation instruments on board. We might be able to—"

"He turns them off at the best of times," Sinead said dismissively.

"Why?"

"You know why."

"Sneaky beaky bollocks," Áine muttered. "So how does he know where he is?"

"He seems to use the compass, and paper maps and charts. He can tell by the depth, I think. He's got funny double rulers and a spikey yoke with legs that he walks across the chart. I dunno. I watched him a few times when he was showing Isla how to do it, but I didn't, like, want to get in the way."

"Worth a go, though, isn't it, in case he did use electronics in the fog?"

"Yeah, but he's—"

"I know. Private. I'll try to ping his phone too."

"He won't … he didn't …"

"What?"

"He didn't have it on."

"You tried to ring him?"

Her tears ran heavily now and she just nodded slowly.

"You changed your mind?" Áine said, as gently as she was able.

Sinead shrugged, then covered her face with two hands.

"I just wanted him to know, even though I couldn't go. I wanted him to know."

Áine rolled her chair over to her sister and gave her a hug.

———

SINEAD TOOK herself off for a lonely walk – her one authorised exercise of the day. She could see families on the North Wall coping with scooters and small bicycles. The traffic was so light because of the curfew that she could also hear the cries of the children from all the way across the river as they tumbled and jumped. Before the lockdown she wouldn't even have been able to hear a car horn from the other side. Inevitably, the sounds of little people made her think of Isla. Sinead berated herself for having imagined they could, perhaps, have forged a family from the wreckage of Sam's life. Or from her own. It had been a stupid, fanciful notion. He was not built for that kind of conformity. She knew he would always crave closeness to some edge – that he was unable to sit still and be content. He could be so rational and calm, yet somehow felt drawn to reckless, hopeless situations; like there was a need in him that could only be addressed through extreme actions. It was impossible. It *would be* impossible to live with. Wouldn't it?

But she couldn't deny that it was exciting. That unpredictability.

How were Sam and Isla managing in this lockdown? she wondered. Would they just sail aimlessly? She knew in her heart that they could, and probably would. That was their way – they didn't really need or want anybody else. Except, maybe, her. *Maybe.*

But if they did that, they would need to be stocked up,

and she doubted Sam had had time to provision the boat before he'd left the north. He'd been running, and before that he'd been working every minute God sent.

So what would they do?

Sinead knew he had cash. The job he'd been involved in before he'd had to cut and run had been lucrative. Babysitting, she smiled at the memory of his withering description. She wondered about the father of the wealthy heiress he'd minded, John, who had become a confidante and one of Sam's few friends; his supplier of kit.

Would he have contacted John?

She pulled out her phone to text Áine: *Maybe try John if poss? Might have been in touch.*

She walked over the Grand Canal, across the Dodder and up to the East Link, the last bridge to cross the Liffey. She stared out towards the port walls and beyond, into the Irish Sea, putting herself in Sam's boots.

What would you do? Where would you go?

She thought about Europe, about Europol, about arrest warrants and international agreements. She thought about his escape, that he'd thought – probably still thought, that the police were on to him for murder. Quite a few murders, in fact.

Wherever he's gone, she thought, it won't be somewhere with an extradition agreement.

She turned her attention to the places he'd travelled before. Where had he said he'd liked? The realisation irritated her as it made Áine's point strikingly relevant: *I don't know him at all.*

She thought again about Isla – what she would need that she didn't have on board. She drew out her phone and tapped again: *Check his Amazon account. And check other harbours. He will have stopped. Please. Xx*

"YOU SHOULDN'T USE SMS to ask me questions." Áine was irritable.

"Why?"

"Think about it. He thinks he's on the run, right?"

"But we know they're not looking for him."

"We *think* they're not looking for him."

"So?"

"So if we're wrong, they will be chasing down every lead. And what are you?"

"Not a lead, anyway. They won't know about me."

"You only think that."

"Ok. Even if they do, they are technically in Britain and I'm in Ireland. They can't bug my phone."

"You can be bloody sure they will."

"Serious?"

"Shit, Sinead. What world are you living in?"

Sinead slumped down. "Ok. I just didn't think."

"Three *Scooby-Doo* movies, craft videos, *Horrible Histories*."

"What?"

"Downloads. Tonnes more."

"How much more?"

"What does it matter?"

"If we know how much media he took with him, maybe we can guess how far he was planning to go."

"Fair enough, but that's not the real value in this."

"What?"

"You didn't ask *where* it was downloaded."

"Right, so," Sinead said, exasperated, "*where* was it downloaded?"

"A harbour on the east coast. Waterford."

"Ok?"

"Some of it was sent to a Kindle from an Amazon Prime TV account in a false name and to a dodgy credit card. Did you know he had a credit card in someone else's name?"

"I know he sometimes acquired cards from criminals."

"Stole them, you mean."

"Liberated, he said. But you'd think they'd have been cancelled by now."

"Unless the criminals had stolen them, and the person they stole them off couldn't report it for whatever reason."

"Like they were stolen in a brothel − punters, you mean?"

"No, like dead, I mean," Áine said.

Sinead bristled. "You have a very low opinion of him."

"Well, how many people has he seen off in the last six months?"

Sinead couldn't really argue with that. It did appear that Sam may well have dispatched quite a few people. "The police don't think it was him."

"But you know, and I know, sure as eggs are eggs, it was him."

Sinead fell into silence while Áine typed.

"So you think these downloads are his?"

"I'm certain. Isla loves *Scooby-Doo* and *Horrible Histories*."

"The BBC account was a fake too. He'd even jimmied the IP address so it thought he was in the UK. He's got better at all this, hasn't he?"

"Well, you showed him most of it. How did you find it?"

"You told me to check other harbours. There's a Wi-Fi router that shut down because someone violated its fair usage. There were fourteen hours of programmes downloaded before he was locked out."

"Isla's Kindle wouldn't have enough space."

"Multiple devices – a laptop, an iPhone, all fairly secure bar the Wi-Fi, which he appears to have turned off as soon as he was shut down."

"So just kids' TV shows?"

"Hard to say. There was a large file from a site I don't know. It will take me a while to work out what it was. It's still mining away here." Áine gestured to a buzzing tower on her right that had a fan pointed at it. "You told me to check Amazon, but I looked at all the main providers, and these are the only major media downloads in east or south coast harbours."

Sinead thought for a moment. "Can you see if the credit card was used anywhere else?"

"What, you think they went for a meal?"

"I think they'll have needed food and water."

"Does the boat not have a water tank?"

"Yes, but he prefers to drink bottled water. There is a water maker, but it's slow and it breaks down."

"A water maker?"

"It does something to saltwater to make it drinkable."

Áine scrolled. "The card was used in a shop in Dunmore East. It was declined twice for a four hundred euro spend, then it was cleared for three hundred."

"What does that mean?"

"Bank must have put a daily limit on the spend. Maybe there was a purchase queued on the card or it just had a really low spending limit."

"Whose name was the card in?"

"Mitcik Vistok." Áine peered into the small data.

"Could be anyone."

"Could be a dead man." Áine all but snorted.

"Ok, can we leave out the constant comments about dead people?"

Áine said nothing.

"Can you see what he bought?"

"No, but it's a supermarket, so groceries, I'd say."

"Is there CCTV down there?"

"If there is, it's not on a network, so I can't get into it."

"We can't be certain it's him, then?"

"If you're not sure about the videos and stuff, then, no."

"I'm sure."

"Then that's bad news," Áine said as data appeared on a new screen.

"Why?" Sinead sounded alarmed.

"Cos that other payment detail says," she paused as she read, "it was for weather modelling for the North Atlantic and charts of the Eastern Caribbean."

Chapter Three

SINEAD LOOKED MISERABLY at the swirls and numbers of the isobars. She had little idea what they meant – her interest in the weather was limited to how it would impact people's behaviour, and therefore what effect it would have on her clients. Sunny evenings and long warm weekends inevitably led to a surge in appeals for shelter on Sunday nights as vested rednecks beat their wives and girlfriends into that final decision: to get out, to seek the help they had been too afraid to get caught asking for.

She tried to snap out of it – thinking about what Áine had said. She lifted her phone and called the convent.

"Tearmann," a fraught voice answered.

"It's Sinead," she told her ageing colleague. "How are you, Grace?"

"Wrecked," her friend said, with uncharacteristic frustration.

"You're getting it tough?" Sinead said.

"Unbelievable. Ten calls a night. This bloody lockdown is bringing out the worst in people, it really is." To hear even the hint of a swear word from this devoted, devout employee was telling in itself.

"Look, Grace, I'm coming back to work."

"Ah, no, no, you're not well. We'll be fine, honestly. You just caught me at a bad moment. There's a young one here – little more than a child, really, and she's had it rough. Then there's an older woman who has done nothing but complain and cause mayhem in the refuge in the few hours since she arrived. God, forgive me, but she's an ungrateful wagon of a woman."

That really was out of keeping with Grace's normal patter.

"Listen, I'll be back this evening. You can hand over all the open cases and then take a break. I'm sorry I haven't been around."

"Did you have the virus, Sinead? I know you took leave and then after, when we didn't hear, I didn't like to ask – but others have been pestering me and I didn't know what to say."

"No," Sinead faltered, "it wasn't the virus, Grace."

"Oh, thanks be to God. That's good, that's good."

Sinead could tell that Grace felt entitled to an explanation, but she knew the older woman would never ask for one. "So, it's domestics mainly, is it?"

"Yeah. No sex workers, really. This lockdown seems to have put an end to prostitution. Dear knows what those poor women in the brothels are being subjected to now instead – probably the internet. I doubt their fine masters would suffer the loss of income."

Sinead could imagine. "In a way, that's safer for them, Grace."

"I'm totally out of options because there's no beds anywhere. Most of the houses are full or closing because of

Covid, and there's no admissions where there are spaces because people in there have symptoms. The women we have now are staying in the convent, but, sure, you know the age of the nuns – we could wipe out a whole Holy Order if we're not careful. Honestly, it would be more humane to … God, forgive me …"

"What?" Sinead asked, genuinely interested in what Grace might be hinting at.

"To get your friend from the north to go round the women's houses and sort their fellas out once and for all. At least then it would be them that deserves it heading for the hospitals rather than these women and probably a convent full of decrepit nuns."

Sinead would have smiled at the suggestion were it not for the sadness it summoned in her. "He's not around any more, I'm afraid."

Grace was quiet for a moment, and for a split second Sinead wondered whether her kindly friend had been fishing as to the cause of her absence and was putting two and two together in the silence.

"Well, I'm sorry to hear that, Sinead," Grace said in a sympathetic but brusque tone, as if confirming to herself all that had been left unsaid.

"I'll be in this evening, Grace. Then you can take a rest. Sounds like you need it."

———

"I'M GOING BACK to work this evening," Sinead said.

"Mmm hmm," Áine hummed, without turning from the screen bank.

"Can you get me one of those letters?"

"I'll get you a letter from the president if it means you

come out of the doldrums. What do you want – critical worker, frontline staff? You'd probably even qualify as a delivery driver, to be honest, ferrying all those girls around."

"You're hilarious."

"I am an antidote to self-pity."

"Just get me the bloody pass so the cops don't send me home."

"Ok, boss. Oh, by the way – have you thought about what you're going to do if we actually manage to find them?"

"What do you mean?"

"Sam and Isla."

"I know. I mean—"

"Like, you can't just travel to wherever they are, with the lockdown and the restrictions."

"Obviously," Sinead said, but in truth it was a question that had been rattling around her head without an obvious answer.

"The travel ban won't last forever, but it could be for the rest of the year, couldn't it?"

Sinead felt her heart sinking again, hurting even. "If that's the antidote to depression, then you'd want to work on your chemistry."

"Seriously, though. If I find them, you'll be like a dog chasing a bike."

"I was thinking you could find some way for me to talk to them."

"Hmm, risky."

"How?"

"Well, he's on the run – or not on the run, depending on where that investigation is. You'll be a target, or not, depending on how much they want him. So if I do find him, they'll want to be listening in, won't they?"

"But you designed a system for him when he had that business."

"The Charlie thing won't work."

"But you were able to set up that encrypted yoke. You said that was for clients to get in touch with Charlie secretly."

"That was three years ago, sis. That was before the Snoopers' Charter came into force."

"The what?"

"Investigatory Powers Act. It's a British thing. It basically lets the government hoke into anyone's system."

"But we're in Ireland and he's – wherever he is."

"It's the Brits who want him, though, so *if* they're still looking for him, it won't stop them. It just means they won't be able to use it in any sort of court case. Not that any court is going to concentrate on *how* law enforcement might have found him. They'll not have some barrister asking, 'And what means did you adopt to track the defendant?'" Áine affected a plummy English accent.

"So you're saying that the old app you set up is no use?"

"Not if you want him to stay under the radar."

"And the phone is out, I assume?"

"Phones are the easiest thing to rip, Sinead. They've been around so long that every workaround has been nailed."

"Well, then, I don't know," Sinead said, frustrated. "I'm going to work. I'll have a think. There must be a way."

Carrier pigeon, thought Áine, but chose not to say so.

———

SINEAD TOOK A HANDOVER FROM GRACE. There were nine women in the convent now but they had placed thirty-nine since the lockdown had begun. Hostels had stopped taking calls, never mind clients; they were more up against it than Sinead's rescue charity.

"Perhaps ..." Grace started, looking up at her boss with uncertainty.

"I'm not going to send some Conor McGregor round to beat the husbands into hospital." Sinead smiled at Grace, hoping to warm her a little.

"No, no, not at all. That was a silly suggestion," Grace said apologetically. "I was thinking, maybe I could take a few of them home with me?"

"You know the policy, Grace – four steps, nothing more. Take the calls, find a way to get the women out safely, place them in a refuge and then work on finding them an income."

"I know, I know ... but these aren't normal circum-stances and, sure, we all know that the benefits system is inundated with calls and emails just now. I haven't been able to get through all week. I don't know how the girls we've already placed are going to get by."

"Calls, extraction, placement, benefits or asylum – the four strokes, Grace. We must stick to that otherwise our funding gets questioned and we have women in our spare rooms every night with men beating down our doors to get to our guests – and that's a slippery slope."

"You're right. The men can track us, but not them." Grace repeated a mantra that had been drummed into the small staff a thousand times. Each of Sinead's team had extra security measures at their homes to prevent them being used as leverage to find escaped women.

"You've done an amazing job, Grace. I'm really sorry I haven't been here to help, but I'm back now and you need some rest, so I don't expect to see you for at least two days. Ok?"

Grace reached out and rubbed Sinead's arm. "You are ok, aren't you? It's not like you to miss a day's work let alone a few months."

"I am now, and glad to be back, Grace. Now get yourself home and get some sleep. And thanks for holding the fort."

She took the file and began working her way around the rooms in the old adjacent convent. They were often still referred to as cells – and they looked every bit of it. Heavy solid-timber doors, the names of long-departed nuns still hanging from a hook on the outward-facing side. Sinead knocked heavily, waiting to be beckoned inside, but the doors were so thick and the stone walls so dense that she had to try the enormous handle and open each door a crack to announce her arrival.

The first cell had an ancient timber floor – the only warmth in an otherwise gloomy, sparse square. There was a table, a chair, a sink with no mirror and a metal bed with an ancient mattress covered in itchy blankets.

"Hello, I'm Sinead, I'm the manager. Can we have a chat?"

A middle-aged woman rose from a foetal position and sat on the bed, her fingers curled like the talons of a hunting bird around the edge of the mattress. "Thanks for coming to get me. I'd have been in Glasnevin if it wasn't for ye."

Reference to the local cemetery was not lost on Sinead. "That's what we're here for," she said soothingly. "You're Clodagh?"

"Yeah."

"Now, you know we're having trouble placing people

because of the virus, so these rooms are all we have just now. It's a bit basic."

"It's grand," said the woman. "I'm glad to have it. I'm glad to be out."

Sinead could see that the woman was a keeper. So often women rescued from abusive situations willingly went back despite not having the slightest hope that the situation would improve. This woman had fly stitches on her right eye socket and bruising on her neck and upper arms – Sinead could see where the fingers of someone large had gripped her.

"Thing is," Sinead began, "you could be here for some time."

"Longer the better," the woman said.

"Were you working?"

"No, he stopped that. Jealous, he was."

"What did you do?"

"Cook at the local school. Three hundred lunches a day."

"That could come in handy," Sinead said, "if you're willing?"

"Ah, yeah, course. Anything at all, really. Got to earn me keep."

Sinead left Clodagh various forms to fill out, confident that the woman wouldn't require guidance.

She worked her way around the rooms. Some of the women hadn't been attacked but had been incarcerated. There was one young woman who had been manipulated and eventually assaulted by her girlfriend. Her hair had been torn in lumps from her scalp. She had been hard to reach, sobbing endlessly and explaining that her parents would never take her back because they objected to her sexuality in the first place.

The last room presented the greatest challenge, and Sinead got to it just before midnight. She knocked heavily and didn't wait for a noise before she gently opened the door a little. "Hello?"

"What?" came an abrasive bark from the darkness.

Sinead stopped. "I'm the manager. I have some things to go through with you."

"What time is it?" snapped the voice.

"It's after eleven," Sinead said, lifting her phone.

"And you want to do this now? I'm in here all day and you want to start the housekeeping now?"

"I didn't mean to wake you," Sinead said apologetically.

"You didn't," growled the woman.

Then what's the issue? Sinead thought. "I can come back tomorrow."

"Ah, just come in now," the woman said.

Sinead wished she'd closed the door and left it until morning. The room was black dark, not even a sliver of light from the high window.

"Leave the light off," the woman said.

"But I have paperwork," Sinead said, reaching for the ancient heavy thumb-flick of a rocker switch.

"Don't you—"

The light came on and the woman swept a sheet up in front of her face as quickly as she could.

"Sorry," Sinead said instinctively.

"What the fuck?" the woman said. "Turn it off."

But Sinead's patience was at an unnatural low. "I'm Sinead, I manage this charity. There is very little I have not seen or heard. Whatever your situation, I'm here to help – not to judge. We need to talk. It can be tonight or it can be tomorrow."

"Then piss off and come back tomorrow," the voice from behind the sheet snapped.

"Ok, see you in the morning," Sinead said, berating herself for the things she was thinking.

———

SINEAD SLEPT on top of a fold-out camp bed she kept for such occasions in the small office, beside an electric fan heater. The deal the charity had with the nuns was that there would be someone on-site when abused women had to be accommodated there. There had been a time when the nuns had the woman-power to deal with almost any eventuality, but a fall in vocations had meant that their population had dwindled. The surviving flock were of a vintage that rendered them incapable of managing outbursts and even occasional violence when some disgruntled, drugged or drunken husband turned up at the door.

Curiously, Sinead slept quite well for a few hours – perhaps through relief at being back doing something useful. The creak of the heavy front door was what woke her, and she reached out to quieten the low hum of the heater.

She was sweating lightly in her sleeping bag as she unzipped it quietly – clicking slowly over one pair of teeth at a time, trying to remain silent. She swept her legs gently to the floor, reaching for her trainers and looking at her own door – part frightened that it might open, part hoping that whoever was moving around would try her room before any of the cells.

She crept behind it and listened, thinking immediately of Sam and the advice he had given her to place a small wedge beneath the door: *Better than any lock. Means any intruder has to take the frame out in its entirety.* He had given her a lump of rubber the size and shape of a small cake slice. She looked at it now, sitting on the shelf less than two feet from the handle. The thought hurt her heart a little as her hand pressed the noisy spring down and the latch flicked back into place with a thunderous click.

The corridor walls were clad solid in tile, and no matter how soft her trainers the echo bounded down the cold hall and back to her. She walked on the outsides of her feet, grimacing at each squeak on the polished floor. She hadn't thought to bring anything with her – not that she had anything passable as a weapon in her office anyway. She was dressed, as ever, in black, and kept to the edges as she imagined Sam would, seeking cover and darkness. The thought of him somehow morphed from sadness to courage – a distraction. She hunted ahead for movement, scanning the cell doors, listening for any disturbance.

The end of the hall was a deeper black, the only light from an ancient overhead inspection hatch faded to black as the corridor extended. She crept on, her hand softly feeling the wall, open palmed, then leapt in fright as a door behind her opened.

She turned, pacing backwards – her back arched and hands outstretched. Even as she did so she thought, what are you going to do with those paws?

"Is there someone there?" a firm voice rasped, making a good job at masking any fear.

Clodagh, the school cook. Sinead tried to gather herself.

"It's ok, Clodagh, honestly. Go back to bed."

"Sinead? What are you doing creeping around? You'll scare the life out of the women."

"Sorry, I, I thought I heard someone."

"Yeah, yer one down the hall. She was up."

Sinead instinctively knew who she was talking about. "Well, where is she?"

"I dunno."

"I need to find her. We can't have the nuns woken or there'll be hell to pay."

"I'll come with ye," Clodagh said. "Sure, I'll not be able to sleep knowing you're skulking around." Sinead was about to argue but felt buoyed by the company.

They walked more confidently now, comforted by one another's presence. They headed up to the nuns' quarters, all the way into the convent and as far as the chapel. Sinead guiltily checked the altar and the locked cabinets, fearing any intruder may have had an eye on the gold candlesticks, or worse. She lifted the Trócaire box – it was still heavy.

"Occupational hazard, I'd say," Clodagh said wryly.

They made their way back down the corridor, past the cell doors once more, half expecting some man to leap out at them. Then they crept down the stairwell, keeping eyes on the enormous, heavy front door, where their fears were confirmed. It stood, just slightly ajar.

"Shit, we'd better check her room." Sinead turned and began to run – up the stone stairs and down the hallway, Clodagh pattering and panting at her rear. Sinead saw the door she was looking for in the gloom and stopped, unsure as to what she would do if the woman's partner had her by the throat or had harmed her.

"Mind yourself," Clodagh said, somehow giving her strength, and she plunged the handle down and pushed the door inwards.

Silence. Stillness. Darkness.

Sinead thought of Sam again, and placed one foot forward lest someone should jam her arm in the door, and reached around for the heavy light switch.

The room lit up, disturbed. A choking mixture of perfume and cigarette smoke filled the otherwise empty room.

"She's gone," Sinead said.

Doors were cracking open down the hallway; some lights came on and filled the corridor with streaks of yellow.

Clodagh turned around. "You're grand, ladies. Someone just left in the night," she said. "Go on back to bed. Everything's grand."

Sinead stood motionless, surveying the room. The woman had used the small mouthwash glass as an ashtray, despite having been told by posters and laminated notices on the wall that there was to be no smoking in the rooms. There had been no smell of smoke earlier, but night time made fag breaks outside less attractive. There was a burn on the sheet she had used to cover her face when Sinead had tried to do her induction. The pages she'd been supposed to fill out lay untouched on the end of the mattress.

"Tramp," muttered Clodagh, which surprised Sinead.

"She's probably had a rough time," she replied distractedly.

"Or caused one," Clodagh said.

Sinead didn't think to inquire what she meant. She was staring at the one thing the woman had left behind – large and expensive looking. "She's left her phone."

"And a mess."

"No. She must have been scared. If she left it behind, she must have been in a hurry. A panic. Ach, I hope she's ok."

"That one will be fine," Clodagh said, turning towards her own room once more. "I wouldn't worry about her."

"How do you know?"

"I knew her a bit. Back in the day. She was in me brother's year at school. She was never any good."

Sinead set about drawing the sheets off the bed, noticing a dark red staining on part of them. She sniffed it at a distance – blood, she thought, with something else smudged into it. She was familiar with drug users, needles, nosebleeds and all the usual excretions, but this stain baffled her.

Sinead sent Clodagh back to bed, secured the front door and returned to her own room. She found her own phone and called the police, but once the preamble began she knew it would prove a waste of time.

"So was there a forced entry?"

"Not so far as I can tell."

"Sign of a struggle?"

"Not really."

"Yes or no?" said the surly guard.

"No, just a mess."

"Well, we can't send a car out on the strength of a woman leaving a mess."

"I know," she said, exhausted, sitting again on the camp bed.

"Is the front door secure?"

"Yes, it is now," Sinead said, thinking of Sam's wedge currently kicked firmly under it.

"Any way of identifying the woman?"

"We hadn't had a chance to do the paperwork."

"Busy are ye," it wasn't so much a question as a snarl.

"She didn't give an address, just a first name," Sinead read from a sheet and her heart sank.

"Which was?"

Grace would have not have known to question it, she had no point of reference.

"Alexa," Sinead sighed.

"Alexa," the guard repeated, her voice laced with irony.

"I know. They often give false names. But if you see anyone walking the streets, she may be bleeding a little."

"How?" the guard sounded interested for the first time.

"There was blood on the sheets."

"From an attack?"

"I don't think so."

"What does she look like?"

"I don't know." Sinead sighed. "She held the sheet in front of her face. I didn't push it."

"Sounds more like one of your people just got up and left of her own free will."

"Maybe."

"Do you want a reference number for the call?"

Sinead scribbled the number down, ended the call and clambered back into her sleeping bag, setting an alarm to raise her before the nuns got up. It would give her less than two hours' sleep. On the floor beside the camp bed was the woman's phone, in case anyone should call looking for it.

She closed her eyes and thought of Sam. She was drifting when it came to her – his overbearing worry for his daughter exemplified by his last job - babysitting an undeserving heiress. He'd been thinking of her father when, prudishly, he'd gone to great lengths to prevent the woman getting a tattoo. She knew he'd been imagining how he'd feel if his own child had returned branded. And then she knew what had caused the stain. The woman behind the sheet hadn't been injecting needles, she'd been marked by one.

Chapter Four

SINEAD HEAPED herself wearily into the luscious sofa of the apartment. Her sister heard the puff of the cushions and came out from her office to lean on the door frame.

"Coffee?"

"Too tired. Need sleep."

"Tough few nights?"

"We're understaffed and over capacity."

"Whiskey?"

"Maybe one. Maybe that will put me out."

Áine clattered in the kitchen. Sinead heard the spin of a bottle top, the glug of two pours and she returned with two measures large enough to tranquillise a horse.

"Slàinte," Áine said. Sinead braced for the burn.

"So how was it?"

"Ah, you know. But I was thinking, could you check Isla's school?"

"Sinead," Áine groaned. "I thought work might be a distraction from all that."

"All what?"

"You know – finding a fella who doesn't want to be found and is well able to keep below the radar. Literally, as it happens."

"You don't think it's a good idea?"

"I didn't say that."

"Then what are you saying?"

"Just that, well – I don't want you to be disappointed."

"You don't think you can find him?"

"That's not what I meant. I just, well, I'm worried."

"About what?"

"About whatever he was before. I didn't realise you knew so little about his past."

"Why does it matter?"

"You know why!" Áine suddenly barked. She hadn't intended to say it, but it had tumbled out and it was too late now. Sinead retracted, her head sinking into her shoulders. Áine scrabbled to atone. "What is it you think her school could tell you?"

Sinead was silent for a while and took a long draw of Jameson. "Stupid idea, really. She'd missed so much school already I doubt he'd have bothered."

"Bothered what?"

"Notifying them that Isla was leaving, or would be absent or whatever."

"Not a chance."

"But what, like, if the school had emailed him or tried to call him?"

"So what?"

"So what if he opened the email out of, like, curiosity? Or to tell them she wouldn't be back? Or to even ask for homework? Whatever you might think of him, he wasn't negligent about her learning – even if it wasn't in school."

"Really?"

"Yeah, he was determined she would get a good education, but a lot of what she learned was, you know …"

"How to kill people and get away with it?" Áine scoffed, immediately regretting her snide remark as she looked at the empty glass that had loosened her tongue. "Sorry."

"Isla was never exposed to that."

Thanks be to God, Áine thought, but said nothing.

"I meant the education she got wasn't on the curriculum – he taught her history, reading, told her stories. Literature."

"Literature?" Áine tried not to sound mocking.

"Yeah," said Sinead defensively. "He's mad about books."

"Well, there you go," said Áine, baffled.

"And he taught her how to use her hands. There was barely a tool on the boat she didn't know the name of. She understood how to do stuff with the engine, she could sail the boat, steer it. He taught her about the sea, tides and stuff, astronomy."

"Astronomy?"

"I think so," Sinead closed her eyes in recall. "The moon and the pull of the sea. Sums to work out – I don't know, depth or something."

"All sounds like perfect preparation for the Inter Cert."

"They do GCSEs up there."

"Maybe celestial navigation's on the physics course in the United Kingdom, eh?"

"Ah, Áine, give it a rest."

Áine fell silent. Sinead knew her sister was waiting for her to calm, as she always did – which had taught Áine that she could get away with almost anything.

"What if," she said after a silence, "you were to take a look, and if the school emailed him, or called, and he replied – or even if he didn't, you might be able to see where he was when he got the message?"

Áine pursed her lips, her head gently rocking from side to side. If, if, if, she thought. "Ok, I could take a look," she said absently.

"Now?" Sinead sought to capitalise on an apology she knew she was due.

"Ok," Áine sighed. "Come into the control room, so. And bring the bottle."

———

THE TWO WOMEN stared at the screens; Sinead hunting for something she might understand, Áine humming gently.

"Ok, so they did ping him. But only once. About seven weeks ago"

"What did they say?"

"Does it matter?"

"Eh, well, I don't know?"

"Here." Áine opened a Word document and pulled it onto a screen closer to her sister.

Dear Mr Ireland,

I am required to write with regard to the continuing absence of your daughter Isla as I now have no choice but to inform the authorities. I do hope that all is well with Isla, and would note that her period of recorded unattendance at school now exceeds forty days this academic year. I would be grateful if you could revert soonest.

Yours sincerely,

Ms McKracken,

School Principal

"Well, that's hopeful," Sinead muttered.

"Hopeful how?"

"There's no mention of the police."

"The police won't search for a kid who's bunking off school."

"No, but the headmistress would surely have mentioned if the police had come looking for information about them."

"Ah, right, so you reckon that means they're not searching for him?"

"Hopefully, but you could find out for me."

"And I will. I just need to time it right."

"Why?"

"Because the cops will do routine maintenance on servers and push out software updates, and when they do there might be an opening for me to get in without triggering any alarm bells."

Sinead said nothing but there was a fuzzy logic to what she was being told.

"There were other emails — just generic school information."

"No follow-ups?"

"None, which is weird. Why would the principal not try him again?"

The two women looked at one another.

"Surely the school would try more than once to get an explanation?"

"The virus," Áine said suddenly.

"Of course! The school's closed, so they don't know who's in and who's not."

"You could disappear at the moment and nobody would know."

Áine's comment hung between them for a moment, as if

37

there was something else in that realisation, then they returned to the search.

"What other emails were there?"

"Round robins from the headmistress to all parents." Áine scrolled. "Updates, advice, yada yada. He didn't open them."

"How can you tell?"

"They're sent using a provider."

"A what?"

"You've heard of Mailchimp?"

"Yeah, sort of."

"Well, like that except another version. It tracks who has opened and who hasn't, and he hasn't."

"I see."

"So because he hasn't opened them we've no location from the email server. We can't use this to track him."

"Ok."

"There are notes," Áine said, reading.

"Notes?"

"The principal's correspondence with … EA?"

"Education Authority?"

"Yeah, of course," Áine said.

"And?"

"And she says she has tried to call him but the phone is switched off."

"Probably at the bottom of the Atlantic."

"If he has any sense."

Sinead suddenly found herself pushing back tears, the whiskey making her maudlin. "That reminds me," she said weakly, fishing in her pocket. "A woman ran from the refuge last night. She left her phone. Can you find out where she lives and I'll send it back to her?"

Áine looked at the device, turned it over and selected a

cable to place into its only socket. A window opened, requesting a passcode, but instead Áine opened a piece of software with a skull-and-crossbones icon and sat back.

"We'll need to crack the nut," she said.

"Fine," Sinead said.

It took less than one pour of golden liquid to supply results.

"Where do you want to start?"

"Contacts, I suppose."

Áine scrolled. A mixture of foreign and suggestive names appeared. There were fewer than twenty stored. "Bit weird," Áine mumbled.

"Try emails."

"Wow," Áine said when the subject titles appeared. "She likes the smut."

Sinead watched the constant feed of filthy references pass up the screen. Many were reviews.

"Ah, no," Sinead said.

"She's a prostitute," Áine said.

"Seems so."

"The obvious next place to look is in photos."

"Ok." Sinead shrugged.

The images that appeared were a grim reflection of Ireland's underbelly. Multiple men and women had been captured – there were even videos.

"Are you thinking what I'm thinking?" Áine said, turning to her sister.

"Yeah, she wasn't a prostitute. She was a madam."

"Oh, right. That wasn't what I was thinking."

"We should send this to the police. She could be in danger. She'd had a tattoo – it was bleeding badly. Maybe it had been forced on her. Judging by some of the photos and the nationalities in them, I'd say she might be involved in gangs. Triads maybe."

"Or," Áine rolled the "r" around her mouth, posing an alternative.

"Or what?"

"Well, this is a pay-as-you-go phone and it's got two hundred euros on it.

"So?"

"So if you want to make contact with anyone – who may or may not be on the run – this might be a smart way to do it."

Sinead looked at her sister, temptation tingling up her spine. "We should give it to the police."

"Only you could be worried about the well-being of some oul wagon who runs hookers."

"What if she's being coerced?"

"Will the cops even look at it?"

Sinead thought about the phone call with the guard a few hours previously. "Probably not."

"Then, what's the harm? She's probably a nasty bitch who is happy to run a bunch of young ones to men and take the money. You need a clean way of communicating with lover boy and – here, one has landed on your lap."

"I dunno, sis."

"I've got the GPS and Wi-Fi disabled, so there's virtually nothing to trace that phone to this apartment apart from you bringing it here in the first place, and this is a big block in a city centre. It's as clean a way as any."

"But we don't know where they are, and Sam isn't likely to have a phone, is he?"

"I doubt it – he's a cute hoor. But if we find him you will need some way of making contact. Oh, and I checked the father of the heiress."

"Well?" Sinead piped up, expectant.

"Don't get excited – there's nothing."

Sinead slumped, her mouth pressed closed. She had an overwhelming urge to cry.

"Look, sis – we have a clean phone for you to talk to him if we do find them. At least we have one end sorted. It's a start."

Chapter Five

SINEAD LAY AWAKE for the third night in a row. She knew she was exhausted, irritable and very probably on the cusp of becoming unreasonable. She also knew that there would be a hangover to deal with in due course, so she gave up, got up and went for a walk. To hell with the curfew, she thought.

Her mind numbed by inebriation, she took the Beckett Bridge and padded into the northside, where life changed considerably. Once the home of native working Dubliners, the north-east of the inner city was increasingly mixed with migrants, and she knew that those on the streets at this time of night could well be up to no good, or forcing said migrants into it. Local gangsters exploited foreign arrivals, but the more confident and brutal of those arrivals managed to scare the shit out of the native scumbags and were confident enough in their brutality to do their own thing. Her hurt was giving way to anger – she knew it, and in that moment she was content that it should be so.

Sinead ignored the fancy banking quarter, preferring to

skirt the Royal Canal, drawn somehow to the water. She thought of him then, beckoning her, and her refusal. An incredible reaction given all that had gone before.

She moved east, her way impeded by her own poorly placed feet and a propensity to bump off the walls of unfinished monstrosities, ill-fitting with what Dublin was supposed to be. Nude glass cages, see-through buildings, exposed, just like the seediness of the city with its gang murders and drug wars, prostitution rackets and subjection of women.

Her mind ranted without an audience and she knew it and enjoyed it; imagining revenge for all but Skibbereen and lamenting the loss of the one person she knew who was prepared to satisfy a lust for justice. He had sailed away, with his one true love, and she had declined the offer to go with them. Her choice – possibly the second worst of her life.

Before she knew it she was standing at the end of Alexandra, no road left between her and the Irish Sea. "I am pissed," she said aloud to herself, immediately deciding that the sea looked appealing. Three steps later and she was over the rocks and slipping into the water, wading to her waist without so much as a gasp – determined to crush the hurt in her head and her heart and to just swim a little.

"Ah, c'mon, sweetheart!" She heard splashing from behind and felt a heavy pant of smoky breath on her cheek as someone landed on her, forcing her under for a split second and drawing the air from her lungs in shock at the cold. There was a luminous flash and a stocky arm flipped her onto her back and was dragging her back to the rocks. "Look, darlin', it really canny be as bad as all that," the man panted. Sinead thrashed around and caught sight of "Stena" emblazoned across the man's jacket.

"No!" she tried not to shout. "I'm not, this isn't—"

She felt the rocks on her legs and struggled to her feet, her clothes stuck to the outline of her body.

"Why do youse always choose here, aye?"

"You're ... Scottish?"

"Aye," he said.

"I wasn't trying to—"

"Aye," he said again, knowing better.

"Really, I was just—"

"Having a wee dip? I know."

Sinead gave up.

And then she realised what she had overlooked.

"WHAT THE ACTUAL FUCK?"

Áine stared at her, damp and dishevelled. She had left without her key fob and the buzzer had gone unanswered for a full half hour. Sinead knew that her sister was lying in bed hoping she would be the one to get up and answer the door – unaware that it was Sinead pressing the button. It had been bad enough waking the doorman to let her in off the street.

"Sorry," she said.

"Are you ... wet?"

"I've got an idea."

"You got an idea – in the rain?"

"Sam had this friend – Mini, Min."

"I remember. You met him in Scotland. His bessie."

"Yeah, him. And, yeah, he's Scottish. So he might know where Sam's gone."

"He'd have told Min – why?"

"No, he wouldn't have told him – in case it compromised him, but Min might know instinctively, like, because they served together. They know each other inside out. If Sam's gone somewhere, he might be able to guess where."

"That's what you went walking in the rain for? That's the best you could come up with?"

Sinead suddenly realised the uselessness of what she was saying, the shedding fug of drink exposing a brutal realisation. The indestructability of the inebriated was no longer with her.

Áine reached out and placed her hand on her sister's shoulder. "Come in, sweetheart, and get dried off. I'll make some coffee."

"But if I wanted you to, could you?" Sinead tried desperately.

"Wanted me to what?"

"Find Min?"

"This is the marine, right? The fella who's still in the forces?"

"Yeah. He's based in Scotland. I forget the name of it."

"I'd say Google would be enough to find him."

"Really?"

"Well, it's better than trying to crack into some MOD frame. All I need is his real name."

Sinead looked at her sister, despondency and desperation dripping off her with the residue of Dublin Bay. She didn't need to say anything.

"D'ye know his rank even?"

Sinead shook her head and tears joined the dampness of her cheek.

"Ok, I'll see what I can find. You do the caffeine." Áine swaggered off towards her tech room. Sinead squelched towards the shower.

WITH A PERCOLATOR POT in one hand and two mugs in the other, Sinead sheepishly peered into Áine's office. The screens were full of camouflage fatigues.

"Ready for coffee?"

Áine ignored her. "There seems to be two options. Faslane Naval base on the West coast – that's a bunch of marines protecting nuclear submarines. They're fit." She nodded at a screen packed full of young men, some shirtless, on exercise in a jungle.

"Maybe. That's not far from where Sam took me and Isla a few times," Sinead traced the map on the screen, "but I got the impression that Min had come from further away."

"Well, there's a base called Condor. It's on the east coast of Scotland. It has a crowd called thirty commando."

"Thirty?"

"From what I can gather they might say three zero, cos that's what they say with other units – like four five or four three, but this thirty bunch are a different type of thing altogether."

"How?"

"Their job is called 'information exploitation', and they have a group, and you'll never guess who set it up."

"Min?"

"Not in 1943 he didn't."

"Right." Sinead sighed, realising that she was going to have to listen to the full explanation. "Who, then?"

"Ian Fleming."

"Who is?"

"Yer man who wrote *James Bond*."

Sinead looked puzzled, although something here seemed to fit. "Really? He wasn't just a writer?"

"This crowd stole the Enigma machine during the Second World War – thirty commando, or IX, or so it says."

"Go way."

"They're an intelligence unit. IX is the information exploitation bit. Thirty IX, I think."

"That's it!" Sinead shouted, then tried to calm herself. "Sure, it was Min who Sam asked to sweep the boat when I first met him."

"Sweep?"

"For bugs – or a tracker, or whatever. Remember those bastards were always able to find him?"

"That paedophile ring?"

"Yeah, they knew every move he made. Sam couldn't work out how, so he brought Min in to give his boat the once-over."

"Right, yeah," Áine said, recalling the difficult period. She wondered how different things might have been if she had just forced her sister's hand back then and refused to help. It might have prevented all the hurt that followed. Back then Sam had just been a kind of contractor for Sinead, rescuing hookers from brothels for money. He was little more than paid muscle. Áine never imagined they would develop a relationship – if that, indeed, was what they had kindled.

"Sam asked Min to find out whether they were following him through his GPS on the boat."

"He didn't do much of a job of it, though, did he?" Áine muttered scornfully.

"Well, Min had one of his blokes sweep the boat while he and Sam went off for lunch, but the boat keys with the tracker were in his pocket."

"Well, if this intelligence commando crowd do know what they're doing, we'll have to be careful."

"This is the right unit – I'm sure of it. What's it called again?"

"30 Commando IX Group."

"I never heard the name," said Sinead, looking again at the screen, "but all that tech and surveillance stuff fits the bill. You want to see the big speedboat he had. Apparently it could, like, mask itself."

"Like the Klingons?"

"What?"

"Cloaked. Stealth mode."

"What are you talking about?"

"Sounds like Star Trek."

"Don't be sarcastic, and have some coffee."

Sinead cradled her mug.

Áine paused, spreading her hands out flat on the keyboard.

"It's not raining," she said, chewing her lip, as if terrified of the statement.

"No."

"It … hasn't been … raining."

"No," said Sinead again, fixing her stare at the screens.

"You're scaring me," Áine said, blunt and to the point.

"I'm not back in that place, Áine."

Neither looked at the other for a long time, until Áine could contain it no longer.

"Sinead, did you jump in the Liffey?" she blurted out, a whisper short of anger.

"No," Sinead said, turning her head slowly. "I told you, it's not like before."

"Because if this prick is going to drag you backwards, I'll fucking—"

"You'll what?"

"I'll kill him."

Sinead stared at Áine for a long moment, then placed her hand on her twin's. "I can't explain something I don't really understand myself, but I know you don't hate him – I think you might even like him, even if you hate some of the things he's done. I honestly know that he's a good man, despite how everything seems. And, Áine, I made a mistake, and I need to fix that, and I need to tell him."

For the first time since childhood that Sinead could recall, Áine's eyes welled. Her hand turned beneath her sister's and gripped it tight. They had been one half of each other forever. "I just don't want another—"

"I know, but he's not, Áine. I know he's not."

Áine nodded – a comfort to herself as much as her sister. "But if he is, I will kill him."

"I know, and thank you."

Áine shook herself like a wet dog. "Right so, make the call."

"What?"

"Call the base. There's the number." She pointed at a screen.

"And say what?" Sinead was astonished.

"Ask for your man – the little marine fella."

"What?"

Áine's uncharacteristic softness was pushed aside. "For fuck's sake, Sinead, shove over that phone."

"You can't use a phone!"

"It's grand for the likes of this. It's an IP phone and it's VPN'd all over the planet."

"I dunno what you just said." Sinead pushed the cradle towards her and looked on as Áine dialled.

"I-X group, please," she said after a few moments. There was a long pause, then her chin twitched as she threw out her line, hoping for a bite. "Hello, is Min there, please?"

Sinead look at her with incredulity.

"Ok, can you put me through, thank you." Áine's politeness was on the edge of its range. "It's a private call." There was another pause before her lower lip curled in surprise and satisfaction.

"Ah, hello, is that Min?" Sinead could hear a gruff one-word response. "Could you hold one second for Sinead, please. Thank you."

Sher handed the receiver to her sister.

Chapter Six

"WHAT DID HE SAY?"

"He said, *woah there*."

"Woah there?"

"And, *haud yer wheesht.*"

"Who is he, Billy Connolly?"

Sinead rocked her head a little. "Not a million miles away."

"Did he know who you were?" Áine pushed, desperate for information.

"Yes, he's met me – he's in charge of some specialist intelligence unit. The Irish accent, the name, he's not an imbecile."

"Then what the hell did he say!" Áine's eyes bulged in exasperation.

"Well, you heard me. I told him it was about Sam."

"Yes, *I'm* not an imbecile. I *can* listen to one side of a conversation." Áine shook her head in bewilderment.

"And he said not to say anything on *the blower*, and that he would come and see me."

"That's it?"

"Yeah."

"Well, how's he gonna come and see you in a lockdown?"

Sinead blew her cheeks out. "I dunno."

"Does he even know where you live?"

"No," Sinead said, her heart sinking for the fiftieth time that day.

"What a waste of time that was."

"Maybe not," Sinead said. "He and Sam – there's something between them. I think he was really pleased to meet me after ... you know."

"No, I don't know."

"Well," Sinead started, unsure of herself. "He obviously knew that Sam's wife had been killed."

"You would hope so if he's Sam's best friend."

"And, well, Sam left the military because of, you know – the murder. And I got the impression he'd fallen off the radar, Sam, with his friends, like."

"Except for Min."

"Well, maybe Min as well. I think he may have only seen him once since the funeral. I thought that, maybe, Min kind of missed him, or had been worried about him. Then he shows up with me, on a kind of holiday."

"But he knew you weren't shagging, didn't he?"

"Áine," Sinead groaned, her face contorted in revulsion.

"Sorry. *It's not like that*," she parroted a previous conversation.

"I don't know what he knew. You know how little Sam speaks, so I doubt he said much. I only met Min for dinner, once, on the boat, but it was in a special place and Min had obviously come a long way, and it felt kind of like Sam wanted me to meet him. That's what I thought at the time, anyway."

"What special place?"

"Tinker's Hole. Near an island called Iona. It was so beautiful."

"Sounds weird."

"It's got rocks either side and you can almost touch them on the way in. Then it opens up into this kind of sea oasis, all sheltered and warm, with rock face rising sheer out of the sea. It's kind of cosy and, like, intimate."

Áine puckered her lips mockingly. "Feels like I'm intruding."

"Ah, will you stop." Sinead scowled, before settling back into the memory. "The boys went off for a while, and I wondered if they might be—"

"More than just friends?" Áine couldn't help herself.

Sinead growled and shuttered up.

"I'm sorry," Áine said. "Sorry, I'll give it a rest. You wondered if they were what?"

"Maybe talking about me. Like, maybe he was seeking some sort of blessing."

"From Min?"

"I just wondered. Min would have known Shannon, Sam's wife. They were all close friends. So if Sam was thinking of starting again … ah, I don't know. I think back sometimes and wonder if maybe that's what they were off discussing."

Áine said nothing.

"Wishful thinking, I know, but it was not long after that he finally asked me to go with him and Isla − after all that time, so I wondered if the meeting with Min had changed things, you know?"

"Yeah, I can see what you're saying."

"Still, as you say, the lockdown's made an ass of all that."

"You've waited this long, sis."

"Yeah," Sinead said absently. "You wait for one, then two arrive at once."

"The kid?"

"Yeah."

"Isla means that much to you, does she?"

Sinead looked up, considering. "Ah, yeah. At least as much, in a way."

"Are you sure …"

"What?"

"Nothing."

"Bloody hell, Áine, we've come this far and it's not even breakfast yet. You might as well get all your reservations out."

"Are you sure it's not that you …" Áine couldn't bring herself to say more.

"Want the child more than the man?"

Áine said nothing, confirming her thoughts.

Sinead sighed. "I wondered about that – the idea of being a kind of mother, of minding her, but I think it's more that you can't separate them. They're a package. It's like they're the same thing."

Áine looked at her sister and conceded.

Chapter Seven

SINEAD PULLED long hours at the convent. It was a vain hope that immersion in work would serve as a distraction and lessen the longing she felt from the moment she woke until she eventually slept. Even then she found herself shuddering from her sleep at night – the darkness somehow exacerbating her fears. The chances of finding Sam, with all his experience in concealment, were next to nil. She dreamt of waking alone, an old woman, with nothing and no one to reach for.

The lockdown dragged on and the convent cells filled up. Clodagh, the school cook, proved to be an organiser and flourished in the old kitchens, feeding both the nuns and the exiled women. The fare was basic but good enough for the Mother Superior to offer to pay for supplies. Graced with a shopping list from Clodagh, whose growing confidence, Sinead knew, was in danger of becoming an irritation, she spent hours online ordering tonnes of potatoes and vegetables, queuing for delivery slots. She clicked between supermarkets, searching for the best deals and comparing basket prices. The nuns were nothing if not frugal – and it put the time in.

A calm gradually wrapped around the convent – most of the women not having set eyes on a man for longer than they could remember. Sinead knew the beats: they would find solace, initially, in one another's stories; would offer comfort accompanied by hugging and sympathy. If the lockdown endured, cliques would form, kindred spirits drawn into huddles, and the chat would start. Eventually, at best, there would be cattiness, but there was always the potential for disputes to descend into physical fights. If or when that happened, the nuns would have a quiet word and Sinead would have to manage the expulsions, which would tax her mind days and nights in advance of eventually mustering the courage to ask someone to leave. But, for the moment, there was peace, and she used that time to be a manager and adviser, filling out the forms for housing and refuge, administering finances and trying to think of anything and anyone but Sam and Isla.

And then the vibe shattered.

"Sinead, there's a man at the door!" Clodagh hissed through the cracked office door which she had neglected to knock. The dinner lady had taken it upon herself to act as the inmates' spokeswoman – a role she clearly enjoyed.

"What?" Sinead looked up from the Tesco delivery screen.

"Did you not hear it? Nobody's answered but we've all taken it in turns to sneak a look out the window in case … you know."

"And is he anyone's husband?"

"No."

"Boyfriend?"

"No."

"Then what's the problem?"

"He's built like a shithouse and looks rough."

Sinead looked at the screen again. "He could be the Tesco delivery driver?"

"Well, he didn't arrive in a van."

"How did he arrive?"

"Nobody knows. There's no car."

Sinead didn't like the sound of that. She thought of the woman who had scarpered. She thought of the phone and its incriminating contents, and the fact that it was currently concealed in her bedside cabinet back at the apartment. Had some pimp come to retrieve it? She pushed her chair back and went cautiously to the window, clinging to the old curtain and edging her body forward to take a glance beneath, but the angle was too acute to see anything other than a shaven head.

"I'll go down," she said. "If there's any trouble, call the Guards immediately."

Clodagh nodded vigorously, scared and excited at the role she had been appointed. As Sinead left the room, Clodagh moved her hand to hover over the phone handset.

If she wasn't feeding the five thousand, Sinead thought, I'd speed up her placement. She went down the stone stairs, one hand stroking the wrought-iron railing, failing to mask the noise her soft trainers made as it echoed up the wall. She could imagine the women above, leaning over and peering down.

Probably just the postman.

There was no point trying to shout through the door – it was two inches of ancient Irish oak. Her voice would carry only to the women and unnerve them further. She strapped the galvanised intruder link across from the frame, turned the heavy key and pulled the door back quickly to demonstrate the chain.

"Hello?" She saw the outline of a man shimmy to the side, trying to get a look in.

He's as broad as he's long, she thought.

Sinead stepped back a little. "Can I help you?" She panicked as the face appeared right into the crack of the door, one eye catching hers.

"Are ye under siege in there, hen?" the voice almost chuckled.

Sinead's muscles softened from a bind she hadn't been aware of. "Min?" she said, baffled.

"Were you not expecting me?"

"Eh, well, not in lockdown. It's—" She rattled the door shut and took off the chain. "Thanks for coming. How did you …?"

She stepped back a little as he moved forward. "That chain's no worth a rat's ass," he muttered as he stood in the hallway looking at her. Sinead was acutely conscious of the bounce of his words up the tiled walls.

"It's ok," she shouted, "it's just a friend of mine!"

There was a murmur above as the women began to withdraw.

"What's going on?" Min said. "Are yis under threat or wha?" he said, only half joking.

"Can we …" Sinead faltered, looking above, expecting one woman in particular to be listening, "take a breath of fresh air?"

"Aye," Min said, curious. "Aye, whatever suits."

They walked down the pebbled path and out into the green field opposite the convent. Sinead knew there would be women watching from the windows above and deliberately kept her back to the building, hoping to lead Min down a path through the trees to the old disused vegetable garden.

"Thank you so much for coming," she began.

"No bother, no bother at all. I was glad to hear from you, to be honest."

"Oh?"

"I've been wanting to get word to our pal, but havnie been able."

Sinead was desperate to hear why, but wanted to get away from the building before they discussed Sam.

"How did you get here? The flights—"

"It was tricky enough. Normally I'd just borrow a boat and find an excuse for an exercise, but British military in Ireland is still a big no-no."

Sinead was not oblivious to the politics of the peace process. "So how?"

"Flew to Belfast, stayed at the barracks one night, pretended to do a bit of work, then took a bike down unapproved roads in the middle of the night."

"You cycled?"

"What? No – a Honda. The police aren't gonnae stop a bike. They're only interested in social distancing – passengers and the like. Helmets are handy too. No way of telling who's under the lid. So I took a bike from the base and here I am."

"You must have left …" Sinead left the question open, still surprised to see him so soon.

"Just after you called. Like I said, I was pleased to hear from you. How's Sam – where is he? I've been trying to—"

"Oh, Min, I was hoping you'd be able to tell me."

"Why?"

"It's a long story."

"I wanted to let him know he's off the hook."

"How do you mean?" she fired out quickly.

"He's no under suspicion of all that … have you a phone on ye?"

Sinead patted her pockets, somehow keen to offer proof. "No, it's back at the—"

"Ok. Well, those killings – they were a bad bunch of bastards, by the way."

"I know."

"They were the people behind the bomb that nearly killed his wee lassie. There's no question, I've seen the intel. After they brought me in for questioning, that became a perfect cover for me to take a look – to help, in fact. Made it seem like I was trying to piece together why I'd been hauled over the coals, y'understand?"

"You were questioned?"

"Aye, before I met you, after the first dissidents were killed. They suspected I was passing information to a boy."

Sinead's heart sank. "So they knew Sam was killing them?"

"No, they suspected someone else – a Scouser me and Sam served with back a while. Doesn't matter. They couldn't prove anything and a lot's happened since, hen, it's hard to explain."

"Tell me, Min, I really want to know."

They reached the old sleepers of the vegetable garden, now overgrown and messy.

"Well, where is Sam?" Min paused to look up at Sinead.

"I don't know. He's on the run – he thinks they're on to him."

"Right. Ok." Min turned and thought for a moment, strolling again, wondering where to begin. "Well, this man – the Scouser they thought was doing the killings – he was our ops officer way back. He got himself arrested."

Sinead stopped, confused. "This is all …"

"I know, it was a mess," Min looked at her, shaking his head. "It wasnae the police who lifted the Scouser, it was essentially British Intelligence."

"For the killings, of the terrorists?" Sinead had stopped moving as she struggled to comprehend what she was being told.

"Aye. Anyway, it looked like he was going down for it, but, instead, the head of intelligence in Northern Ireland was removed and the scouser was released. They've concocted some story for the press that the murders were part of an internal feud – the IRA killing each other. Plays well for the police and intelligence."

"So do they know about Sam?"

"Only one person did, but it seems she's dead."

"They killed her?"

"Who knows? Maybe, maybe not. The intel I've seen suggests that they genuinely don't know."

"Could Sam …?"

"I've checked and it couldnae have been him – times don't work. This woman was a spook, so it might've been her own."

"What?"

"It could have been her own team knocked her off."

"Seriously?"

"I don't know, darlin', honestly. It could also have been a freak accident."

"So they still suspect Sam?"

"No," said Min. "That's the bizarre thing. There is no mention of Sam in any of the intelligence, and it's not as if it's been erased or whatever. It seems he managed to avoid them altogether – .apart from this one woman, and she's dead and never filed any paperwork or told anyone else."

"So how do you know?"

"My Scouse pal. This spook – she told him, alright, but he's safe as houses. He'll never say a word. Me and Sam and him, we go way back."

"This is all very weird."

"None of it's important. All that matters is that Sam is not on the hook for this. They don't even have a file on him any more. Far as they're concerned, he retired a few years back and is out of everything."

"So they're safe?"

"Who?"

"Sam and Isla."

"Oh, course, aye, they're safe."

"They ran for nothing?"

"Aye," Min repeated.

"We need to tell them."

"That's what I'm saying! That's why I was glad to hear from ye."

———

THEY SAT in an unexpectedly easy silence in Sinead's car. She had rushed into the convent, called Grace to arrange for her to take over the day shift, placed the grocery order, grabbed her keys and returned to Min.

"What if we get stopped? What will you say?"

"To the Guards?"

"Uh-huh."

"I have a frontline worker pass."

"I gathered that. I mean, about me."

"I'll say you're a colleague."

Min grunted his doubts but said no more until after they got parked and were standing in the lift.

"Swanky, this, for NGO staff."

"My sister bought it. She's in blue-chip tech. You might have heard about her," Sinead tried, half curious to see the extent to which Sam and Min had talked; half hopeful that he would be braced for the inevitable impact of Áine. Min shook his head, barely detectable.

"Bloody hell," he muttered as they entered the apartment – a reaction Sinead was accustomed to.

"I'll go and get her."

Min slowly turned, looking upwards and then almost involuntarily stepping forward to the front-facing room to stare across the Liffey.

"That's like a tube of beer on a tilt," he said when he heard footsteps behind him.

"It's the Dublin Conference Centre," a new voice informed him. He turned to find a similar – if shorter, version of Sinead. Her face was not as open; even the way she stood gave her a chippy air.

"I'm Min."

"I know," she shot back.

"You must be Áine."

Sinead hustled in before her twin had the opportunity to ignore their visitor. "Shall we get started? Min, would you like a coffee? You've had a long journey."

"Just flew in on a Chinook?" Áine's eyebrows arched. Sinead note that Min seemed fit to ignore her.

"Coffee would be lovely, darlin', thanks."

"Through here," Áine tossed behind her as she walked away. Min relished the challenge and followed.

"This is tricked out," he said, admiringly, as she drew him into her cave.

"I would hope so," she said, softening at his appreciation of her meticulously designed workspace.

"You could land the shuttle with this kit," he murmured.

"We can do almost anything with this rig."

"I'd say you could," he nodded, gazing around. "I'd say you probably could."

"How's it going?" Sinead entered juggling mugs.

"Haven't started," Áine muttered.

"Started what?" Min said.

"Finding Sam." Sinead rolled over a chair.

"Are we, eh …" Min rocked his head in query.

"All good. There's nothing Áine doesn't know. She and Sam have worked together for a while."

"If you can call it that. I don't get paid," she said, "and I've copped a lot of shit, so it's that kind of work."

Min pulled in his lips, apparently deciding not to inquire further.

"So where do we start?" Sinead leaned forward with happy anticipation. Áine and Min looked at one another.

"Well, where did he leave from?"

"Last I saw them, they cast off the pier in Dún Laoghaire in thick fog."

"Good, he'll have had to use navigation kit if the vis was bad."

"Uh-uh," Áine said. "He powered everything off."

"Prick," Min muttered. "That's typical, that is, navigating in fog without the mod cons."

"Even with Isla on board?" Sinead said.

"Well, you make a point. He must have been convinced they were on his tail then."

"He definitely was. He was in a desperate rush."

"So he could be anywhere." Min shrugged.

"We did make some progress," Áine interjected. "We tracked his downloads, and we think he went down the east coast. There was a Wi-Fi hit at a harbour in Waterford and a dump of Eastern Caribbean charts."

"Oh, really?" Min was suddenly interested. "Good effort. A specific download?"

Unconsciously, Áine straightened. Sinead could see she was pleased at the compliment, that here was something about this man that made her keen to impress.

"A specific search and direct download – not a stumble or an impulse buy, not as a result of an advert served."

"Very good. But why would he go to the Caribbean ahead of hurricane season? Normally its these next few months people get out of there in their yachts?" Áine and Sinead shared a glance – this was the sort of knowledge neither of them naturally possessed. "And how would he land anywhere or manage? Sure, all the sea borders are closed, aye?"

Again, Sinead and Áine looked at one another. "You mean, they'd turn him back?" Sinead asked.

"Depends where he went. One of the bigger islands could very well send a ship or their coastguard out to chase him off."

"So maybe he'd have gone to a smaller island?"

"Aye, but even though he could probably anchor up, he wouldn't be able to go ashore."

They all looked into the middle distance, unravelling what that meant.

"What would they eat?" Sinead asked.

"Fish, I suppose, but that's not enough if you've a bairn aboard."

"They'd need to go ashore."

"Aye, or …" Min was thinking, kindling a notion.

"What?" Sinead pressed.

"Or he'd go somewhere he could get help."

"Like where?"

"We had a pal, back in the noughties. He was part of a team we had. It was a tight wee unit."

"For the betterment of humanity, no doubt," Áine sniped, and then drew her jaw in. Sinead distractedly wondered if she was berating herself.

"Well, it was effective, I'll say that. There was five of us, and one had joined from the recruitment of the Caribbeans." Seeing the confusion on their faces, he elaborated. "Something the Marines does – offers a few spaces to folks from Commonwealth countries on YO training in Lympstone."

"My universal translator got about two words of that." Áine attempted.

"It's in Exmouth, the commando training camp."

"Full of little Rambos."

"Pretty much." Min smiled at her persistence but still didn't rise to it. "Young officer training. Some are not so young – like me and Sam, when we eventually gave in and went for it."

"And the Caribbean connection?"

"Well, a lot of the time the lads frae the West Indies are not there to join the corps but they get the training if they can stick it – most don't. Some are useless layabouts and end up going back."

"Typical," Áine snapped. "Colonialists still looking to exploit the natives as cannon fodder."

If Min was perturbed, Sinead couldn't see it. "Like I said, they're not expected to serve, and it costs a fortune to put them through it. It's a year's worth of brutal graft."

"Sounds like an act of extreme benevolence, so." Áine caught Sinead's imploring stare.

"But there were a few who came through really well,

and some were exceptional. Oxen they were – kept going for days without dropping their heads. Aye, the Caribbeans were a mixed bag – some who just wanted to lie in the sun but some who were outstanding."

"And?" Áine said with exasperation.

"And one went on to go through selection with us, and we kept tight after. Then we were put in the same squad."

"What's selection?" Áine asked.

"Special Forces," Sinead answered when it was clear Min wasn't inclined to.

"Oh, great, another robot killing machine enters the frame."

"Áine!" Sinead hissed.

"This man was from Dominica," Min recalled.

Dominican Republic, Áine turned and began to type.

"No, no—"

"It's ok, this rig is VPN'd," she said. "Nobody will track any search from here."

"That's not what I mean, love."

"Call me *love* one more time and you're out on your ear, commando or no commando," Áine said. Sinead knew such familiarity actually translated as affection in her sister's world, but Min was proving excellent at ignoring her feigned hostility. "No, I mean it's not the Dominican Republic. Daniel would go off on one if anybody mixed them up."

"Daniel? Daniel from Dominica?" Áine was sniggering sarcastically.

"You wouldn't laugh if you saw him. He's bigger than three men."

Áine was typing and reading. "Well, bloody hell."

"What?" Sinead, excited, rolled her chair closer to the monitors.

Áine pulled the same image onto the screens in front of each of them. It was a newspaper article: Man suspected of robbing visiting yacht claims he is the victim.

The headline immediately seemed to fit.

"Look at the date," Áine said.

"That's ..." Sinead thought for a moment. "Thirty-four days after Sam and Isla left. How long does it take to cross the Atlantic?" she turned to Min.

"Piece of string. Depends entirely on a range of things, but that's totally possible."

Áine clicked into the article and they read.

A man arrested for breaching the Covid curfew claims he was attacked by a visiting yachtsman while fishing at night. Derek Amoah was picked up by police on a road close to a beach on the west of the island and immediately taken to hospital where he was treated for wounds apparently inflicted by a harpoon. The yacht that Amoah claims to have been the base for the attack has since vanished, but newspaper records show that Amoah has a previous conviction for stealing from visiting boats.

Without further evidence the police say it is unlikely he will face any charges other than flouting new legislation aimed at curbing the spread of coronavirus. Amoah claims he was shot with his own harpoon when a sailor found him snorkelling close to an anchored yacht on Tuesday last.

Áine turned to her companions. "Sound like anyone you know?"

"If it is him, that robber's lucky to have got away with a flesh wound," Min said.

————

THE WOMEN STARED at Min as he shook his head.

"I can't mind, ladies. I'm sorry."

They'd chimed off the names of every port, town and village Google Maps could offer, but all Min's expression returned was exasperation.

"So you probably killed alongside this bloke, slept in tents, I imagine, probably cuddled up in the cold, but you never thought to ask him where he was from?"

"Dominica – a small island. It wasn't a big topic of conversation, love." Min stared at Áine, who, Sinead noted, quickly decided not to pick a fight.

"What *did* you talk about?" Áine said, more softly than she was accustomed to.

"The task in hand, and not getting slotted, mainly. And you're right, we were close, close enough to do things you'll never want to know about, but circumstances at home were always pushed to the back of our minds. Easier that way to get on with the job."

Áine turned back to the screen. "Daniel Joseph. There are so many of them. And this one with a Facebook profile—"

"Too young – and too old to be a son. He doesnae even look like Danny."

"It shouldn't be this hard. Dominica only has a population of seventy thousand."

"He was big into the environment, mind. Way before all that green stuff was a thing."

"Oh?" Sinead said.

"He was a brilliant diver. He'd been into scuba before he joined up. I mind him passing the diving course and then being made up to an instructor. Sam asked him for extra help. We called Sam 'Corky' – he had wild trouble staying under."

"Do you think he could be a diver on Dominica?" Áine

was typing again.

"Mebbe," Min said. "He was always banging on about swimming with whales. On the courses he took, you know."

Áine pulled up a website and shared it across the screens. There were videos and underwater images of huge creatures, constantly interrupted by a reappearing advert for GoPro cameras.

"Sperm whales," Min murmured. "This is what he was into. Protecting these beauties."

"Would Sam have known that?" Sinead asked.

"Aye, Danny and Sam were tight, you know. Extra diving lessons until Sam was good enough to make the grade. Like I said, he was better on the surface than under it. I never saw as buoyant a boy in all my puff."

Áine was beavering away with the trackpad and an unusual keyboard she had pulled over on an extending arm. Min watched over her shoulder. "Clever girl," he said.

Sinead was baffled. "What are you doing?"

Min shook his head gently in admiration. "She's only just got into the staff gateway of the Environmental Protection Team."

"Not just a pretty face," Áine said.

"You are quick, lass. If you ever want a badly paid job with the military, gimme a shout."

"Guess who works with whales?" Áine said with pride.

"Daniel Rosseau Joseph," Sinead read off the screen. "Is that his middle name?" She turned to Min.

"I have no idea, darlin'," he said, "but that'll be him. He was mad about they whales."

———

"SO WE CALL HIM!" Sinead was as animated as Áine had seen her in months.

"What?" Min's head tilted a fraction on his trunk-like neck.

"Call Daniel – at the whale centre base, or whatever it is."

Min did all but hold his palms up. He wanted to whoa her gallop to a canter. "And … say what?"

"Ask if Sam's there?" Sinead said, bemused.

"We canny do that."

"Why?"

"Yeah," Áine butted in, "you said the police aren't looking for Sam, so what's the issue?"

"Sam's the issue."

"What?" the women said collectively.

"You need to think it through, girls."

Áine's finger came out then. "I am not a girl, and neither is she."

Min shook it off. "Sam's no gonna take a call from me, is he? And he's no gonna take a call from you either."

"Why?"

"Look, put yourself where he is. He's running, right? Or at least he thinks he is."

"Yeah?"

"And he thinks he's clear, so far."

"Yes." Sinead wanted the whole thing to speed up.

"And then it's you who finds him. What's he gonna think?"

"That Áine's tracked him. He knows how good she is."

"Aye, but he also knows how good *they* are."

"They?" Sinead's exasperation was at the point of anger.

Áine helped her out. "The spooks – MI5, MI6."

"But they're not interested!" Sinead tried not to shout. "You said so!"

"But he doesnae know that. He thinks he's on the hook for multiple murders."

"Then why can't you call him?" Áine said.

Min sighed deeply. He was evidently conflicted.

"Did something happen between you and Daniel?" Sinead asked.

"No, no. It's ..."

"You rode his wife?" Áine was getting frustrated. "You crashed his car? You owe him money?"

"Ah, for goodness sake," Min spluttered. "Sam's gonna wonder if I'm compromised."

The women sat back in their chairs. Their expressions said it all: *explain.*

Min looked away, wrestling with the need to tell them and the desire not to. "I gave Sam a wee hand. On his last operation."

"Taking out those bombers?" Áine asked.

Min said nothing.

"I didn't know that," Sinead said, pieces falling into unwelcome places. "Is that why you visited us – in Scotland?"

Áine looked nervously at her sister and changed the subject. "So what? What's it matter if you helped him?"

"If I call out of the blue, asking Daniel if he's seen Sam – Danny's gonnae tell Sam, isn't he?"

"Well, yeah? That's the point, isn't it?"

"So if I was Sam, I'd be wondering if they're using me to get to him. See?"

"But he trusts you," Sinead said quietly, as if suddenly doubting everything.

"Aye, but he knows and I know that anyone can be

compromised. Him and me have seen that happen often enough."

"I don't get it. You're such good friends …"

"Anyone who has anyone who they care about can be leveraged. It's just a fact. We saw that up close and personal. We worked in that world for a while. It's not pretty."

Sinead nodded. Sam had alluded to as much in a rare, slightly drunken conversation.

"So let me get this straight," Áine began, haughty and bolt upright. "If you contact them, Sam's going to think that someone's putting pressure on you to identify where he is so that they can arrest him?"

Min nodded slowly.

"And *she* can't contact him because he'll think that if *I* can track him down, then so can MI6?"

"It's more than that. He'll be certain they're involved because the only way to do this is through Daniel – and, sure, how could you two know about Daniel? He'll run all this through his head in a matter of seconds, and if I was him, I'd take off."

Áine's forehead creased. "Will he, though? He trusts both of ye."

"He knows that we both have things we won't risk," Min said quietly.

"You've got kids?" Sinead asked.

Min said nothing.

Áine turned to her sister. "What about you?"

Sinead gave her a long look.

"Me?" Áine spluttered. "Sam will think they're using me to turn you against him," she said, flabbergasted.

"Makes sense," said Min. "And what's the one thing he will never compromise?"

Sinead sat back, accepting the logic. "Isla. He'll never allow himself to be separated from her."

"So, explain this to me," Áine said, "what was the point of finding Daniel if we can't contact him?"

Min looked blank for a moment, as if a fundamental flaw had been identified. "We just need to think," he said eventually. "If we go in like a bull, he might run. He might not, but it's a risk. D'ye not think?"

Sinead nodded slowly. "He's right. If Daniel hands him a message – or even hands him the phone – Sam's likely to hoist the sails and head for the horizon."

"Assuming Sam's even there at all," Min said.

"No question, then, Sinead said. "We need to tread softly. We can't have them shooting off into the Atlantic. We'd lose them again for sure."

Chapter Eight

IT WAS late by the time they finished up, despondent, in front of the bank of screens. Large and plush as the apartment was, it only had two bedrooms. Hotels remained closed and, strictly speaking, Min wasn't even permitted in the apartment at all.

"I can kip on the floor, don't worry," he said. "I'm well used to worse."

"You will not," Áine replied, which earned a cocked head from Sinead. "She's got a spare bed in her room. Isla slept on it when she stayed here before."

"Oh, no, that wouldn't be right," Min replied.

"Not for you, you eejit. For me."

Sinead, stunned, was slowly stacking it up. Her twin, who abjectly refused to allow anyone close, was offering her inner sanctum to a man she had just met.

"I'll just sort a few things and put on some fresh linen." She walked off.

"Really, darlin', that's not necessary—"

"Call me *darling* once more and you can sleep on the street," came Áine's inadequate defence as she vanished.

Min turned to Sinead, shaking his head, "I really can kip on the couch."

"Take it as a compliment," she said. "She obviously wants you to have a comfortable bed."

"Aye," was all he said, looking at the empty space through which Áine had travelled.

Sinead's shoulders tightened as a line of worry developed for her twin. "Is there anyone at home you need to call, a wife or girlfriend?"

Min smiled, understanding immediately. "No, thanks anyway, there isnae a woman waiting for a phone call."

"A man, maybe?"

Min laughed at that. "I may be in the navy, Sinead, but I dance at the other end of the ballroom."

Sinead allowed herself a smile and fleetingly imagined a different, happier life bundled into one extremely unlikely outcome. Min unwittingly shattered the thought.

"We've made a lot of assumptions," he said, staring at Áine's bedroom door.

"How do you mean?" Sinead asked, thinking he was about to elaborate on his lack of a love life.

"About Sam, about Dominica. It often happens when you're desperate. You grab onto the skinniest of threads and you pull. But really, we havnae a clue whether he's even in that part of the Caribbean – or if he's gone to the West Indies at all."

Sinead looked down at her hands, suddenly fighting an almost overwhelming urge to weep. She sucked her tongue onto the roof of her mouth, unable to respond. Min realised his mistake.

"Sorry, love," he began, "I sometimes forget who I'm talking to."

Sinead shook away the apology as unnecessary. "You're right," she said softly, and rose to head for her own bedroom. "Night, Min."

Sinead lay on her bed and listened to the murmur of Áine and Min. She heard a clink of a glass and the two of them moved into the living room. She could imagine them looking out over Dublin, getting to know one another a little better. She was still awake three hours later when Áine's over-exaggerated foot placements crept through the room. Áine didn't even undress, just threw back the covers and clambered in. Within minutes Sinead heard a gentle snore from her sister and rolled over.

IT WAS pitch-dark when she woke, dragged, again, from her sleep by the pain of her mistake. Her dream bore different characteristics but it came down to the same thing: she had let him go. Her decision, and the consequences were hers to bear. Her imagination had conjured Sam and Isla on a beach with someone else, dark and beautiful, playing in the surf, laughing. She'd woken when the woman took Isla's hand to lead her up the sand. The darkness in the room made her loneliness and her ache worse. Only once before had she felt her heart physically hurt within her body. As quietly as she could she sniffed back the tears and the loss.

ÁINE NEVER COULD SLEEP WELL for long with drink in her. She lay, stone-still, and listened to her sister sob as

FINN OG

silently as she could. She knew that this was very likely a nightly occurrence, and while it frustrated her, it upset her too. She waited until the sniffling stopped and Sinead's breathing regulated, then as quietly as someone quite pissed could manage, she crept from the room.

The way forward seemed so clear to her. She told herself she would do the same if she were sober. She punched in the code to her office keypad, and her arms reached out and flicked the systems into life, drawing up the information. Her fingers were slightly sluggish on the keyboard, but muscle memory helped her crack back into the environmental agency's staff gateway. Within five minutes she had found a country code, a number and scribbled it onto a Post-it. She slid the phone her sister had brought from the convent into her pocket and wobbled to the front door, making her way down in the elevator. Two blocks of apartments up the street, she switched the phone on and held it aloft, searching for a Wi-Fi signal that didn't require a password. Frustrated, she connected to Dublin's city bubble and began punching the number for Daniel Joseph into WhatsApp, overly careful to ensure the fug of drink wasn't making her forget any important steps. Áine smiled as she was treated to an image of a man in a tiny circle – a handsome, rugged face with the wake of a wave in the background. She tried an internet call.

"Hallo?" a rich, deep voice answered eventually.

"Is that Daniel Rosseau Joseph?" she said.

There was a moment's silence. She looked at the clock and vaguely worked out the time difference, wondering what the man must make of the slurred use of his full name on what, for him, was a midnight call.

"What has happened?" he asked, and she could tell he was afraid for someone.

"Nothing." She tried to shake herself. "Nothing to, eh, worry about."

"Who is this? Do you know what time it is?" She thought she could listen to his Caribbean lilt for hours.

"I'm calling from Dublin." Áine closed her eyes in realisation that she had not thought this through. "My name is Áine, and I desperately need to talk to a man called Sam. If you've seen him, please, tell him I need to speak to him urgently about Sinead." There was a long silence. "Hello? Daniel?"

She heard a rattle and a bump but at least the man hadn't hung up. The noise increased and Áine considered ending the call, fearing that she may, in her inebriation, have precipitated the worst of all outcomes by blundering in. Sinead would struggle to forgive this one.

The phone was muffled, as if a hand had been placed across the handset, and Áine could hear two drones – like conversation. Alarm caused her to hover her thumb over the red button in readiness to end the call.

"Áine?" a breathy voice suddenly burst through her speaker, whispered but urgent.

"Sam?" she said, excitement swelling through her.

"What's happened?"

"What?"

"Is she ok?"

"Yes, she's ok." Áine struggled to get a grip of herself so as not to spook him.

"How did you …? Is this …?"

"Everything is fine. Everything. Do you understand? *Everything* is ok. Not what you think." She bit her lip in frustration at her addled explanation, suddenly conscious of her inability to speak sensibly. There was a moment's silence that she felt the need to fill. "There's stuff you need to know

– things have changed." She pulled the phone momentarily from her ear in frustration and caught the image of Daniel Joseph on his boat on the screen. "Your fish isn't on the hook any more." She screwed her eyes shut at the stupidity of what she'd just said.

"Stop," he said. "Not on the phone. But she's ok?"

"Yes, fine, all fine."

"Ok, ok." He paused. "But not on the phone."

The line went dead and Áine realised she hadn't said the most important part.

Chapter Nine

MIN WAS SITTING at the breakfast bar when the twins ambled through into the kitchen. Áine looked like she'd been hit with a digger bucket; Min looked like he'd been out for a run.

"Have you …?" she began.

"Sure, even in lockdown you're allowed one bit of exercise a day, aren't you?"

"Unbelievable," Áine muttered. "Bloody machines, you lot are." She rattled a spoon into a mug and flicked on the coffee machine.

"Thanks for the bed."

"No problem," she said absently, but Sinead could see that there was a dismissiveness designed for her rather than Min – a protective mechanism posing as nonchalance.

"I'll have to head back to barracks soon."

Sinead was looking at Áine's stiffening back, noting that she poured her coffee before it had percolated. The fizz of the drops hit the hotplate in a mirror of her sister's temperament.

Sinead tried to brighten the mood. "What else can we do – before you head off?"

"I went for a jog to clear ma heed – to try to think of something. I still havnae come up with anything."

"There must be some way to get a message to them." Sinead tried not to sound like she was on the cusp of desperation.

"There will be. It'll come to one of us. Only it's not … obvious just at the minute."

"Maybe this is the way it's supposed to work out. Maybe he was meant to, just, disappear."

Áine slammed the mug down, spilling coffee and turning angrily. "D'ye know how much you overthink things?" she barked at her sister. "For fuck's sake, like."

"What?" Sinead was startled.

Áine's head was banging with the after-effects of the whiskey. "He's there. He's exactly where we thought he was."

Min looked at Sinead. Sinead looked at Min. They both looked at Áine.

"We can't be sure of that," Min said gently. "It's a bit of a wide arc. Likelihood is he's in South America, bumping round rogue states, far out of the reach of British extradition treaties."

Áine seized upon their dithering and made her confession "He's not," she growled. "And you know how I know? I spoke to him last night." She leaned back on the counter and crossed her arms in an aggressive stance. Min and Sinead stared open-mouthed.

"You what?" Sinead's neck stretched forward, appalled.

"Well, feck it, anyway, Sinead. Ye pair were going to noodle around for ages, just like you did when you should have got on that bloody boat before they left. Instead, you got your priorities all bollixed about. I heard you last night—"

"Áine," Sinead warned through a clenched jaw, imploring her not to go further in front of their guest.

"I did, and I'm sick of it. Your moping around, you being so upset. So, yeah, to hell with it – I rang him."

"Who?" Min asked.

"Daniel. I got the number from his work's back end and I rang him, and within two minutes I was speaking to Sam."

There was a stunned silence for a full ten seconds.

"And what did he say?" Sinead's eyes were enormous, suddenly wet and full of fear.

"Hang on." Min's authority suddenly surfaced. "Be clear. You rang him on a phone from this flat?"

"Course not."

"Talk me through what you did," Min said calmly, but with a hitherto concealed sternness.

"Am I a child?" Áine snapped.

"Just explain," he said firmly.

"We have a phone. Sinead got it from some hooker at the refuge—"

"She wasn't a—"

Áine held her hand up to halt the interruption. "The phone is a pay-as-you-go, loads of credit and disabled for all but internet calls. I walked towards the city centre, hooked onto the town Wi-Fi and used an encrypted service to make a call."

The corners of Min's mouth turned down and he gently nodded his approval. "Fair enough."

"What did he *say*?" Sinead cut in, patience exhausted.

"Very little, actually." Áine could not abandon her hostile stance. "But I tried to tell him he was in the clear."

"You didn't?" Min said.

"I bloody did," Áine turned to face him, "cos what's the point in finding him if we can't do anything about it? Like eating soup with a hammer."

"Bloody hell," Min muttered.

"What will he do?" Sinead asked Min.

"I've no idea," Min said.

"What would you do?"

"Well, I'd either stay put or go to sea." He looked at Áine's now-turned back. "Depends on what you said, exactly."

Áine held her forehead and tried to quieten the pain. "I told him he's off the hook and everything is ok."

"And what did he say?" Sinead asked.

"He said, *Not on the phone.*"

"Then what did you say?"

"I said you were ok."

"Me?"

"Yeah."

"He asked about me?"

"Yeah."

"Then what?"

"Then he hung up."

———

MIN WAS unaccustomed to his advice being disregarded. At first it stirred an irritation in him just short of anger, but he rapidly altered his thinking. Of course, the women weren't military, and Áine's actions couldn't be thought of as insubordinate. He quietly reminded himself that he was out of Arbroath. Nonetheless, he was preparing to leave within fifteen minutes.

"You travel light," Áine said.

He didn't know her well, but could see her sheepishness. He looked at his little ruck. "Aye, well, don't need much, and I'm on a bike."

"Oh?"

"Aye, it's at the convent. Sinead—"

"She drove. I know. She'll drop you back."

"Aye," he said, looking at her.

"Will we see you again?"

Min thought about what to say for a moment too long, spurring her to speak.

"I fucked up," Áine said. He could see she was angry only at herself now. She sighed, turned from the hallway and marched towards her office. Min looked at her and failed to grasp one sensible or useful word to throw at the pleasant sight of her retreating transom.

"Right, so." Sinead appeared with a rattle of keys, noticing the look of despondence on his face and closing her eyes in familiar irritation as the control room door slammed. Min shrugged.

———

THE DRIVE WAS slow despite the absence of traffic. Sinead, without realising it, was delaying Min's departure while she struggled to get a question out.

"Look, darlin', just ask whatever it is that's on yer mind."

She breathed in, locked her arms against the wheel, and began slowly. "When we first met …"

"You and Sam?"

"No, you and me, in Scotland."

85

"Aye?"

"And you and Sam went off in that fancy boat."

"Uh-huh?"

"I don't know if you ... maybe you don't want to ..."

"Just ask, Sinead."

"What did you talk about?"

"How d'ye mean?" he said, genuinely confused as to the line of questioning.

"Well, did you ... did you talk about what Sam was going to do ... with those terrorists?"

"Just be mindful," Min said, his broad palm out in a calming gesture, before sweeping the air. Sinead admonished herself but was perturbed that a man like Min was still cautious of loose talk in a car with only two people in it.

"Sorry," she said, shutting up.

"The answer is no. That wasnae really on the agenda. There was something I needed to tell him, but the rest was not discussed."

"Then what was discussed?" she blurted out.

"I can't—why? I'm not following what you're on about?"

"Did you talk about me and him, Min?" she fired it out before it got jammed. "Did he mention anything about maybe taking me with him – or was it all just spur of the moment, something he hadn't thought through?"

"Ah, right," the penny plummeted. "You're worried it was just a kind of a – like, an impulse thing when he asked you to go with him?"

"Yeah. And you're his closest friend, and he never explained anything – well, hardly anything, and I'm just so fucking confused."

She could feel Min assessing her turmoil. Swear words did not fall easily from her lips and she felt vulnerable having succumbed to such emotion in front of a man she barely knew.

"Yes," he said softly. "We spoke about you."

Sinead's heart began to hammer and she stared straight-ahead at the road, resisting the urge to look at him. She waited, her exasperation building at the lack of elaboration.

They turned a corner and were already driving along the walled road that led to the convent entrance.

"My bike's in that copse over there," he said.

Sinead couldn't slow the car any further as they drove into the estate, bumping along a path ill-suited to vehicles. She came to a halt and pulled the handbrake harder than was necessary. She kept looking ahead, making out a motor-bike hidden among the trees.

Min readied to leave, his fingers on the handle.

"Am I making a mistake?" she said, as firmly as she was able.

"What d'ye mean?"

"Áine says I know nothing about him – and she's bloody right." Sinead was shaking her head, staring without focus deep into the copse.

"He's no' easy to get to know, I'll give you that. But it is worth the effort."

"What is?"

"Taking the time to find out."

"There's been a lot of time, Min." She eventually turned to face him, before looking back into the darkness of the trees. "Time wasted, maybe."

"Look, I don't know how much you know about – you know – before. That's for you and him to discuss. But if you mean, are you doing the right thing in finding him and sorting it all out?" Min struggled for the right phrase. "Then I'd say, absolutely, darlin'. No question. That man's full to the lid with demons, but he's as decent a bloke as I've ever known."

He pushed open the door and Sinead yearned to hug him, but within seconds his head was in a helmet, the bike was rocked backwards and a gloved hand waved as he drove off.

Chapter Ten

ÁINE WONDERED who she had damaged more – herself or her sister. There had been times during their childhood when bickering had morphed into long periods of silence – Sinead refusing to be drawn into the vocal arguments Áine was inclined to favour. Instead, her twin would withdraw into maudlin reflection, a type of depression. Áine called it "the gloom". She'd use the word to their mother – "Sinead's in the gloom" or "Oul Granny Gloom's in the house". She'd dismiss the mood and almost completely, successfully, ignore it. Áine also had a capacity for avoiding repentance, knowing that eventually Sinead would surface and gradually their relationship would right itself without much of a word said in reflection. If it did affect Áine, she simply refused to admit it.

For almost three weeks Sinead wallowed in the gloom, acknowledging her sister but not sitting with her in the evenings, not allowing herself to be drawn into conversation. She politely declined suggestions that they watch a movie or have a drink. Not once did she accept the offer of a coffee or share a dinner. In fact, she didn't eat very much at all. Áine considered it her sister's way of punishing the offender, hitting back at her for having called Sam despite the risks, but as the gloom dragged on she began to realise that Sinead was not capable of sustaining such intended vengeance or spite. This was not retribution – it was hurt.

One evening, in the fourth week of gloom, Sinead's mood altered. She bustled into the apartment in a hurry, clutching the post. Áine had given up offering a "Hi, how was your day?" She had grown to expect nothing in return, yet today she received one unbidden.

"Hello," Sinead said, and the curt utterance gave her sister hope of an emergence. Sinead left down three letters, kept one and vanished into her room.

Áine stared at the space left by her twin.

———

SINEAD EXAMINED THE ENVELOPE CLOSELY. For a long time before opening it she lectured herself on not allowing her hopes up, afraid it would contain nothing other than some work issue. It was unusual, and in so being gave her an excitement she struggled to contain. There was no address, no stamp, no hint of its provenance, yet hand-written in the centre was one word: Sinead. Many things passed through her mind as she turned it over and held it to the light bulb – Min? One of the nuns? They wrote letters all the time rather than using the email she had set up for them.

If it wasn't from either of those quarters, then how did it get into their letter box, inside their apartment block's main doorway, without an address on it? Without a flat number, the concierge wouldn't know which locked box to select, would he? The old man never used her name when she left home or returned. In the end she packaged her hopes, prepared herself for disappointment and gently slipped the leaf with her thumbnail.

Hello,

Please excuse the lack of names and whatnot. I just need to know what way the land lies because I don't really understand what's going on. It's taken a while to follow up but that's only because I needed to find a way of doing it without, well. Anyway, after a lot of thinking I found a way that makes sense.

First, I hope you're ok, better than ok. I hope you're really well, and that the other one is too. I got a shock when I heard from her, but in hindsight perhaps I shouldn't have because I know how handy she is. What I don't get, though, is what it was all about. That's why I'm being so opaque here. I don't know what or how much can be said just now.

But we're fine. We'll probably keep moving, so, and this isn't to put you under any pressure or anything because you maybe don't want to, but if you do want to reply, then I've made an arrangement with someone. I know this should reach you without interference, so to reply – if you'd like to, that is, leave it in a plastic wrap taped to the underside of the lid of your recycling bin. All a bit mad but I can't think of a better way. It's kind of pressing, though, so if you do want to, if it could be soon, then we won't miss it.

I don't know what else to say because I don't know where you're at, but hopefully you know you're being badly missed. You-know-who is asking about you all the time.

Best to burn this or whatever after reading and that will hopefully keep us all between the hedges.

Sinead flicked over the page, incredulous. She knew she would find the other side blank. No signature, no handwriting, just plain type printed out. She sat stock-still and didn't know whether to smile in delight or hit the wall in anger. Confusion furrowed her brow and she tried not to cry.

What the hell is this? What is he thinking? Is this supposed to make things clear?

Her mind went blank for a few minutes, stunned perhaps. Then she decided: all this excuse for a letter did was make things worse.

You're being badly missed. By whom – by him? He suggested it was by Isla – or did he mean both of them? She growled in frustration and was tempted to tear the page apart, as instructed.

"Fuck's sake." All this time – and *this* is it?

She read it again, hunting for solace between the neatly printed lines. She found none despite scrutinising the words again and again. If it had been her, she'd have found a way of saying what needed to be said without compromising them all. But this – what was this? A letter? A note? A bloody memo? It had the feel of something put together in a half-assed rush. She knew he wasn't much of a communicator, but still. She closed her eyes, willed herself to be calm, and then the exhaustion of wondering and weeks of sleeplessness eventually took over and she slept until her 5 a.m. alarm summoned her to work.

———

ALL SENSE HAD DESERTED CLODAGH. Her self-appointed exalted status within the convent was dinging the other women like a fairground striker. Sinead had tried to put off addressing the obvious in the hope that the situation would resolve itself, but when one of the senior nuns approached her, she knew she'd have to whack the mole.

"The young lady from Clontarf," the nun began, her approach befitting the gentle nudge that was intended, "is rather determined to have her own way, we've noticed."

We've conveyed her meaning perfectly. The nuns were not part of a silent order, but they didn't, as a rule, say a great deal, so if they'd been talking about the dinner lady, then her time was definitely up.

"Has she stepped out of line, sister?" Sinead asked, feigning ignorance.

"She is rather overbearing, dear," was the reply, "even with some of our religious visitors." The nun nodded knowingly, as if imparting crucial direction without feeling compelled to issue orders. Sinead knew her charity's endurance was only a given with the support of the nuns – both financially and for accommodation. She closed her eyes in acquiescence and thanked the old woman for the unwelcome command.

The news did not go down well.

"Hi, Sinead," Clodagh said brightly, turning with a massive saucepan in hand as she entered the kitchen.

"Hello," Sinead said with an awkward grimace. "Can we have a word, do you think?"

"If it's about the state of the place, then I'm tired telling them. This pan was supposedly washed before, you know, but I'll get them in order, Sinead, don't worry!" she said brightly, as if it were these two women against the tardiness and lethargy of the world.

Sinead's patience was not as inexhaustible as it might have been on a better day, in a better month. Her anger with Sam made her think of a few things about him – his uncanny ability to be listened to when speaking, his no-bull-shit attitude when getting things done. His style and approach flitted through her thoughts and she immediately adopted a tone she had heard him use.

"Sit down," she said, drawing her chin into her clavicle.

Clodagh placed the pan on the counter, her smile flattening immediately.

Oh, this works, thought Sinead.

"Have you had issues with your manner before?" she said, not sternly, but adopting Sam's occasional detachment.

"Eh, how do you mean?"

Sinead resisted the urge to buckle and use pleases and thank yous and I'm sorrys.

"I think you know what I mean," she said dully.

Clodagh's hands came up in front of her face and her elbows reached for the table before her. "I'm sorry, Sinead," she said, "I just ... I get carried away."

The day before, Sinead would have reached out for her, stroked her bare arm and given her another chance – knowing even then that it wouldn't work, but she was tired of lost causes, and wondered if she, herself, might be the worst of such cases.

"I think you're ready to find a place outside the fold," Sinead said. "You're clearly strong, you have the will, and we all know you've got the drive. So think of it as good news. You're ready to stand on your feet again – be proud of that."

The woman's hands parted and her reddened face looked out in shock. "You're ... you're throwing me out?"

"Everyone leaves," Sinead said. "That's the purpose of this place. We help people get back on the road and live independently of what they've escaped."

"But who will run the kitchen? Who will keep the women in order? The place will go to the dogs," she said.

If there was one thing Sinead detested, it was a lack of

self-awareness in people that made them feel superior to all around them.

"Nobody asked you to keep anyone in line," she said coolly. "That is not for you to do – that is barely even for me to do. This is a safe place for women and children to come to escape domestic and sexual abuse. We facilitate placements and help people get back to work and into the community. This is not a regime."

"Are you saying I'm running it like a regime?" Clodagh bristled, sitting upright, her annoyance morphing into anger.

"I'm saying *you're* not supposed to run it at all. You've taken that upon yourself and it isn't going down well."

Sinead was surprised at how tough she was being – it felt as alien as it was invigorating.

"Hardly surprising with the state of some of the women in here," Clodagh spat.

"Excuse me?" Sinead was immediately riled, and although she knew her anger was really deserved of someone else, she hadn't the energy to temper herself in the face of this reaction.

"Some of these women," Clodagh said with ice scraping in her voice, "brought their circumstances upon themselves."

Sinead forced herself to suppress what she was thinking. She let the hypocrisy of the comment pass and with as much zen as she could muster said, "We do not judge in here. We do not decide who has brought what upon themselves. It is time you moved into the community. We have a space at a women's refuge in Rathmines, and you can spend two weeks there. You should already have all your applications in order if you have followed the guidance given when you arrived. All you need to do is notify the agencies of your change of address, and we will forward any correspondence that comes here for you."

"On your head be it." Clodagh shoved back the chair. "You'll be sorry when you see the state of the place this time tomorrow. You won't be able to run it without the likes of me."

Sinead stared at the woman as she stomped off. I've been running it for years without you, she didn't say. But she did think about how the Sam approach had saved her an hour of tearful apology for her decision. It had prevented her backtracking from a position she knew was correct and would have resulted in a repeat eviction in any case. And this way, the abrasive reaction had left her feeling less bad about her chosen course.

Perhaps there was something to be said about being a hard-ass after all.

———

I'VE HAD A LONG DAY. I'll follow your patter, so, in not using names and "whatnot".

I'm tired, though, of beating around the burning bush, and I need to tell you that I'm cross – angry. And at the same time I'm worried that in telling you that, even this inadequate communication will close down. Therefore, as far as I'm able to via this means of conversing, I'm just going to come out and say to you: I'm pissed off.

Sinead reread what she had typed, slightly surprised at the formality of her tone, her lapse back into a training she had thought long forgotten. She shuffled forward, slouched – exhausted, and started again.

Could you not have said more? It's been months. Really, could you not have explained? I mean, for it all to be like,

"This is it. Will you come with?" was a total shock. I didn't even know there could be an ultimatum between us. Whatever "us" is – is there even an us?

I know I'm rambling, and I know I'm not in a good place, but at some stage I have to say this to you. This has been going on for so long now – if, in fact, anything has been going on, and, to be honest, I can't even answer questions from you-know-who about anything, really. I think one minute that I know you to your core, but I don't know the first thing, not really. Most of what I know I only "think" I know – robbed from snippets or unguarded moments before you shutter up and close the bloody shop for the night and I go off to my bunk and you go to who knows where. And the worst of it is – I can put up with all that vanishing into the night, disappearing and whatever the hell else, and I don't bloody think there are many who would. Underneath it all I somehow agree with what that's about, even though I can't say it because it's you who sets the rules, always. And the rule here seems to be to say nothing. So, for the record, I'm in agreement with all that – even though it seems to go against everything I've ever stood for or worked for or believed was right. But I can see that you have a kind of logic and sense to what you do, and I can live with that, in the same way you can't live without it, it seems.

What I can't live with, is not knowing. I'm all out of rope here, and it's not just the screamingly bloody obvious. It's being able to have a sensible conversation with 'the other one' as you put it. For crying out loud. Like when she says, "What do you really know?" What am I supposed to say? Seriously, I don't even know where you went to school. I couldn't tell her if you'd been to college or what led you to go off and do the things you do or did – whatever they are. I don't know the most basic things. I don't even know what age you are. Or if you've got a middle name. I don't care if you have a middle name or whether you're forty or fifty-fucking-five, but the more I think about it and write this, the more I realise that I just don't know anything about you personally.

I do know I'll always be second, and I know that many women wouldn't like that, but I am ok with that – more than ok with that. Much more than. You know all about my feelings there, and if you don't, then you're blind. And I know you're not blind because you somehow see things and know things that I could never see or know. I don't get how you instinctively work stuff out or notice shit that just about anyone else never would, YET you don't seem able to see what's staring you in the face.

Maybe I'm just typing this to get it out of my system because it's been a bad day and I need to vent. I hate people seeing me cross or upset and that's happened recently and I struggle with it. I can see you have struggles too – even a blind man can see that, but you won't share and I can't ask. I dunno. I doubt I'll send this, but this is how I feel. Pissed off.

And I don't want this to be the first thing you hear from me, I really don't, so I will probably write something else tomorrow when I'm in better form, but you'll probably have cleared out by then.

What I wanted the first thing I told you to be is this – all of this is so bloody unnecessary cos the other one has checked in all the right places and your trusted person (from Tinker's - yeah, we've spoken) has confirmed it. There is no one connecting any dots. To cut a long story short, all that last-minute will-you-won't-you head-wrecking stuff was not bloody necessary at all. It's been dealt with and no worm cans are about to be reopened. What do you think? It should be good news, so why is it making me so bloody angry?

––––––––

SINEAD LAY in bed for a long time the following morning. The thought of going to work on the day that Clodagh was due to leave was deeply unappealing. She normally wouldn't duck such a difficult conversation. If she felt responsible, she would flagellate herself before the nuns, taking all that was her due and much that wasn't on the tip of her chin. Yet, today, she was exhausted, thinking bad things about everyone she cared about, and chose, instead, to find a film on her phone and lie there. She didn't even ring to let Grace know.

After an hour she heard the front door open and close, felt the vibration of the elevator shaft working, and knew Áine had left the building. After twenty minutes the lift gently buzzed again and she pulled the duvet close, resolved not to answer whomever the concierge had allowed up.

The door opened again and a strike of alarm ran through her. Áine never collected the post or went to buy milk – that was down to Sinead. She tensed and worked out what she would do with an intruder, thumbing her phone ready to dial the Guards. Her worry was allayed when the keys were dropped – as was Áine's custom, in a porcelain bowl filled with gnarly scentless potpourri by the kitchen door.

Two crap films later she slunk through to the kitchen in her pyjamas, flicked on the kettle and looked at the door to the control room. Only then did she remember what she had left in there the night before. She tried not to run to the door, but, relieved, found Áine pouring through screeds of code on multiple screens.

"Hi," she said.

"Hi," Áine said without turning.

Sinead's eyes darted over the desk and hunted the screen bank.

"I left some papers in here last night."

"Over there." Áine's arm craned out, a stylus in her hand.

Sinead retrieved the page and the envelope and hovered.

"Did you …?"

"Started to, then realised it was from him."

"There isn't much of it, so if you started, you probably finished."

Áine said nothing.

"I used one of your computers last night."

"I know," Áine said.

Sinead faltered and made to turn away, but she longed for an opinion, some reassurance, at least a discussion. She felt, in that moment, deeply, horribly lonely. She faltered, then slowly walked away.

"That's the most you've said to me in a month," Áine said, no detectable tone to her voice.

Sinead paused. "I'm not angry with you," she said.

"It's worse than that," Áine said. "You're disappointed."

"I'm disappointed with a lot of things," Sinead said. "I just don't know what to make of it." She started to move again but Áine refused to let their dialogue re-enter the deep freeze.

"What you said was right, you know."

"What?"

"What you wrote in response."

"You read it?" Sinead turned to find her sister swivelled towards her.

"Of course I fucking read it. You haven't spoken to me for four weeks. You may not realise it, Sinead, but I love you. You are all I have and maybe all I'll ever have, and he needed to hear that from you."

"No, that was just anger – it was over the top. I had a bad day and I was just getting it out."

"You could have spoken to me. We had a deal after last time."

"Don't!" Sinead held up her hand. "I'm not going there, not now."

"I thought you were going there over these past few weeks, sis. I have been worried out of my fucking mind that you were going there, and you wouldn't talk to me. So enough's enough."

Sinead looked at the tears welling in her twin's eyes and suddenly realised what she'd done.

"No!" she panted.

Áine stared hard at her.

"No, Áine. This is not the time for tough love. You didn't – tell me you didn't?"

Áine crossed her arms but her eyes showed how unsure of herself she was. Sinead knew she had not expected to be rumbled.

Sinead tore for the door, pushed the elevator button repeatedly and hopped gently waiting for it to arrive. She slipped in before the doors fully opened and slammed her palm against the -1 button. Áine arrived just as the doors were closing and stepped in, standing like a lamped hare in the corner of the mirrored box. There was nowhere to look where Sinead couldn't see her sister wrangling with what to say by way of justification, so she stared at her bare feet.

The door opened and Sinead stepped out and ran past parked cars to the enclosure behind which the bins were stored. At the front of the bay Sinead lifted the lid of the one with their number melted onto the face of it. On the underside was a torn triangular remnant of parcel tape where something had been ripped from it.

She turned to Áine, who held up her hands. "He had to know. You've been too, like, permissive or something – too backwards!"

"You. Complete. Bitch," was all Sinead could say. She walked slow and stunned to the lift, returned to the apartment, packed a case, and left.

Chapter Eleven

SINEAD GAVE NO MERCY. Her day couldn't get any worse, so she watched as the dinner lady left the stone steps, crunched along the pebbled path and climbed into the taxi, glaring back at her as the car pulled off.

Her own case hammered and thumped as she dragged it up the steps, and Sinead decided to make good out of bad, seeking out the Mother Superior.

"I just want to let you know that with the place full, I'll be staying here to keep a better eye on things. I understand that with the lockdown it was getting a bit out of hand, so I'll be in the office at night, and any more issues just let me know. I'll make sure they are dealt with immediately this time."

The nun looked at her searchingly, almost with suspicion, then softened a little. "I'm sure there is no need to take you from your home, but if that is what you think is best, that's up to you."

The other women milled around and chatted, breaking for the door for smoke breaks on occasion. Sinead hid her case behind an old bookshelf, looked around the room and decided she would make the best of living in this dreary office for the next few weeks. Then she would find a place, somewhere, ignoring the fact that she paid herself next to nothing. Dublin's rents had been shoved beyond the reach of ordinary humans thanks to Airbnb, but perhaps the lock-down absence of tourists would allow some space for nego-tiation, she thought.

———

ÁINE LOOKED at the phone belonging to the woman who had run from the convent. She handled it cautiously, making a long-overdue decision to wipe it with alcohol sani-tiser; bottles of which Sinead had deposited all round the place. Despite rarely leaving the apartment, the Covid warnings were at long last finding their way into her consciousness, and she had a sudden urge to clean the face of the handset, given the muck stored within.

A debate was raging in her head: second contact to clear the air, or let the hare sit and hope for the best? She knew she had gone way too far this time in Sinead's eyes. She was as confident that what she had done had been for the right reasons as she was unsure that Sinead would forgive her within the calendar year. But there was more to it than that. Áine couldn't sit back and watch the degradation of her other half indefinitely. She knew her sister's damage was deep. Nobody knew the whole story, but nobody knew it better than Áine. It was Áine who had found her, and Áine who had the greatest investment in her repair – until Sam bloody Ireland had shown up with hope and promise and uncertainty and danger. Always with that man came ladles of danger.

She'd hated him initially, for the precarious position in which he'd placed her twin. That had lasted for a while, until Sinead had explained that their first contact had come about as a result of him helping her, and that he had, in fact, saved her from an attack. That made it hard for her to maintain her loathing, and Sinead had made it more difficult by repeatedly engaging his help. Áine knew that in the following months and years she and Sinead had become complicit in his reclusiveness, aiding and abetting it. It had happened again and again – with Sinead clinging to hope without expressing it, that her life might change to become a part of something that remained, somehow, always just out of reach.

Áine had always denied that she any regard for Sam; she found it easier to manage that way, but she knew it wasn't true. Had he been different – had he the ability to let Sinead be a part of his life instead of using her as a babysitter and leading her to the point of expectation before evaporating into the air, Áine might have been content. Sinead's happiness would bring her happiness, if loneliness. Maybe then Áine would get on with her own future, but not until she was sure that Sinead could manage, again, without her. Too much had happened, too much to allow herself to think about.

Áine took the phone and wandered aimlessly outside, making her way through the city's southside. She passed *The Irish Times* building – all but empty. There was little traffic noise save for the odd reckless hurtle of a long-wheelbase Ford delivery van, no doubt ferrying an Amazon package the size of an envelope.

She went up Merrion Street, where art would normally be displayed on the wrought-iron railings, past the Dáil, where a government was yet to be formed. She was surprised to find the park open and wandered past the memorial where she stared for a while at Oscar Wilde. She read his quotes that people had written on the pillars opposite his lounging.

Every saint has a past, and every sinner has a future.

Áine stared at that for a long time and tried to take from it some kind of affirmation that she had been right to send the letter.

Life is not complex. We are complex. Life is simple, and the simple thing is the right thing.

To which she found herself crying, silently, for a sister she was terrified of losing, for a relationship she desperately wanted her twin to obtain.

Always forgive your enemies; nothing annoys them so much.

Áine closed her eyes and asked that she might be forgiven. She wanted – more than anything in that moment, for Sinead to annoy her through forgiveness, yet she would not ask for that. She lifted the phone, inputted the code she had cracked and changed the settings. She waited for a moment to allow it to find a wireless connection, then sent a message to Daniel Joseph. Plan complete, she dropped the phone into a rubbish bin and took out her own handset: *I've done the only thing I can to make this right. I've explained that I sent your letter – that you didn't intend to. I don't know what else I can do.*

She tapped the send circle and walked the slow, lonely road back to the apartment.

Chapter Twelve

SINEAD STARED AT THE WALL. It was easy to ignore the flutter of the notes she'd Blue-Tacked to it. Beneath them a little three-bar burner agitated the papers as it vainly attempted to heat the office. Her hideaway was a twentieth-century afterthought, bolted on but never connected to the clanking pipes of the convent.

She knew things were bad when the nuns showed signs of worry about her. There was no real way to define a nun. It had taken her a long time to get her head around the fact that they were just people, like anyone else, subject to the same proclivities and weaknesses of any woman or man. Their uniform gave them structure and even their names could offer superiority, but she imagined they harboured the same urges and thoughts, generous and wicked, as the next person. Perhaps they were better at suppressing their dreadful side – for everyone possessed that, in Sinead's opinion; that willingness to imagine the demise of those who had done you harm, who had treated others poorly, or appallingly. Sinead had willed and even prayed to avoid such delicious thoughts of comeuppance and retribution, but had grown to accept them as part of the intricate weave of the mind – perhaps offering protection from the vile follow-through that such imaginings quenched. Unlike Sam. Sam did not leave those instincts in his head. He did not satisfy his discontent by simply dreaming of vengeance. And she admired that, wrong as she knew it surely must be.

Sinead's had been an existence of arguing against many of the building blocks of Christian society – using its own logic against itself while still adhering to the faith. The black-lipped bar debates of her student days in which she had levered rudimentary knowledge of the scriptures against her adversaries; an eye was not to be removed – rather a plank. Ours was not not to judge – God had made that clear, surely? And where Sodom was destroyed because of baying mob hostility, not because of a wilful misinterpretation of the exact same mentality.

The paper notes on the wall were about as important as her degrees, now. Thinking of her university days, her bold years of conviction and surety made her realise how little Sam knew of her. They had never discussed her teenage years, her own education, the career she had abandoned – perhaps against her will, perhaps because it had been ordained. She wondered whether her suffering had had purpose, and if so, why was she being subjected again?

Sam had never asked about her past – did that mean he hadn't cared, or was he content to know her as she was? A leopard cannot change its spots, she thought, but scars and burns can alter them.

"Is everything alright, Sinead?" the Mother Superior had inquired, having made an unusual journey to the office on the outskirts of the cold, austere complex. Sinead had been embarrassed to be discovered, fully clothed, in her sleeping bag on the camp bed. The nun could see she had been crying.

"Yes, thank you. Has something happened?" She'd rolled herself bolt upright, catching the zip in the thin fabric of her sleeping bag in her effort to manoeuvre. Snarled shut she was forced her to lie back down again and kick it off in the most ignominious fashion.

"Did you have a long night?" asked the nun, looking pointedly at the clock that read midday. Sinead knew the old women rose at five.

"I've been up and down. Sleep has rather been eluding me," she muttered.

"Confession," the old woman quipped. "Confession is what you require, young woman."

Only one as old as her could call me a young woman, Sinead thought, or one who had long since abandoned hope of intimacy.

She fell back upon the cot when the door closed – may as well be hung for a sheep as a lamb, she reckoned. She prayed then, that he had moved on before the letter had arrived, that he had taken to sea. Then she prayed that they would avoid hurricanes, that her sadness had not sent them towards the storm. Darkness folded in upon her and she felt – for the first time – bereft of a family that had been offered to her and that she had refused, and she was angry only with herself.

———

DAYS PASSED without major event at the refuge. Clodagh's absence had instilled a temporary equilibrium. Paperwork was filed and placements for the women slowly secured.

"Missus, missus." Sinead was working at the computer

when her door opened a crack. She recognised the voice of the youngest woman taken in since lockdown began; an inner-city kid from the Liberties who had – as yet – refused to explain how the marks down her back had been inflicted.

"Yes? Come in, Macy."

Sinead lamented that girls who had been named after music acts of her youth were already adults.

"Missus, your sister's here for ye," she spluttered.

"Take a message!" Sinead called at the closing door, unsure whether Macy had heard the instruction.

She waited, still, at her desk, wondering what would happen next. Would Áine be shown up? Would she refuse to have a message ferried and instead march in causing a holy show in front of the women and the nuns?

Long minutes ticked by as Sinead tried to work out what she would prefer. Then, before she had decided, the door cracked again and Macy's hand came in.

"Letter for ye, missus," the hand waved.

"Just come in!" Sinead barked, and the door pushed open a little further, the grey roots of her bowed head leading to a sheepish peering as she waited for further direction. Sinead fleetingly wondered whether the greying at such a tender age betrayed stress and hard upbringing - her body if not her mind old before its time.

"Thank you," Sinead said as Macy handed over an envelope.

"She's went off," Macy said, nodding without knowing what to do next. "Your sister, yeah. Went off."

"Ok. Thank you, Macy," Sinead said, willing her to leave now.

"I was wondering," Macy whipped up some hidden courage. "I was wondering if, like, I might be allowed to try for me qualifications, you know?"

Sinead's heart was hammering. The envelope was exactly as before – blank but for her name, handwritten. This time, though, heavier, thicker. She exhaled and drew her eyes reluctantly to the young woman.

"What qualifications are you thinking of?" she said distractedly.

"I dunno. Anything, really. Anything would be good seeing as I haven't a one, like."

"No Inter Cert?"

"Naw!" Macy said, her brows creasing as her head shook, accompanied by an incredulous laugh.

"Well, what might you like to do – as a job?"

"Ah, you'll think I'm mad, like."

"I won't," Sinead said, suddenly torn between interest in what her ambition might be, yet touching the envelope and trying to regulate her breathing.

"I was thinkin', I might like to do a bit of what you do."

"Oh," said Sinead, with a surprise that earned her an immediate look of embarrassment in return.

"Stupid, I know," Macy said and pulled the door closed in front of her. Sinead leapt up, compelled to explain herself. She opened the door and called down the hall to the escaping woman. "You don't understand," she said. "I've never had anyone want to do something I do before. I'm … really flattered, I think."

Macy paused and almost turned. "Naw, it was a stupid idea." She began to run.

"Come back this evening!" Sinead called. "We'll get the ball rolling." But she wasn't sure Macy would listen.

———

I'M NOT good at this, I know that. I hadn't meant to annoy you, really. It was stupid and I know that now, I can see that now. But when I wrote first, I didn't understand all that was going on. All I really knew was that you didn't want to come with us, and I totally got that, but I didn't really think through why, or register that it was the suddenness of it all that had been the problem. Not that that was the only problem – I get that, I've always known that.

But I promise I will do my best. It might take a bit of getting out, and bloody hell I haven't written a letter in so long, so long. I haven't spoken to anybody, not properly – apart from you and a priest in Italy, believe it or not, in years. So, please, bear with me. I'll try to fill in some blanks, and although I'm happy enough that this way of getting word to you is as tight as it can be, nothing is infallible and so, again, please stick with me here. I'm still checking things but I get what you're saying. I'm treading softly but thank you for looking at the dots and who may be joining them.

I don't know where to start now. It might take a bit of prompting – maybe when I was a young fella? I had a great wee life, to be honest. I was reared by the sea, half on it at times. The shore was a play park, and although I'll not go into locations just yet, it was in the north and family was strong and kind and fun. There were a few of us. I'll not go into specifics but we had the craic and most of what I remember is being afloat and messing and building huts and roaming the beaches and building boats.

We worked from early doors, fish or at the boats, learning stuff, and we learned to drink our wages and – the hard way – not to bet them on a horse race at lunchtime with old boys who would take your envelope from you on payday. I got a pound an hour on my first job, and the kids next door couldn't see the point. Forty quid for forty hours of stiff back on the seabed at low tide. The neighbours just messed and played, but we got a flavour of real life, all life, really – of working men and growing up fast. I loved it. Pints on a Thursday, wages gone by Saturday, taking second jobs teaching squaddies how to sail.

You'll remember the place was full of soldiers back then, and there was a place where they came to do water sports, and I showed them how. The regulars were dead on – nice fellas out of their depth, not much older than me, but they were carrying guns when they worked and most of them couldn't understand why the locals hated them. Then there were their bosses, and I'm telling you all this cos maybe it'll make sense later, but they were a different breed altogether. "There's nothing in there for you," I remember one of them shouting at me, pompous prick, as I went into a shed to get his boat ready. He assumed I was some scally in to pinch stuff. He got some shock when I turned out to be his coach. He couldn't take direction – more brains in a mackerel, yet he was in charge of a whole brigade.

Anyway … we were handy at it, the boats and that. We competed and did ok, and then people asked us to race their big fancy boats for them and we did that and we got about the place, seeing and sailing and getting a few quid in the pocket. And we were sent to a school with a great reputation that cost the folks a fortune, but that's the way they were – all about giving us the best opportunities and options and letting us think for ourselves, but guiding us, gently and almost imperceptibly at times, to just do the right thing and let the rest of it look after itself. They were workers too – the most decent people. Spent their lives working for other people when, in all honesty, they could have done anything and been anything, but that's what they chose. We were really proud of that. It was good, all that time, as a youngster. It was better than good. Sometimes I look back on it now and fail to think of how it could have been any better.

I'm just checking your letter, and it was fair enough – in case you're worried. I got the message from the other one, that you didn't send it and hadn't meant to, but maybe it's what I needed to realise. I was being thick and I'm sorry.

Right – middle name. I'll tell you that and my age when all is sorted. It just never occurred to me, not once, that you didn't know. But I don't think that was the point, was it? Or am I being thick again? I'm probably being thick again. I can see you-know-who looking at me sometimes, shaking her head as if mine has wandered off. I'm read like a book, my failings all laid bare in one look from her.

College, you asked about college. I didn't go to university. I was meant to, alright, but then something happened. It wasn't great and I'll go into more detail another time. Please understand I will tell you about it (if you want to hear it, of course) when it's more, kind of, appropriate (you understand what I mean?) to get into the weeds with all that. But it happened at school and it was ugly, and even though you were very kind in throwing me a bone over some of the stuff I've been involved in, this might test you. So, there you have it, or don't, but I promise you will.

That's what led to the ultimatum I got. It was one way or the other, and although I would never have considered the track I took otherwise, there was really no other sensible option. You broadly know where that ended up, and I have to be honest, there are very likely to be cans of worms I will never open here. I don't know how much of an issue that will be for you – and I know I'm making assumptions here cos maybe it won't be an issue because maybe you won't want there to be more conversations or letters or anything and I'd understand – I really would, but since I left the quay I know that's not what I want.

I don't really know where to go next. I feel kind of hamstrung until these checks come back – not that I don't trust the other one, just that for obvious reasons I have to be sure.

I'm nervous about saying this next bit, but you had the courage to put down some stuff that needed to be said, so I ought to too. I know I haven't asked that much about your past. Agh, how to explain this? I know that we both have stuff in the locker. I knew from the first time we met and you flinched when I was making sure you weren't injured. I don't want to upset you. I'm a blunt enough instrument at times, and I'm not sure you will ever want to go to wherever that leads. I don't even know how to say this, but if you ever did – want to go there – I'll go with you.

I hope that came out the way I mean it.

Sinead smiled and a tear ran down her face. She traced her finger down the page, turned it over, and lifted her phone.

Thank you, sis.

Then she flicked the mouse, woke the screen, and began.

Chapter Thirteen

SOME OF THE stuff I said was harsh and you were never meant to hear it (she's a bitch for sending it), but it has made me think. It was unfair, in a way, because I just assumed that my past maybe wasn't that important, that maybe you don't really care about anything from before. To be honest, I'm not sure you care about it still, but maybe that's not a bad thing. I've been confused, I said that last time, but gradually I'm coming out of it – at least I think I will, after I got your letter.

I have no idea how this is working, by the way. How your letters just turn up and everything. And it strikes me now that I don't even know who is writing my name on the front because I don't know your handwriting. But that seems inconsequential now, in light of what you said. But you're right – we have befores that either need excised or not. There I am again – talking like a fecking lawyer.

Which is probably as good a place as any to explain that part, at least. I was a lawyer, half a lifetime ago now. Me and that wee bitch grew up in Dublin, not far from the

beach, as it happens. I wish we still had that house now –
it'd be worth a fortune. It was small and only one part of it
was really ours, but it looked fantastic and we could be
down on the long sand in ten minutes. We used to walk to
Lansdowne Road on match days and sell Mars Bars and
Twixes, three for a pound, well, punts they were then, long
before the euro arrived. Mum caught us at it once and took
the money, but she gave it back when we went on holidays.
Do you want to know this stuff? I'm just writing away
because I asked you and you answered, but maybe you
don't? There were other things, to be honest, that you didn't
answer from that letter I never meant to send – just by
the way.

I've been taking a leaf out of your book, kind of, and it's
paying off. I'm being more hard-ass. I kicked a one out
yesterday – she was being a pain in the hole – and I used
your approach. It's quite fun, to be honest. I think I might
keep it up. And I'm swearing a lot more now too. I
blame you.

It's almost easier to talk to you in a letter. I don't know
why. Sometimes I find you so silent. Not that that's a bad
thing, but I do wonder what's going on in there. I do think
that for me it will be important to know more, even if it isn't
for you. I have a kind of … not sure about this, a sort of
need at this stage for reassurance. That probably doesn't
make sense, but, you're right, there has been stuff, and I'd
maybe get into it only for fear of it giving too much away
about who we are and spooking something or making you
take off. But you did go into some detail yourself – and why
is it that talking to you in a letter makes me waffle? Is it
waffle or whaffle? I don't care, but I'm definitely doing it
right now and you're however many miles away and making
me feel like a schoolgirl.

And, yeah, I was a convent girl. I don't even know if you're Catholic. I'm guessing not if you were allowed to teach British soldiers how to sail. Maybe that was permissible – I have no idea. That was all so alien to us down here – the Troubles. It was just stuff on TV. Not real. It was … black and white, I want to say. Black-and-white TV, it reminds me of. Those women and their bin lids and green army everywhere, even in black and white. It's like it was all camouflage and really long, long rifles and checking driving licences. I was never in the north before we met. Not once. Mad, really. Before we met is weird too. Feels like I'm somehow going too far. Did we have a "Where did you meet?" Sort of feels like you only have that if, you know, agh … whaffle, waffle, maple syrup.

My father worked all over the country – still does, to be honest. Does really well, and they have loads of friends. Every corner. They're popular, well regarded – even though people don't know the half of what they do for folks. Like your oul ones, they're kind people, and I'm really proud of them. Our mother has brains pouring out the side of her head. There's probably nothing she couldn't do if she set herself about it, but all she's interested in is grandchildren. I'll maybe talk about that another time.

We were both convent girls, like half the country. Unremarkable, really, school. The other one was always a handling, but brilliant – as you know, even before her trade was a thing there was very little she couldn't do, but there was very little she would do, if you know what I mean. She wouldn't lead nor drive for anyone, until it suited her, and then she could turn failure into triumph overnight. She was always saucy, though.

I went off to Trinity. I loved it. It was mad and interesting and kind of sophisticated and grown-up. The first three years were amazing, then I qualified the first hurdle and went on my placement year and things changed. But maybe that's as much as you can take for this instalment given that you didn't ask for it, and maybe that's all I want to write for now.

So what do I do now? Throw it in the bin? That's what I tried to do last time, lol. Feck it, new, sweary me. Caution to the wind. Who knows? Take care and a massive hug where it is more deserved. Make sure they get it.

Sinead debated whether to sign it. Her name had been attached to the front of the envelopes she had received, but it occurred to her that Sam may not have been the one to write it. She left the letter blank.

Chapter Fourteen

ÁINE READ the text message and very nearly wept. She never cried in front of anyone, yet still she forced herself to wise up and hold it all back even though she was alone.

Thank you, sis.

Sis made all the difference. Had it just been *thank you*, she could have interpreted that as a cold enough acknowledgement of receipt. She debated whether and what to reply. Responses were unusual enough for her unless a specific question had been posed. She was not prosaic, gushing, ebullient or particularly friendly; she knew that, and was reconciled to the fact that at forty years old she was unlikely to change.

Shrugging hope away she set back to work, wondering aimlessly whether she might meet the mini marine again at any stage, and how she would feel about that. He was different to Sam – more open, curiously, for an intelligence expert. He didn't give the impression of carrying a bag full of black memories either, despite having served alongside Sam. She found herself thinking about the night they had chugged whiskey – him complaining that Irish was for cooking while Scotch was for savouring. Didn't prevent him licking half a bottle into him, she smiled at the thought. She'd matched him drop for drop, which he seemed to appreciate. But, then again, she didn't go for a jog the next morning.

Yep, remember he's a psycho.

It was a nice feeling, all the same. One that she hadn't had in … how long? Since that time when Sinead came back. Before that, even. She knew she couldn't blame her reclusiveness on Sinead, but it helped to do so, and in it there was a grain of truth.

Áine had a pile of work to do resolving issues set out by some junior business analyst and product manager at a major multinational. The development sprint was already a week old and she hadn't done a tap, but the fixes would be easy if she set her mind to it for the week she had left to louse the bugs. She had, thus far, managed to avoid the Zoom meetings about her team's progress by simply not logging in. Her reputation was good enough to get a pass, but she knew she was taking the piss.

Yet instead of getting stuck into the fixes and code, she found herself drifting over the website for Min's commando unit, the images, the pretence at openness hiding a dearth of real information. She cautioned herself against meddling with the back end and records. Fooling around with MOD frames was a silly, dangerous business and should be reserved only for emergencies.

The door knocked and for a moment her heart lifted wondering if it was Sinead – then realised Sinead wouldn't knock. Her mind flitted again to Min and in that split second she wasn't sure who she would prefer to see standing outside. She rose and sprang merrily to the door without wondering how someone had managed to knock the actual timber rather than buzzing for entry from the foyer below. She pulled the tall oak back and was punched hard in the face.

———

ÁINE SCRAMBLED backwards on the marble floor. A man and woman walked in and the man reached down to grab her but she flipped onto her front and crawled at speed away from him, trying to regain her feet and lashing round as he grappled her upper arms and shoulders. She knew if she got as far as her control room she could lock herself in securely and call the Guards, but he hammered down hard on the side of her head, swivelling her round and punching her again with a brutal uppercut. She felt her tongue mangle between her teeth and saw blood fly upwards, then she fell back further – in slow motion, her head cracking on the tiles.

She lay still and panted, a blackness veiling her sight, shaken by heavy blows to her exposed ribs and trunk – her elbows raised, instinctively, to protect her head. There was noise, but she couldn't make out what it was – voices, perhaps, then a stinging ring in her ears. Her hair was torn as her head was lifted upwards, and she was treated to two livid faces, both shouting – yet she still couldn't hear what was being said. Her head was dropped again, and their feet moved away. She rolled her head to find furniture crashing to her eye level, feet moving backwards and forwards, the ringing growing fainter as the movement continued.

Where is the concierge? Where are our neighbours?

She saw the man put his shoulder to the control room door, again and again. Somewhere in her head she almost smiled, knowing he would fail. Then someone stood on her hand and from the other side a woman's face appeared.

"How do we get into that room?" Áine's own phone was held up to her face. "Where is it? We know you had it!" The woman screamed so loudly that Áine couldn't help but suddenly grasp what they wanted.

She suddenly realised how complacent she'd been. The screaming continued but Áine couldn't find the ability to respond, which encouraged the blow that flicked her lights out.

———

"DON'T PANIC. I'M OK."

"Why are you talking like that?" Sinead panicked, as predicted.

"Bit my tongue," Áine said.

"First time for everything."

"Sinead," Áine slurred. "Sinead, I need to see you."

"Look, Áine, I'm glad you sent the letter on but—"

"It's not that. I know you don't want to, but something's happened."

"What's happened?" Sinead's voice rose in range. "I can barely make you out. Have you got it – Corona?"

"No," Áine muttered, exhausted, the pain leaking into her voice. "Just come when you can."

She hung up, knowing she was barely intelligible, pleading quietly that her sister wouldn't fall foul of the same people who had beaten her purple.

———

"HOW IN THE hell is this your fault?" Sinead asked, once she'd Dettoled and Savloned the cuts and applied an ageing tube's worth of arnica gel to the bruising.

Some innate sense in Sinead had clicked when she'd opened the apartment door and found her sister bleeding gently on the long couch. She'd not asked many questions, just checked her over, performed all the correct tests – concussion, dilation, bleeding on the brain, and insisted that she go to hospital.

But collectively they'd agreed on observation at home – because of Covid, Áine had claimed, but Sinead knew there was more to it than that. She waited as long as she could and then pressed her sister to explain.

"Nobody can bring this on themselves, Áine."

"I dropped the ball." Áine struggled to speak through her jarred jaw and swollen tongue. "I was ditching that bloody phone and should have wiped it and powered all tracking off."

"What phone?" Sinead shot back, but in her heart she knew the phone her sister was talking about.

"The one from the woman who ran away from your place."

"The madam," Sinead said. "Was it her who did this to you?"

"I dunno," Sinead said, barely able to form the words, "but you need to listen to me."

"I am fucking listening!" Sinead exploded.

Áine looked stunned. "I'm ok, sis, I'll be ok."

Sinead exhaled deeply, upset and angry and worried. "Listen to what? Why would they do this?"

"I was thick," Áine started. "I took the phone into town and sent a message saying it was me who posted the letter to Sam."

"A message to whom?"

"Joseph," she said. "I mean Daniel – Daniel Joseph."

"So what?"

"So I switched everything on again – Wi-Fi and that, to send the message, cos it didn't really matter when I was gonna dump the phone anyway, and I was a distance from here – Merrion Square, so another reason it didn't matter."

"So why does it matter?"

"Cos like a thicko, I then sent a message from my phone to you."

"So what?"

"From the same spot."

"Yeah – so what!"

"So they're not just ordinary bloody criminals. They must have been looking for the phone."

"Áine, I'm lost here."

"You brought that phone here ages ago – well over a month ago, right?"

"Yes, but you said this is a big city block and they wouldn't be able to narrow it down."

"That's right, and they still managed it, so they must have used other information."

"Like what?"

"The only time GPS and location services were used again on that phone was when I took it to Merrion Square. Then I dumped it and used my own phone from the exact same spot seconds after." Áine was struggling to explain. "Look, they must have pinged their phone and the time, then my phone and the time, talking to your phone, and drawn a triangle of links. Their phone to mine, mine to yours, yours to the convent. That's how they tracked us here."

"That's … that's mad. That's totally mad."

"Yeah. They're well resourced, or they're not just running girls."

"How do you mean?"

"This is sophisticated." Áine slurred the word with saliva dripping from her torn lip. "This is smart. Having the tech is one thing, but thinking to search for it this way is more worrying."

"How?"

"They must really have wanted that phone. It must have serious shit on it we never looked at."

"You dumped it, so it doesn't matter."

"You don't understand, Sinead." Áine was shaking her head again.

"Understand what, Áine?"

"They'll be able to see who we called."

Chapter Fifteen

THE TWO WOMEN sat silently for a while, Sinead desperate to ask questions but keenly aware that her sister was in too much pain to deal with her much-too-basic queries about tech and what it all might mean. Áine held the fingertips of one hand to her temple, desperate not to move a muscle lest the pain increase.

"There's an infirmary at the convent. I want to go and get you some co-codamol or something but I don't want to leave you here."

"Drugs would be good."

"I know, but what if they come back?"

"Drugs, sis."

"How did they get up here? Where was the fucking concierge?"

"I'll be sure to ask him when I can reach for the bastard, Sinead. But drugs, please."

You could come with me?"

"Is that a joke?" Áine pained herself by looking up at her sister. "I am not moving a muscle." She was too sore to argue further, to say that her attackers were unlikely to return, but she was afraid – not that she was about to admit it. So she stayed still. Only her eyelids moved and even they brought horrendous pain to her bruised sockets.

She heard Sinead stand and move about in aimless frustration, before going to the bathroom. Áine could hear her pulling out boxes and creams from the cabinets for a third time, searching for painkillers that they both knew didn't exist. She stomped back, fell into the two-seater sofa and began to think aloud.

"I wish ..."

Áine was supposed to say "What" but didn't want to flinch.

Sinead filled the silence, "I wish one of them was here."

Áine's interest warmed a little. Her eyes darted to her sister but she refused to move her neck.

"Min or Sam," Sinead said.

The thought of it pleased Áine, although she doubted it would go anywhere.

"They'd know what to do," Sinead rambled, prompting a sarcastic snort from Áine.

"Bust heads," she said through thin unfluttering lips, but not in her normal disapproving manner. Áine could very much see the attraction of a few busted heads.

"Maybe I'll ring him." Sinead's thoughts were all one-way traffic. "Min," she clarified an unasked question. "Maybe I should just see what he thinks."

Ordinarily Áine would caution against an open call and explanation, but her mind was filled with as much fury as her body was with pain, and she was tired and groggy and wanted someone else to make the decisions. She may not have been beyond caring, but her concentration was focused on not moving and waiting for her sister to locate drugs from somewhere.

"Pharmacy," she muttered.

Sinead looked up. "But—"

"Ten minutes, there and back." Áine closed her eyes and said reluctantly, "You could use one of your old prescriptions – see if they'll take pity."

Áine opened her eyes to see Sinead stiffen at the reference to her past requirement for such medication. She looked at Áine's misery and stood up to go in search of an old script.

Áine's mind blanked. She wondered if she was on the edge of consciousness and fleetingly considered whether she would care if she blacked into a coma and never surfaced. The pain was everywhere – chest, chin, lips, mouth, her head was screaming at her and her neck felt like it was rusted solid.

Sinead returned with a shoulder bag, from which she produced an odd piece of rubber. "I'm going to need you to use this. You'll have to get up, sorry. I'm not leaving unless you force this under the door."

"What?" Áine said, utterly exasperated.

"It's a wedge. Unbelievable really, but it will stop anyone getting in. Just force it under the door."

"Are you serious?" Áine tried to snap.

"If you don't do it, I'm not going." Sinead tried to be stern.

"K," Áine said, and Sinead moved to help her up, bringing a yelp and a tear shed in pain.

"Áine, I still think it's hospital time."

"Drugs," was all she said in return.

They hobbled to the door and as it closed, Áine went

through the agony of moving her leg to kick the dropped wedge under the frame.

She would live with the pain, she thought, just as she would live with what Sam might do to the bastards who beat her, if he ever turned up again.

————

SINEAD FISHED another piece of paper from her back pocket with a trembling hand. She was upset at the sight of her twin, for sure, but she knew that it was the idea of requesting the meds, the notion of pleading that she needed them because of old afflictions, that was the more pressing and disturbing issue. The elevator pinged and opened two floors above ground, frightening her that someone was about to enter the lift.

She found herself holding up a hand in a manner completely alien to her when a man attempted to walk in. "Please, social distancing. It'll be free in a moment." She hit the button to close the doors and watched the neighbour she vaguely recognised nod apologetically.

In the foyer she looked around for the concierge, anger building in her, but the desk was empty. Frustrated, she made to leave for the street but changed her mind. The wedge would have to suffice for half an hour. Instead, she turned for the stairs to the underground car park. She walked towards her car and then wavered, thought for a split second and turned towards the bins. She lifted the lid of the one nearest her and saw that her last letter had already been removed, and dropped it in surprise. The noise echoed around the car park and back to her. What the hell, she reasoned, and lifted the lid again, using the remnants of the tape already there to affix a new letter. She turned and went to her car.

Fifteen minutes later, she entered the convent grounds. She parked on the stones where she wasn't supposed to, ran up the stone steps and shuffled quickly along two corridors and another flight of steps to the landing with the infirmary. Inside, the musty smell of old, empty beds and disinfectant reminded her of unpleasant nights when women had been treated for similar afflictions to those sustained by Áine. Sinead was no nurse, but she had seen the sisters busy themselves at the various cabinets, readying bandages or plasters.

She opened cupboard after cupboard, quietly reciting a plea to not get caught. She hunted the cupboards for the heavy stuff and eventually, low down, found a locker filled with regimented boxes of diazepam, tramadol and paracetamol. Only that one of the nuns was a registered nurse, such stashes would not be allowed.

"Feeling unwell, Sinead?" the condescension in the query filled her with dread. She turned to find the Mother Superior standing in full headmistress mode. How had she crept up on her so quietly?

"My sister, she's had an accident and she's in a lot of pain."

"Those are prescription medications, I'm afraid, Sinead."

"Are they?" she tried. "She's been attacked. I need to give her something."

"Attacked? Sounds like she needs to go to accident and emergency." The way she enunciated "emergency" conveyed extreme scepticism.

"Not with the virus, Mother – that would just make a bad situation worse."

"Well, you'll need to be care—"

"I will," Sinead said, stepping around the old woman, trying not to compare her to a witch, but all out of patience.

"Well—" she heard the nun say as she hustled through the door.

"Gotta go, Mother, sorry. It's an emergency!"

Sinead ran down the small flight of stairs, back along a corridor and bumped into Macy.

"Came to see you," Macy said, timidly but with some faint trace of accusation.

"Sorry, Macy, something urgent came up. Someone needed my help – couldn't be avoided, but I do want to go through all the qualifications stuff with you."

Sinead moved to dance around Macy and was treated to a "Yeah". She had weathered all the doubts she was prepared to in the space of a few minutes. "Look, Macy, this really is someone who needs my help. If you want to do this kind of job, you need to be prepared to drop everything to go to those who need it, *when* they need it. Now, I will help you – I promise you that, but there is someone who needs my help a whole lot more right now."

"Sorry," Macy muttered, as Sinead ran down the stairs and opened the door. Macy stared over the balcony, keen to apologise properly.

And that made Macy the last person to see her.

Chapter Sixteen

"SO WHAT YOU'RE SAYING, SISTER—"

"Reverend Mother."

"Sorry?"

"I am the Mother Superior here. Mother will suffice."

"Right, well, what you're saying is that you caught the refuge manager stealing drugs from the cabinet?"

"Well, I didn't think she was stealing them, guard," the Mother Superior bristled. "I simply—"

"But she's not allowed to distribute drugs, is that right?" The officer's thick Dublin accent was distasteful to the pompous nun.

"That's right, but—"

"So is she, or is she not, allowed to take drugs from the infirmary?"

"Well, no, but I thought your inquiry would focus on the manager being missing?"

"She can't really be missing if she's only been gone twenty-four hours, sister."

"Mother."

133

The guard ignored her. "She's an adult – it's allowed, but if she's been stealing prescription medication, that's suggestive of something else altogether."

"Like what?"

"Exactly, sister."

"What?"

"Like what?" said the guard, who much to the nun's irritation was proving as intelligent as he was disrespectful.

"Who reported her missing?"

"Again, sister," said the guard, "not missing. Just never showed up. Her sister, as it happens, who is not prepared to open her door to speak to us, which is odd, don't ye think?"

"Why will she not open her door to you?"

"Yes," said the guard.

"What?"

"Yes, sister, why will she not open her door to us?"

The old nun was tiring of the smart shenanigans. "Well, I'm not sure I can be of any more use. I've told you what happened and you've spoken to Macy, so you can let yourselves out." She coated the silent female guard with a long disapproving look and left the room.

Macy stood sheepishly as the guards turned to her again.

"And what was the reason, would you say, that the manager didn't take her car when she left?"

"I dunno." Macy shrugged.

"And it was parked where it is now?"

"Yeah," Macy said. "I saw it just as the door closed."

"And does she often park on the footpath? Those pebbles aren't for cars are they? Most of the other cars are parked further away."

"Don't know," said Macy.

"And you didn't see anything else?"

"No."

"Can you tell us anything else? Is …" the guard checked his notebook, "Sinead well liked here? Is there anyone in this place," the guard circled the air with a finger, "who doesn't like the way she runs things?" Macy looked guiltily at the cop, who tilted his head slightly. "You need to tell us. We need to know what's happened here."

"Well, Sinead did ask someone to leave a few days ago?"

"Oh?" said the guard, leaving that wide open.

"A woman."

"Aren't ye all women in here, Macy?"

"Eh, well, yeah."

"So?"

"She was a busybody, annoying everyone. Sinead got her another place, in Rathmines, I think."

"Alright," said the guard. "We'll get the details from Sinead's number two when she comes in later, then, will we?"

"S'pose so," Macy said, "I wouldn't have a clue about that stuff."

The guard looked to his colleague. "It's too early to do much more. All we know is she's cleared off with a load of drugs. Let's call her assistant later and keep in touch with the agoraphobic sister on the phone."

———

ÁINE'S PAIN was gradually being replaced by fear. The Guards had treated her with little more than hostility when she'd explained that Sinead had gone off to get her some painkillers.

"Ah, yeah?" the guard had said, knowingly.

Áine's defences had gone up immediately.

She lay back on the sofa and stared out the huge window, unable to register anything. It was easier just to let her focus blur. Then the landline phone rang and she had to drag herself up, pacing gingerly around the back of the sofa, using it as support. She reached for the receiver and held it to her ear, a shot of pain from her elbow coursing up to her brain.

"This is Garda McKenna. We called earlier but you wouldn't open the…"

"Any news?" Áine cut across him.

"Hard to get gear at the minute, isn't it?" he said.

"What?"

"Does she often raid the convent for the fun stuff, then?"

"What are you talking about?"

"Your sister."

"She went to the convent?"

"Looking for drugs, apparently."

"Painkillers," Áine corrected.

"See, that makes me wonder why you wouldn't open the door to us."

Áine bit her lip and nearly yelped at the pain. "The virus," she tried.

"If my sister was missing, I think I'd chance it to see the guard investigating it."

Áine closed her eyes. She hadn't wanted to let him in, to see the mess of the attack, which would have demanded an explanation that was not hers to give. She'd stood on the inside of the door, still wedged shut, and listened to the guard ask her questions. Her mind had struggled to make sense of what to do. To reveal her damage and tell him about the vicious beating would lead to an admission that the attackers were looking for the madam's phone. The phone would be connected to Sam and had, in effect, been used to conceal contact with a possible fugitive, wanted for murder. Her mind had muddled, it had all suddenly become too confusing. She'd decided then and there that she couldn't have Sinead completely disown her for spilling it all just because she was worried about her twin being missing for twenty-four hours. Áine was terrified that she'd damaged their relationship beyond repair as it was – to say something that could lead to Sam's apprehension would have sealed the deal.

"Are you still there?" the guard asked.

"Yeah," Áine said. "Where did she go after the convent?"

"Exactly," said the guard. "She didn't take her car."

"What do you mean?" Áine's heart sank, sure now that her worst fears had been realised.

"Her car's abandoned outside the door of the convent. Not even locked."

The temptation to tell the Guards everything became almost overwhelming, yet Áine said nothing.

The guard snorted derisively. "So here we are. You call us, but you won't tell us what's going on. You won't even open the door. Your sister leaves her car at her back and goes for a long walk or whatever, and you sit on the phone all silent. I'm not sure this is a disappearance at all. It looks drugs related to me."

"No," was all Áine could manage.

"Tell you what. If you decide you're going to help explain what's going on, you can ring me. You have the number on the card I slipped under the door you wouldn't open. Until then we have a pandemic to be dealing with, OK?"

Áine hung up the phone. She held herself upright against the kitchen counter for a long while, increasingly convinced that she should have just told them the whole story. The ache was everywhere now, inside her head, all down her back and ribs. She needed help, she needed someone else to make the decisions. So she did the only other thing she could think of: she walked slowly to the control room, lifted the IP phone and called Min.

———

A FULL DAY and night without painkillers added to Áine's anguish. She stared into the mirror for a long, long time, the effects of the attack only half on show; the blunt end of the hurt internal. They had made her afraid, deeply sad and anxious in a way she had never experienced before. She was scared primarily for her sister. She knew Sinead would never leave her for this length of time – angry or otherwise, without painkillers, which meant only one thing: they had her. That meant they would be questioning her about the phone and where it had been left, and Sinead wouldn't be able to answer. Perhaps she would relent, eventually, and explain that there was only one person who knew where it had been dumped, and that would bring the attackers back to her door.

Áine felt deeply guilty for worrying about herself, but it was unavoidable. She knew she couldn't undergo another beating – her head felt drunk with vacancy as it was. She imagined it was concussion but she had no idea how to manage it. Nobody had ever hit her before. Not once. Sinead, on the other hand, had a point of reference. Áine had seen the effects of all that, and it wasn't pretty. She found herself fearing that, like her twin, some sort of post-traumatic depression might descend upon her, which brought further guilt and deeper worry.

The television flickered, mute, as she sat and waited for something to happen. She was preparing herself for an incoming phone call to say that her sister's body had been discovered. The tears fell heavily then, her throat contracting, and she wished she had enough sleeping pills to make a job of it. The only time she turned up the volume was when the news came on. She'd sat through four cycles – breakfast, lunch, evening and the nightly bulletins. Nothing.

She woke at four o'clock to a persistent buzzing. It was dark outside and she hadn't pulled the curtains, which exacerbated her fear. She creaked painfully to the intercom panel, terrified that it might be her assailants but more scared that it could be the Guards with the news.

"Hello?"

"It's just me, darlin'," the gruff Scot's voice almost overwhelming her with relief.

"Min," she whispered, "come up." She pressed the button and crouched, wincing, to remove the rubber wedge. She opened the door and waited for the lift.

She heard footsteps and saw his burly form emerge from the elevator. She stepped into the hallway and did something she hadn't done before. She reached for a man she barely knew and began to cry uncontrollably, gushing her thanks for his arrival, sobbing into his neck and shoulder, clinging tight, refusing to let go.

———

"WHAT HAVE THEY DONE TO YOU?" Min said, over and over. He stroked her hair and allowed her to rest against him, there, in the hallway.

She felt his tenderness and thought of Sam –

wondering whether he was capable of similar softness; wishing it for her sister, willing her to live to feel its comfort.

"They've got Sinead," she sobbed. "It's been two days. She would never vanish like that – not when I need her. There's just no way."

Min said nothing, sensing the need to wait and listen.

"It's all to do with that bloody phone. They wanted it – whatever was on it. I should have told them where I dumped it, but I just didn't think. I've led her into this, and she won't even be able to tell them where to go to search for it."

He led her gently in a crab-like walk into the apartment and sat with her on the couch, cradling her head and rubbing her shoulder.

"Can you find them – can you get her back?" she pleaded.

"We need to tell the police," he said gently.

"I did. They don't care. She hasn't been missing for long enough."

"But did you tell them about the attack? That she's likely to have been abducted?" he pressed gently.

She stiffened. She had hoped Min would persuade her that kidnap was unlikely – that there would be comfort and chinks of light to let hope creep in, but realised that wasn't the way these men were built. They were realists, always erring toward worst-case scenario.

"No," she admitted. "Sinead's so cross with me as it is, I didn't want it to lead to Sam. If he got arrested because of all this, that would be the final straw."

"Surely there'd be a way of explaining it without linking to Sam? And that's another thing," Min said. "We'll need to tell him. He'll have to know."

Áine hadn't really considered that – Sam's investment in Sinead's welfare. "But what if ..."

"They're not after him. I've been up and down it with every intelligence check I can think of. He's not on their radar at all. Not even a blip."

"He ran for nothing," Áine said, not a question – just a statement reflecting the irony of their situation.

"We'll tell the police first thing," Min said. "There'll be a skeleton response staff at this time of the morning, so we'll call at nine. Before that, let's see what we can find."

"How?" Áine said. "I don't know where to start."

"Will there be anyone awake overnight at the convent? Is there a night shift?"

"I don't know, but I don't care. I can call anyway."

"OK, give them a buzz ," Min said. "See if there's any CCTV that might show this pimp woman."

"I don't think there are cameras at the convent."

"Worth asking anyway. And we'll get the CCTV from this building too. See if we can work out how the pair that attacked you got in here and what way they left after."

"I can break that from my system here," Áine said, glad of the focus and structure.

"Also – did you plug the madam's phone into your computer?"

"No, I was careful as hell with it," she said. "But I do have a rig that could cope with it – keeping it vanilla and offline." She placed her hand on his chest, pushing herself upright.

"And you dumped it?"

"Yeah, it'll be gone now."

"Are you sure?"

"It was days ago. It was a bin in the park. They'll have emptied it by now."

"Even with the lockdown?"

"I just assumed …"

"Assume nothing, hen. Assume nothing." Min rose. "Where's this bin, then?"

———

BY FIVE THIRTY Min was soaked through with sweat and standing, for the second time, at the apartment door. He wasn't smiling but was shaking his hand in which rested a handset. "This the one?"

"Unbelievable," Áine muttered, stepping aside to allow him in. "You switched off location?"

"Couldn't. It's dead as Hector. Battery's puffed."

They walked without thinking to the control room. Min pulled the light switch with a familiarity Áine noted and from which she drew an odd warmth and pleasure. Then they sat, her pulling a cable from a bank of leads; him drawing a keyboard and mouse towards himself.

"Let's see what's so bloody important, then," he muttered.

It took a few moments for a battery icon to appear, empty, followed by a red bar. "If we can't get the location switched off immediately, they could ping it to this apartment. They could come back," she tried to keep the tremble from her voice.

"I'm banking on it," Min said. Áine shot him a glance – part fear, part awe. "Don't worry, darlin'. You'll no' be here if they come. I'll be the one to greet them."

"Thank you," she said, wondering whether she might already have … don't be stupid, she told herself.

"Now, you'll have to tell the big man."

"What?"

"Call Danny. Speak to Sam. Let him know. He'll be mad as a bull wi' sore balls if you don't let him know what's happening. And that's no place to find yourself, sweetheart. No place at all."

Áine pulled over the IP phone, looked at the Post-it she had scribbled the number on, and dialled. The ring went on forever.

"Yes?" a Caribbean accent croaked groggily.

"Daniel?"

"Yes," the voice said again. "Who is this?"

"I'm sorry to wake you. It's Áine, Sinead's sister. I'm looking for Sam?"

"Not here," the voice sounded defensive.

"It's ok, it's all ok. He's not being looked for – we know that for sure. I just need to speak to him. Something's happened."

"But he's not here," Daniel said.

"I know he's there. Honestly, it's all ok."

Min leaned over and took the phone from Áine. "Dan, it's Min, I'm with her. What she says is right enough. The danger has passed. There's naebody looking for him."

"Min?" Daniel said. "You are with Sam's woman?"

Áine could overhear what was being said, but knew it was no time to rail against the possessive.

"Aye," Min said, "with her sister. It's complicated, but we do need to speak tae him."

"But," Daniel said, "it's not possible. Sam is gone."

Chapter Seventeen

"WHAT DO YOU MEAN, GONE?" Áine's headache, which she'd become less aware of since Min's arrival, returned as she'd listened second-hand to the transatlantic conversation.

"Ach, I wouldnae worry. Sam just, like, pisses aff frae time to time."

"That much I do know," she said without warmth. "If he's vanished, then there's no point in wasting time on him."

"You're not a fan?"

"No reflection on you," she muttered. "He's just … pissed her about a bit. And, as you say, fecked off from time to time."

"He's a good bloke, you know. He wouldn't do that deliberately, or if it wasn't necessary."

"Well, you would say that, you're his best mate."

"I wouldn't say it if I didn't think it, though."

Áine turned her shoulders painfully towards him, and saw that Min was sincere. She felt strongly that he was an honest person, a man who dealt in facts, no matter how unwelcome those facts might be. She relented, a little. "Sinead's been through more than a person should go through in life." She stared again at the screens, uneasy at her betrayal, desperate to explain herself to this solid and reassuring man. "She's … she needs minding."

"There's two of them in it, then," Min said.

"I know about his wife," Áine said. "I know she was murdered and he was overseas. You were probably with him."

"Naw," Min almost laughed. "We parted ways in our service just after he met Shannon. Sam went AWOL, got busted. I stayed in the service."

"I know."

"What?"

"I know – she died, Sam left, you stayed."

"No, no, this was before. Sam was a rare breed – boot-neck first, later an officer. That's no' often that happens, hen. The men loved that. They'd have done anything for Sam, so he was the boy they selected for a fair whack of difficult shit. Then on one op, he disappeared. He sent us all aff safely. We had no choice but tae see through our orders while he vanished. Next thing he pops up in Cyprus, and before we know it he's hitched and ditched."

"Married?"

"Aye."

"And ditched?"

"Back to bootneck – a marine again. No fancy smancy operative any more."

"Aah," Áine nodded, the pennies dropping like an arcade shelf finally pushed to its limit. "You two were special forces."

"Aye. Has he no' said?"

"Not to me, but it makes sense."

"I just assumed …"

"Assume nothing, Min."

He snorted. "Touché."

"Does Sinead know?"

Min thought for a moment. "I … guess so. I don't know. When I first met her I had some fancy toys, so I just thought he'd have filled her in, you know? But Sam can be funny like that."

"Secretive?"

"No, not really, just he never seems to think anybody else would care, if that makes sense."

"Care that he was a killing machine?"

"Oh, aye, here we go."

"What?"

"How do you sleep at night? How do you live with what you've done, etcetera, etcetera?"

Shame ran over Áine in a hot wave. She stammered, "No, Min, I don't mean—"

"It's inevitable. People are bound to wonder. Least you're straight about it. Most folks beat around the bush a bit before they get to the real question."

"Which is?"

"How many people have you killed? What's it like?"

There was a long silence.

"And?"

"I don't know, and it's fucking horrendous. But this isn't helping find your sister, is it?"

"I'm sorry."

"Don't be. I'm glad it's said. I hate when things is left unsaid."

Áine found herself smiling. She lifted the madam's phone. It was still too dead to switch on.

"Let's get a look at this building's cameras, aye?"

Chapter Eighteen

MIN WATCHED Áine closely as she navigated her system. She could feel his occasional nod in gentle appreciation as she broke through two firewalls and entered the frames of a central security agency based in County Cork.

"Nicely done," Min said, "they're a big outfit."

"This company has the contract for a lot of real estate in Ireland, even the big tech companies, so they're not flahoolick with their systems."

"Flahoolick?"

"Careless? Some words are hard to explain."

"Casual?"

"Yeah," Áine said, a little surprised. "But it can mean generous too. It's just one of those words. Doesn't matter."

"They might not be shabby but it still didn't take you long to get in."

"Well, I used to work for some of those big tech companies."

"Used to?" Min asked, as Áine's hands danced over the keyboard.

"Another little something to thank your best friend for," Áine said.

"What d'ye mean?"

"Sam was running around Libya a while back, probably exterminating all in his path, and he got me to do a bit of back-end work for him. Through the jigs and reels it got me pinged by US intelligence and sacked by my firm."

"Oh, shit," Min said.

"Oh, shit, is right. That was a hundred-and-fifty-grand-a-year job."

"No, I mean, you'll be on a watch list."

"Ah, yeah, never mind the top job I lost – *I'm* on a watch list."

"It's a shame about the job, agreed. Sorry. But if you got flagged by the NSA, then you'll be watched."

"And you think I don't know that?" Áine said, offence rising in her like heartburn.

Min looked exasperated. "But how do you function knowing they're watching your keystrokes?"

"I make sure they can't," Áine replied.

"Function?"

"Watch my keystrokes."

"Look, hen, even if you've VPN'd this kit to hell and back they'll find a way if they think you're a threat."

"Precisely."

"What?"

"Tell you what, instead of me explaining all this to you, why don't you get one of your military weirdo hacks to see if they can find me? You run an intelligence unit, right?"

"You know I do."

"Then let's see what you can see."

"Ok," Min muttered, confused.

"And Min?"

"Aye?"

"Call me hen again and you'll be the bull with sore balls."

———

MIN WAS in the kitchen making a call when the madam's phone lit up. Áine reached forward and lifted it, watching the battery symbol migrate to a bitten apple. She quickly popped the device – cable attached, into her black jammer pouch, the lining of which, in theory, should leave its transceiver redundant. The door opened behind her.

"We've got life."

"What's the wallet for?"

"It's supposed to jam the signal. I bought it from China, so it might work and it might not."

"I kinda want them to come back for the phone," Min said.

"I know, but I want to see what's what first."

Min looked at the screen bank as Áine ran software to crack the phone's code. "Why do you have all this kit?" he asked.

"Long story," she said.

The characters went from underscores to stars and the phone opened itself to them. "What do you want to look at first? The images and videos are filth." Áine shifted uneasily remembering what she had seen when she had opened it with Sinead. "Maybe social media?"

"Aye, might be the best way to find out who these bastards are."

The phone had its passwords saved, but required a fingerprint, so for the second time Áine ran a programme against it, which took longer than the first.

"I don't understand how you have this kind of gear. I've never seen these before." Min nodded at the icons on her computer dock.

"That's cos I built them my own self," Áine replied. "And unless you're employing me, you won't have seen them. That's the plan, anyway."

"Are ye a snooper?"

"A what?"

"People paying to have you snoop on their other halves."

"That sort of thing has been requested. But, no, that's not what I do."

"What, then?"

"I mess with code to put the time in. I'm employed by big tech to build security systems. The best way to build them well is to break them. I have a team of developers who stack it all up, then I come in and knock it all down again. They fail better the next time."

"Ok, and then you keep the software?"

"I refine it – quietly, just in case."

"In case of what?"

"In case Sam makes a bollocks of it and I get fired again. It's good to have some intellectual property that might keep the wolf from the door. I don't know how or why I might use the software, but it keeps my hand in and makes me employable if I can talk about what works and what doesn't. And, look …"

Facebook opened on the screens.

"It comes in handy."

Min shook his head gently. She swiped and scrolled at speed, forcing him to hold out his hand.

"Hang on, no' so fast. What the hell is this?"

They were looking at images of young people in various states of repose, all without essential garments.

"Agh, no, child porn?"

"No," Áine said decisively, "look at the age of them."

She rolled down the page at speed, so as not to intrude further into what were obviously private moments.

"They're teenagers – still kids," Min said.

"But it's not teen porn," Áine said. "Look."

A crafted post appeared: *We know what you've been up to in your bedroom, dirty little boy. Here's the video. Two thousand euro and this goes away for good. No money and it gets sent to all your FB friends.*

"Fucking bastards," Min said.

Áine had already opened another screen and was typing a name.

"Who's that?"

"The kid they were blackmailing."

"How fast do you read?"

"Young eyes."

"I didn't even see his name."

"You'd want to pay attention, then," Áine sniped, and immediately felt the need to moderate her tone. "I know this isn't your normal area of expertise."

A page full of results appeared, and the news drew their hearts into their boots.

The family of the Durham teenager whose body was recovered from the River Wear have appealed to young people to keep themselves safe online amid reports he was being black-mailed. It's believed images of the boy had been circulated on various social media platforms in the days before his death.

Durham Constabulary are understood to be investi-gating whether the 15-year-old may have been duped into sharing information with what he thought was a girl of a similar age. Sources close to the family believe the boy was, in fact, targeted by an organised criminal gang.

"Right, we need to find out if this shit is confined to this phone or if it's on a computer somewhere else too."

"This phone isn't linked to any other device," Áine said. "It's possible the whole thing is being controlled from that." She tapped the black jammer wallet.

"So that means we can—"

"Find out who owns the Facebook account? That could be tricky."

"No!" Min said impatiently – the first time Áine had experienced that side of him. "We can contact all the other young people and tell them it's alright, we've seized the phone and they're not at risk any more."

Áine blinked, shocked at her own oversight. "Of course, of course." She began to scroll, looking at the number of people who had been targeted. "There's dozens of them."

"Aye. We need to move as quick as we can. If they're sitting frettin' at home, who knows what they might do to themselves. This is unbelievably sick."

Áine clicked open a profile and began a message, then paused. "What do I say?"

"I dunno – don't worry, we've got the device this was being run from and it's safe?"

"Who is *we*?"

"Eh, well, we could say we're the police?"

"Then the police will be asked about it and say it wasn't them."

"Well," Min was scrabbling, "why don't we say we're, like, internet security folks. We could invent a name or something. But we'll need to do it sharpish."

"A name like what?"

"I dunno – Internet Guardians?"

"Cop on."

"Well, this *is* your area of expertise. You tell me."

"Freelance Cybercrime Specialists. At least then it has a ring of truth."

"Whatever you say. Just get the messages sent."

Áine hammered hard on the keys, copying and pasting to each and every one on the screen. As she did, she spoke.

"I'm sorry."

"For what?"

"Not thinking about the kids first."

"What?"

"I was thinking we should track the owners – for Sinead. I just didn't think."

"Course you didn't – your sister's been snatched. Natural. Don't be daft."

Áine finished. "We can't be sure it will have any effect, or that this is everyone. They could be doing it on other platforms.

"Like what?"

Áine was bouncing through the phone's data. "There's no Snapchat, no Twitter – never has been. No Instagram."

"WhatsApp?"

Áine reinstalled the app and waited for it to gather data. The loading clock ticked round and then the application gathered itself and drew down the information. All the contacts and chats were defined by numbers only. They read together, Min considerably more slowly than Áine.

"This isn't being used for blackmail. This is some sort of …"

"It's like a booking system."

The messages were requests for particular physical

attributes – men, Áine assumed, demanding women of certain complexion and proportion.

"Let's see if there's any consistent place these johns are being sent to."

They read in silence for twenty minutes, but the responses were succinct.

Yes, we have what you are looking for. Send us the address. Payment upfront with cash taken off premises prior to any engagement.

"What does that mean?" Min muttered.

"It means they send women to men's addresses, or hotels, by the looks of things." Áine scrolled.

"No, 'cash taken off premises' – that suggests the women are accompanied, or driven. Maybe the driver takes off with the cash or waits outside?"

"Makes sense."

"So maybe we place an order and speak to whomever is waiting outside."

"In lockdown? Sure, you're not even able to visit anyone else's house."

"You reckon this stuff has just stopped?"

Áine shook her head in bewilderment. "I have absolutely no idea."

"We could try it?"

"How? This is the phone that manages it all," Áine tapped it again, "and it's here – with us."

"Then why's there nae messages coming through looking for sex, or whatever?" Min growled in frustration.

"Good question. They must have stopped it, or diverted it, or readvertised."

"There's a few gigabytes of information on that phone. Between us, it would be proper mental if we can't find a location for where all this is done from."

"Yeah," Áine said, "let's pick it apart."

Chapter Nineteen

AFTER TWO HOURS Min leaned back and turned to Áine.

"Take a break, go for a walk. Something might come to ye."

"I never take a break," she replied without turning to him. "And my sister is missing. You take a break if you want to."

"Seriously, give your head a chance. You can't think straight, staring at the same stuff all the time."

"I'm not some squaddie under your command."

"I know that."

"Then you take a break if your tired eyes need a rest."

Min sighed heavily. "Look, love, I have stuff I want to do and I'd find it easier if you were out of the room."

Áine turned, at last. "Ah, you want to call your team and see if they've found me? You're worried we're being ripped by the NSA or your own spooks."

Min grunted dismissively. "Sure, if I wanted to do that, I'd just walk outside the room and make the call."

"What, then?"

155

"You know what I do, don't ye?"

"Marine intelligence exploitation, whatever that is."

"Aye – well, some of it's tech, but I have folks for that. Most of it's analysis, including images."

"So?"

"So leave me at it for a while and let me see if these old eyes can spot anything. And I'm in my mid forties, by the way. You canny be all that much younger."

"You think you'll see something I can't? And you've years on me, just saying."

Min's exasperation reached the surface. "Look, Áine, I'm going to go through the dirty photos and videos. See if there is anything identifiable that could locate where all this is being done. There are particular things we can look for, and it would be a hell of a lot easier to pick through them if you weren't sitting beside me."

Áine thought for a moment. That meant all kinds of things. She had never imagined this bulky little man could be bashful, embarrassed, uneasy. It also suggested something more subtle that she couldn't put her finger on. And then, she reasoned, it suggested he was trying to … "I don't need your protection, thanks all the same."

Min shook his head in resignation and, in full command mode, said, "Just get out of the fucking room for half an hour."

Áine was taken aback by how firm, yet softly spoken, the order was. She found herself rising and, admonished, headed for the door. Oddly, she quite liked it.

———

ÁINE WASN'T ACCUSTOMED to taking a walk, and she had no intention of leaving the apartment – the pain in her head reminding her of the potential consequences. She found herself uneasy at being more than a few hundred yards from the burly Scotsman on the other side of her control room door.

Idle and at a loss, she found her tablet and considered taking a look at what he was doing in there – the mirroring system allowed her to continue working when not in the room. She often padded through the apartment staring into it – while setting the coffee machine running or, not that she would ever admit it, sitting on the jacks.

And then an unusual pang of guilt overcame her, as if intrusion into Min's activities was somehow indecent. Instead, she opened up the other unfinished task, tapping a window that allowed her to look at the CCTV of her own building. They'd neglected it when the madam's phone had revived itself.

Áine found the date and time and shivered slightly as images appeared in sixteen separate boxes on the screen. She braced a little against the countertop as she watched two people – a man in a baseball hat, the only thing visible from above, and a woman with a very scruffy haircut – loiter outside the building, turning on occasion to glance through the glass frontage. After about five minutes the man appeared to nod and they entered the lobby. She tracked her eye across to the next camera, seeing the concierge desk unattended. Áine immediately began to wonder how they had triggered the elevator, which required a resident's card or code, but the man leaned over the counter and stretched out his arm.

Now, how did they know to do that? she wondered, having seen it done a dozen times before by the concierge when a resident had forgotten their pass or the lift was being cleaned or serviced. The button triggered the release of the stairwell door and the couple pushed through it in a hurry, shortly after which the concierge returned from the lobby toilet.

Áine tracked the couple's progress with a fleeting glimpse offered by the sole camera pointed down the stairwell, but they became lost after a few minutes – which was confusing.

Where have you gone?

She scrolled back and forth, panning across to the other camera images, confused.

Then, after ten minutes, they were back, twisting around the stairs. She followed their slow climb all the way to her own door, which was shielded for privacy reasons by the acute angle of the hallway camera. The rest she remembered better than she cared to.

The whole attack took less than ten minutes. Nine minutes twenty-two seconds, to be exact, to beat the shit out of her and ransack the apartment. Not very thoroughly, she thought.

Then they were back in the hallway, hurrying this time, making their way down the stairs. Áine noted that they could have used the lift to go down – there was no code required to descend, to allow visitors out or for fast escape in the event of fire. Áine thought it interesting that this pair had known about the stairwell door release button, but not the lift protocol.

They rushed to the ground-floor door, peering through the small window into the lobby. There they waited for a further minute before triggering the door and walking out – straight past the concierge who didn't pay much attention, and onto the street. From there they walked – oddly, the man a few paces ahead of the woman, until the cameras had nothing else to show. They had walked upriver, away from the docks, but there was no car to be seen, no waiting vehicle to collect them. No onward journey trackable through the apartment block's CCTV.

Áine threw down the tablet in frustration, its heavy plastic case shielding the screen from damage.

And then a thought occurred: why had they spent so much time off the stairwell? She retrieved the pad and dragged the cursor back. She peered closer into the screen, zooming a little before realising that she had been wrong: they hadn't gone up the stairs initially – they had gone down, to the car park.

She straightened up – painfully – and thought for a moment. Why would they do that?

The car park had cameras too, of course, so she opened the dark frame and watched. The image was black and white – colour and light would only be triggered by movement, but there was none.

So, without thinking, she moved to the door, into the hallway and summoned the lift. Inside she selected -1, watching the iPad screen falter, the signal breaking as she descended. Two steps outside and she was at the car park door, flickering her eyes between the newly established screen image and the door, ready to test when the light would come on. But when she pushed the door, she found the light in the echoey parking floor was already on. She moved inside to see where the camera was positioned and was startled by a sound behind her.

There stood a man at her own open bin, with a letter in his hand.

Chapter Twenty

ÁINE FROZE. Her senses were as heightened as they were confused, like the aftermath of watching a scary movie. For the first time in her life, she was without words and utterly terrified, unable to separate what she'd seen on her screen and what was before her now. Her instincts told her another beating was imminent, yet her body seemed completely helpless to turn or move to prevent it.

The man in front of her was in his fifties, fit looking, with the aura of a burglar caught in the act.

"How are ye?" He feigned nonchalance, confusing Áine further. "Can never remember what day's collection."

On an ordinary day Áine would rip him apart with her tongue – *Can't remember which bin is yours either*, but the sentence wouldn't form. Áine just stared at him.

The man looked at her looking at him and his unease morphed into curiosity as she failed to respond or turn away. He dithered about what to do, plainly keen to take the letter away while wanting to appear as if he was throwing it in the bin. "You ok there?"

Áine looked at the letter in his hand, then flickered her eyes back to his face. The man did the same before looking straight at her.

"Sinead?" he ventured, unsure of himself.

The door suddenly swung open behind her and Áine ran.

———

LOCKDOWN RULES on non-household mixing went out the window as three people entered Áine's apartment, staring at one another warily.

"I think you're going to have to explain yourself," Min grunted at the binman, bundling him into a chair.

"Yeah," Áine finally found her voice, calmed by the fact Min had come looking for her and oddly reassured by the protection he had thrown around her.

The man looked strangely unperturbed, despite having been gripped, twisted and manhandled in and out of the lift by the mini marine. He'd protested, but not wildly, saying only that he hadn't been stealing.

"Look, brother, I think *you're* the one going to have to explain himself. I am a man completely at liberty, and you have taken me against my free will and with no small measure of illegal force, to a contained environment. So, comrade, I think *you* need to tell *me* what that's all about."

"Oh, do ye?" Min said flippantly.

"I am saying absolutely nothing until you tell me who you are and where you come from," the man said. Áine recognised his accent as pure inner-city northside, Dublin.

"Does he live in this block?" Min said over his shoulder.

"No," Áine replied, "don't think so. Never seen him before."

FINN OG

"Alright, sunshine. I'll tell you where I came from – right here. I realised my ..." Min looked round at Áine, who was standing behind his chair, "friend was missing, so I went looking for her and find her running away from you."

Áine realised that Min must have searched the CCTV system. "What were you doing at my bin?" she said.

"Are you Sinead?" the man asked again.

"Why are you looking for Sinead?" Áine shouted. "We don't have the fucking phone!"

"What?" the man said, evidently baffled.

Min shifted a little. "Look, you were in her apartment block, in her bin."

"If it's her bin, she must be Sinead." He looked again at Áine.

"Do you live in this building?" Min pressed on.

"Wow," the man said, as if the idea were preposterous. "Give me a break, here. This place is for fat cats and the non-tax-paying scum of this fine city."

Min looked behind him at Áine. "What the hell is he talking about? What were you doing in the car—"

"What happened your face?" the man asked.

Áine peered out through the bruising, as confused as anyone. She ignored the intruder and spoke to Min, "I looked at the camera recordings and saw the two who attacked me had gone into the car park, but the camera down there hadn't triggered. Then I thought maybe they knew about the letters, so I went down to see where the camera was."

"The letters?" Min asked.

Áine shut up, staring suspiciously at the man again. "Shouldn't we, like, tie him up?"

Min shook his head dismissively. There was no need.

"I'm just a delivery boy," the man chirped in, as if he

were the most innocent man in Dublin. "I have me orders and I follow them."

"From whom?" Áine asked.

"I really can't say."

"You'll find yourself saying one way or another," Min said steadily, but with unnerving menace. "You'll tell us who you're working for and we'll go and get her, that's a fact."

"Get who?"

"Sinead," Áine shouted.

"I thought you were Sinead?" The man was back to bafflement.

"Ah, for fuck's sake," Min spat. "Tell me who the hell you are or I'm gonnae snap your fucking wrist." He got up.

"Wow, brother!" The man held up his hands before whipping them behind him lest the threat should be carried through. "There is no need for further violence. Looks like this young one has seen enough of that for the lot of us."

Min paused. There was something florid and beguiling about the man's overconfident patter that suggested an unconnectedness to the attackers.

"Talk, you little prick."

"Pot and kettle," the man muttered, for which he was treated to a large paw around the throat and a pinning against the Liffey-facing window.

"Alright, alright, fuck it, anyway!" the man said, his toes still dancing on the rug for Min's stretch could hoist him no higher. "I was engaged by a former comrade to perform delivery of certain letters to and from this apartment complex," he gushed.

"Stop talking like an estate agent and just tell us what's going on."

"If you're not Sinead," the man croaked over Min's head, "who are you?"

"Just tell him before I bust his head." Min's patience was exhausted.

"I'm her sister."

"Ah, you're Áine!"

"How do you know that?"

"I, young woman, am Fran. I am a comrade in arms to the young Sam – without the arms, admittedly," he gasped.

Min lowered the man to heel height.

"Have you any identification?" Min hissed.

"I do, brother, I do." Fran fished in his back pocket for a wallet and opened it to display – with pride – a union membership card inside a film-faced pocket.

"I know who he is," Áine muttered with resignation.

"What were you delivering?" Min remained confused.

"Well, that is largely private," Fran said.

"Just tell him," Áine snapped, her back to both men.

Fran held up his hands. "Look, I don't know what's been happening here, but all I'm doing is acting as a courier for an old friend."

Áine placed her hands at shoulder height against the wall, her head dipped between. "Sinead's missing. Min is Sam's best friend. For fuck's sake, just tell him why you're here before he cracks your skull open."

"You make a persuasive argument," Fran said, oddly unperturbed.

"Hurry up, then," Min growled again, "and stop with all the bollocks talk."

"Sam contacted me asking for assistance in delivering letters – old-fashioned style – from his location to this. He suggested a curious means of transportation, but I have become accustomed to his clandestine behaviours and so acceded to his wishes."

Min turned to Áine. "Why does he talk like that?"

"I haven't a clue. I've never met him before."

"How is it that you—"

She sighed. "I know he put work Sam's way. I helped Sam set up the system that kept his work under the radar. He," she pointed at Fran, "was involved in the Libya disaster – before it was Libya. He gave Sam information that led to the sinking of some ship in Egypt – I never got the full story. It doesn't matter."

"You're from a trade union?" Min looked perplexed.

"I am!" Fran announced. "I am the rep for your fine country and this one, and I assist beleaguered seafarers suffering at the hands of the capitalist classes who would exploit the workers to their advantage, caring not for chick nor child."

"Give me strength," Min whispered.

"I have access to a global membership who can ferry goods from one side of the world to another. Now, I'm not at liberty to say from where these letters came—"

"We know he's in Dominica," Áine interjected.

"From Dominica," Fran resumed without drawing breath, "to our glorious green isle. That, I did out of regard for our mutual friend."

"So Sam got you to tape letters inside our bin?" Áine said.

"Look," he brandished an envelope as if it were a golden Wonka ticket, "here is the one I was to leave today before being so rudely man-handled." He stared at Min with distaste.

"How did you get in?"

"Ah, now …" Fran got defensive.

"Answer her!" Min suddenly shouted in Fran's face.

"The man on the front door is a member."

"Of what?"

"The union."

"Right." Min shook his head.

"Are you signed up at all?" Fran ventured, ever the opportunist.

"Not in my line of work."

"So how are the letters getting back and forward?" Áine asked.

"Ship."

"That's why it's so slow."

"Old school," Fran said. "Now, Sinead I have spoken to on the phone, in the line of duty, but I have never actually met the woman, so what's the diddly there?"

Min's tightened jaw could not contain his guttural displeasure.

"He means story," Áine explained. "What's the story."

"It's like I've entered another dimension," Min said.

"Sinead and Sam are – confusing," Áine said. "They have a relationship, of sorts."

Fran raised an eyebrow. "Above my pay grade. Anyways, thanks for the abuse and actual bodily harm, but if it's all the same with you, I need to take this and get it dispatched. I don't suppose there's much point taping Sam's letter inside the bin lid."

Áine turned quickly. "Sinead left a letter in the bin?"

Fran suddenly looked sheepish.

"Did she or didn't she?" Áine shouted.

"I have it here," Fran conceded, fishing a second envelope, complete with parcel tape, from inside his jacket.

"When did she do that?" Áine's mind was whirring.

"Any time from last collection," Fran announced.

"Which was when?"

Fran shrugged. "Few days back – three or four?"

Áine's gaze fell into the middle distance as she started

counting. "That can't be right – that would be the day I was attacked."

"Well, which day were you attacked?" Fran held his hands out and gestured as if to say, how am I supposed to help if you won't tell me what's happening?

"It's … eh …"

Min stepped forward. "Four days ago."

"Four days ago," Áine repeated. "So," she looked at Fran," was it three or four days ago you collected the last letter?"

Fran looked stumped.

"Check the cameras," Min said.

Áine whipped up the iPad and began hitting it with her index finger and thumb. The two men watched her, trying not to look at one another.

"Here she is arriving. That's four days ago – the day they beat the shit out of me." She looked up at Fran. "Well, look at that, she headed in the direction of the bins before she came up."

Min could tell Áine was slightly hurt at her sister's prioritisation. "Right, well, that makes sense," he tried to deflect. "She leaves a letter before she disappears."

Áine wasn't happy. "So if that was four days ago," she looked up at Fran, "and you say you collected a letter a few days back, then what's the letter in your hand?"

"Good question," Fran said.

Min stared at Áine, working it through. "Could she have left two letters? Would she do that?"

"That's not strictly speaking letter-writing etiquette," Fran chimed in.

"Shut up," Áine and Min said in unison.

Min walked over and gently lifted the iPad from Áine. He then scrolled forward, more clumsily than she had.

"Bloody hell," he turned to Fran, tilting the tablet towards him, "you turned up less than an hour after she left it. I assume you took it away?"

Fran shrugged.

"But you didn't leave a letter?" Áine asked.

"Well, no, as I say, usually one person writes then the other person—"

"Stick your etiquette up yer arse and just answer the questions." Min turned back to the tablet. "Aye, so she went that way twice. Seems she left two letters on the same day."

Áine shook her head. "Why?"

"I dunno, but there she is coming down to the car park at the end of the same day – the day you were attacked. Then she goes for the drugs, gets in the car and drives out."

"Shit," Áine said. "I thought for a minute ..."

"What, if you don't mind me asking?"

"I thought she might have returned – after she went missing. I thought she might just be in the gloom and taking time to herself."

"I'm completely lost now," Fran said.

"We can't find her, Fran. I'm really worried. We think she might—"

Min held out his hand to halt Áine in her tracks.

"Ah, right," said the little Dubliner. "This has something to do with drugs."

Min stared at Fran, who held his gaze unwaveringly. Min noted how ballsy the new arrival was. "The drugs were painkillers for her," he jerked his head in Áine's direction, "after she was attacked."

"Right, so." Fran nodded, willing to accept anything rather than be pinned against the window again.

"Timings don't work. She left one letter – you collected

it – then the same day she left that one that's in your hand. Unless you've been back in-between?"

"No," Fran said. "That's it, twice in the last week only."

Min had questions of his own. "So if you were going to put Sinead's most recent letter on some ship, where is the ship going to, cos Sam's left Dominica."

"Not on this occasion," Fran said. "I am to scan it, without reading it – strict instruction – and send it by email."

Min looked at Áine. "Sam must be relaxing. Mebbe the message is getting through."

"What message?"

"That he's not being looked—" Áine began, only to be hushed again by Min with an upturned hand. "Sorry."

"Sounds messy," Fran concluded. "And how is Sinead missing – since when?"

"What email address?" Áine ignored his questions.

"What?"

"What email address are you to use to send Sinead's letter to him?"

"His usual one – the Charlie one."

Min looked queryingly at Áine.

"Charlie was his little company I set up for him. It's been dormant for ages."

"If he's using an old email, it sounds like he's definitely confident."

"Or desperate," she said nodding. "But where's he gone?"

"That, my new, very violent friends," Fran declared, "I cannot help you with."

Chapter Twenty-One

"WE'RE WASTING TIME HERE," Áine said.

"And I have a job to do," Fran piped up, and headed for the door.

"No chance, pal. Leave those letters here. Áine can send Sinead's – she has the email address, and she'll give Sam's to her sister when we find her."

"But Sam trusts me to deliver it and my word is—"

"My word is, you'll leave that with the sister of the woman who wrote it and you'll take your silly sentences and you'll piss away aff, is that clear enough for ye?"

"Crystal, brother," Fran said, "but on your head be it. I will have to explain all to our mutual friend."

"You will say F-all to anyone, pal. She," he pointed at Áine, "can get into anyone's emails, and if you so much as mutter any of this to any other human, I'll sling you frae that bridge out there. Rest assured, Áine will send the letter."

Fran looked at Min, shook his head and made for the door.

"One more thing," Áine said. "Give me your number in case I need to contact you."

Fran took the pencil from her and wrote on the proffered Post-it. He handed it and the letters to Áine. "I wish you the best of luck in locating you sister," he said. "Regardless of what you may think, I am – quite literally, little more than the messenger here and I have the greatest regard for Sam." He let the door swing closed behind him.

Min exhaled noisily. "What a massive distraction."

Áine looked at him. "What made you come looking for me? Did you find something?"

"Mebbe," he said. "But I also got a call from work."

"You have to go back?" Áine found herself immediately anxious.

"Naw, it was one of my tech team. They canny find ye at all. However you've done it, you seem to be masked." Min was shaking his head in amazement.

"Imagine, and me a woman too."

"Don't be going down that feminist tunnel wi' me – it's a dead end. Right, I need ye tae see something."

Min led Áine into the control room where a series of separate images had been arranged on the screen. In each was a well-dressed woman posing, but her heels and a glimpse of tattoo suggested something else. The shoes were ridiculously high and betrayed the business suit as aimed at some sort of fantasy, while the body art was ill-concealed and teasing. All shots had been taken outdoors.

"Recognise anywhere?"

Áine stared first at the women, then dropped focus to the background. She blew up the images and dragged them around the screens. "What are these – adverts?"

"Aye, escort service. Claims to be high class for accompaniment at dinner and whatnot, then in the same sentence lets you pick a nationality, hair colour and interest."

"Interest?"

"Aye, and they're no talkin' aboot walks in the country-side or going tae the cinema either."

"I see," she said, but she couldn't see at all. "There's nowhere I recognise." Áine's head shook in frustration.

"That's a shame," Min replied. "I couldnae even find a green pillar box in the background tae confirm they were taken in Ireland. In truth, they could be anywhere. It's well done, I'll hand them that much."

"But these can't be the only photos on the phone – there's a few gigabytes in there."

"Storage seems mostly internal shots, all filth. You're no gonnae want tae look at them videos and the like. I'll keep going through them, but it's grimy bedrooms, grainy shots. More blackmail, I'd say."

"Why?"

"I think they're taken on a secret camera, or a mobile phone. The angles are poor, the lighting's dreadful. I think it's all done in secret. Maybe from a handbag or a pinhole camera. I imagine there's a bloke waiting outside who shows the video to their clients as the women leave and then demand more money to delete it."

Áine thought of the world her sister worked in - Sinead's motivation for helping the victims of such exploita-tive behaviour, her bravery at doing so despite all she'd been through. A tear fell down Áine's cheek and she felt an arm around her shoulder, pulling her in. Unable to look up she buried her bruised face into the shoulder of a man she barely knew and she wept, in fear, in sadness and in pride.

———

"YOU KNOW the best thing tae be at?" She heard Min after a few minutes spent sobbing into his armpit.

Áine just shook her head against his solid body.

"Work," he said. "Work at it, build a list of tasks and stroke them off, limit the scope for error."

"The photos?" she said, muffled, not keen to remove herself from his muscular embrace. She felt him stroke her hair and knew he was about to push her upright and she wanted him to leave her where she was.

"I'll look after the photos," he said. "I've got one of my unit scraping the data from the phone to see where it pinged."

"You let it find service here, in this apartment?" Áine pushed herself up in panic.

"Not yet. I cloned it and sent the packet to a man I trust. He's a real geek, no' like you. He can barely hold a conversation."

Áine almost smiled. "So what do I do? What's on my list?" She found herself querying the ease with which she was prepared to be commanded by this man, the comfort in being guided – a feeling hitherto completely alien to her.

"I want you tae think about how Sinead will be reacting – how resourceful is she? What would she do? Any way she might exploit to get a message tae ye. Has she any of your expertise?"

Áine wilted a little. "She has no tech knowledge at all."

"Ok. Well, what's her training – will she fight? If she has been taken, will she be able to manage?"

Áine blanched and stammered. "I don't want to think about that," she blurted in panic. "I really don't want to …" She found her throat swelling and almost making her choke with fear, as if she had been blocking the thought from her mind.

"Hey, hey," Min said soothingly, "easy, now, easy." He reached for her arm again. "What's the matter at all?"

Áine gulped air, calming herself. "It's just, I can't …" She shook her head despondently. She looked at Min in desperation, then down at the floor again, and said quietly, "This isn't Sinead's first rodeo."

———

HE KNEW NOT TO PRESS. Some seam of deep hurt had been struck and he was at a loss as to how to react. "I'm sorry," was all he said.

Áine shook her head again. "I don't even know if Sam knows. I can't—"

"Listen," Min said, "don't be thinking about how she'll react. Ignore me. It's probably not important."

"Then why did you ask?"

"It's something we do. Focus can be helpful, usually." He suddenly looked unsure of himself. "When someone gets taken, captured, I suppose, we make an assessment about how they're likely to react so we can plot how any extraction is likely to pan out. The mental state of any hostage is an important consideration."

"Why?" she almost moaned the word.

"Cos a hostage, or a captive, can right royally fuck up any rescue. If they're likely to fight, if they're not fighters, if they react badly to any violence – and it's usually the case that extractions have pretty extreme violence – the hostage can run around and get themselves … injured," he corrected what he was going to say.

"Sinead won't do that."

"That's good. She's smart, she'll tell them what they

need to know. That would be smart. There comes a point when you have to just tell the truth to protect yourself."

"I don't know if she'll do that."

"How do you mean?"

"I don't know if she will talk."

"What would be the point in not talking? She knows the phone was dumped in a bin, doesn't she?"

"Well, she knows it was dumped but—"

"So she'll tell them that, aye?"

"I don't know, Min. I don't know. If they have her, if they lock her up, I don't know what she'll do!" Suddenly Áine was sobbing again. "I don't know what her state of mind will be. She may … she might not. She might not."

"What? She might not what?"

"She might not say anything! She might close down, or she … she might hurt herself. She won't be able to …"

Min was at a loss, faced with mounting distress and unable to understand any of it. "I'm not following ye here at all. Why would she hurt herself?"

"To stop them being able to …" Áine broke down in a flood of tears. "I can't say. I can't … I don't even know how much she's told Sam, so I can't betray her confidence. I can't …"

"Alright, darlin', he said, rubbing both shoulders, inept in the face of her breakdown. "Ok, ok, I'm sorry, I shouldn't have suggested it. We don't need to talk about this, ok?"

"Then why did you ask?" She thumped her fists gently against his shoulders.

"I wanted to give you something to concentrate on, and all information is useful. It was stupid, I'm sorry."

"I'm so scared. What if she—"

"It's ok, we'll find her. We'll find her." Minutes passed as

Min tried to console Áine and she gradually became quieter and gathered herself, eventually raising her head again and turning to the computer screen. "I suppose we can get the police involved now too, now that Sam's convinced he's not being hunted. That risk has gone."

Áine sat upright. "I'll scan the letter and send it to Sam's email address." She rallied as if at least resolved to do something useful. "Then you can start at the photos again."

"You should lie down a while. You haven't slept properly in days and you'll be no use to me if you're exhausted. We need your mind sharp. Get sleep while you can."

Áine grunted. "Go make some coffee for yourself, I'll not be long."

"Alright," he said, "but none for you." He rose. "You need to get some shut-eye."

Min left the room and Áine opened the envelope.

Chapter Twenty-Two

CAREFUL NOT TO LOOK, she spread the first page on the scanner glass. The paper was thin and her sister's handwriting stared at her from the reverse of the sheet. She genuinely tried not read what was written, but one word burned into her retina. She closed the lid and made sure the letter's image appeared on the screen before her, saved it as a PDF and placed it in a folder. She lifted the lid and flipped the page, closing it and repeating until all five sheets were converted and saved. Then she opened an email, dragged the folder across and typed the Charlie address from memory. She turned and met Min as he entered the room, hitting send in haste and closing down the screen. In one hand he had a glass of water, in the other a fistful of pills.

"Swallow these," he ordered. "They're no' painkillers, but they'll help ye sleep."

She looked at the little pile, and, without questioning him, gladly followed his instruction and swallowed them with the water. "Thanks," she said, looking up at him. "Thank you, Min, for coming."

"Get to bed," he said. "I'll wake you if anything comes in."

She knew then that he was confident she would sleep with what he had administered, but she didn't care. He had removed the guilt, the responsibility, and assumed it himself. She was calm at his presence, his solid reassurance, his innate sense of what needed to be done and his ability to see it through.

She moved into the kitchen, swiped up her iPad and went to her bedroom.

And there she lay, numb and awake, staring at the ceiling, one word keeping her awake.

Uganda.

She had tried to avoid the invasion of her sister's privacy. Whatever was said between her and Sam was their business – even a twin had no right to see inside whatever intimacy they had, but it had been a shock – particularly given what Min had asked about Sinead's state of mind - to see it written there. The name of a place, all that was required to describe an awful truth.

Áine rolled onto one side, her mind blurring a little, as if she'd had a strong drink on an empty stomach. But her agitation would not permit sleep. She rolled onto her back, then her other side, and then back to stare at the white ceiling. Where are you, sis? She thought of Min's stupid questions, and how she wished he hadn't intruded into her twin's mental state, and then of how little she really understood about what had happened there.

Uganda.

All she knew for sure was what it had done to Sinead, who'd returned as a shell of her former self.

Mind swimming, Áine reached out and lifted the iPad, located the file and read.

HI,

Something's happened. It's technically your turn, but I need to let you know something cos it might have an impact.

I'm sitting in the apartment looking at the other one who is bruised and hurt and was beaten to a pulp last night, and I wish you were here. I wish you were here to tell me what to do, and I'm angry with you that you're not – because we told you there was no issue but you won't bloody listen. And now I'm here having to work this out without the one bloody person I know who understands how to deal with stuff like this. I'm at the kitchen counter and she's dozing on the sofa and all I have managed to do is stop the bleeding.

Someone forced their way into the flat and hammered her. They smashed her face and hit her head off the floor. They were looking for the bloody phone she used to ring you. And before you start – no, it's not the authorities or anything – it's a bunch of bloody criminals who just want their phone back, but it's gone now, dumped. It's full of nasty photographs, which is probably why they're so determined to get it. Some woman left it at my work. You know the drill – you'll be able to work out what her line of work was. And because the phone was used to call you, we didn't tell the police about the beating yet, but I'm writing to tell you that we have to because these don't seem to be people who will let this thing lie. I need to tell the Guards, and they might be able to trace the call to where you are, which I don't think will matter one little bit because in all sense and reason nobody's one bit concerned and I can't see how it would affect anything anyway. I don't see why it would matter, although I understand, I get it, that you might. But she's my – I'll not say it but you know what she is to me, and I can't not get the police involved because this cannot happen again. This probably makes no sense as a heads-up.

I can't have her dealing with this sort of violence. The legacy of this stuff is horrific. I hope you understand that. I mean, I know you understand that – the violence thing and how it fucks with your head. That's not what I mean. I mean I hope you understand that I can't have her go through that cos I have been through it and I wouldn't wish that on anyone – even someone who reads my personal bloody letters and sends them off without asking. Which is part of the reason she was here alone, and that's my fault – for being so bloody unreasonably upset with her. I moved into a room at work, so I wasn't here when she was attacked. And she lay on the floor and bled for ages before she was able to ring me, and I didn't even want to answer and she needed me.

She helped me, you know, back when I needed it. You spoke about stuff in the locker. Well, yeah, you're a hundred per cent on that, Sam. On that topic you're nail on the head. My locker has its fill, and I will not have that for her.

I've no computer with me – it's at work, other than hers, and, well, obviously I won't be making that mistake again, so it's handwritten. I'll probably type a different version of this at work later and I'll probably leave a lot of this stuff out, but it felt better to write my anger into the first letter, so what the hell? Counselling ... without a counsellor. Cheap. Dear knows how much I've spent on counselling since then. Since Uganda.

Ever been? I imagine you probably have. I can't begin to guess how far and wide you've been, doing what you did. I've been nowhere. Except Uganda. Not really – Disney,

Spain, Portugal, school trip to France. And Africa. One passport stamp. Just one. I wanted to have a passport full of stamps, and now I wish there weren't any.

I went there on placement from Trinity. It was so feckin' exotic. I watched the sunburst sand from the plane – it was mud, really, but it looked clean, red, completely African. I was so excited. The drive from Entebbe to Jinja, the bicycle men – the Boda Bodas, stopping to offer lifts on their little padded parcel shelves. The incredible flies and creatures by Lake Victoria, the weird insects buzzing around. The talk of saltwater crocodiles and mosquitoes. The malaria drugs that were worse than getting malaria, some people said. Didn't fizz on me at all. I was tough and resilient and ready.

It was a dream job, a placement with a human rights firm. I was going to work wonders and shit miracles out there. I was a naive little girl on her first foreign trip and I thought I was going to advocate for the afflicted and afflict the advocated.

We travelled north to where the interviews were to be conducted. They took us through the most amazing countryside in a tiny Toyota with no air con, but the hot air rushed through the vehicle and the buffering kept us cool. We gazed out at the mud buildings and the coffee and banana plantations, sugar cane and fires and the smells – the smells were amazing. The women stooped from the hip from washing clothes in buckets. For the first time I saw someone carry a can of petrol on their head – just like in the old schoolbooks. For two days I was on top of the world.

Now I'm looking at her and I know what she's going to feel soon. And there can't be any follow-up for her. When she comes round we will make full statements and stop this bloody nonsense. She was so good to me when I came back. We had drifted apart a little when I went to Trinity – she took the piss too much and spent a lot of time in her room, training herself, as it turned out, building her own computers. Why she took that turn is a complete mystery – it wasn't something teenage girls did back then. I dunno.

But when I got released she was there, on the phone before Mam or Dad, even, asking how I was. It was a surprise. And she came out to travel back with me. Mam and Dad had been out when the search was on, but it lasted months and the firm I was working for encouraged them to go home. There was war over it. Dad refused to go back to Dublin but eventually visa rules got the better of him and the government didn't want him wrecking the place, so they basically deported him. The whole thing took a lump out of them that will never be properly fixed.

I'm not explaining but that doesn't matter cos I will cut pretty much all of this anyway before I send it. But it helps to write it down to you as if I'm telling you cos this way it somehow feels safer. I don't feel like crying this way. If you were here, I'd probably bawl like a dumped schoolgirl.

Ehm ... the release. No, the kidnapping first. That was a blur. A complete blast of noise and dust. We were with the girls – well, they weren't girls in the normal sense. They were barely teenagers, but they'd all had children of their own and had been brutalised, horrific, horrendous forced and depraved stuff. They'd been kidnapped years before from a school in the north and marched off by Kony and his madmen pretending to do the work of God. The Lord's Resistance Army, evil to the core. They killed thousands of people for absolutely no reason and stole their children and raped and mutilated them and turned the kids into machine-gun wielding maniacs.

So these were the miracles I was there to perform, to help these children use international law. What a joke.

Joseph Kony is probably still marauding around the north or Congo or wherever sowing his seed of hatred and twisted alchemy like some settler medium whipping up a cult.

Why do you make me waffle so much?

It would have been second nature to you, the attack. You'd have known what to do. I would love to have that instinct but I know I never will. The ack-ack of those bloody guns, the people lying dead everywhere. They walked straight up to those poor children and executed them right in front of me. I screamed so hard I couldn't hear myself, and I prayed so hard and they didn't kill me, and I wished for years afterwards that they had just shot me.

We were the only whites within hundreds of miles. I was a mzungu, an object of curiosity, evidently, because they took me as a trophy. Ten girls and me, led off through the bush, loaded into old cars and driven for days in the heat. I didn't care – I thought I didn't, anyway, because I thought, well, what can they do to me now? There's nothing more they can do. They killed everyone, probably because someone told them what we were doing there. Us white legal knights fighting the good fight and all we did was get the kids massacred.

But then they found a way to make it worse. Can you believe that? Actually, you of all people probably can. They made it worse, and then they made it worse again, and then they made it worser and worser and you can imagine and I don't need to elaborate. I don't know if it will make the cut but I feel I need to give you another heads-up in case it ever crosses your mind or in case anything ever does come of whatever we are. I will never be able to have children. That's said now. That's been on my mind. How to tell you. If ever we did manage to cobble something out of this mess, that might be a deal-breaker. I don't know because we haven't even covered the first step yet – you know, a movie, maybe a walk on the beach.

Waffle.

Glad to have said it. Maybe, to hell with it, I will send this. The last letter at least moved us forward, I think. Didn't it?

And now that I've said it, it feels like a hell of a weight off my mind. So here's the other thing that plagues my head: I have wondered whether part of the tractor beam around you is the little person. It's worried me, getting so attached, knowing that I can never…. This makes me so sad to admit, but it worries me that I'm compensating somehow. Does that make sense? You are not one, you are two people, and it worries me that that's part of the draw, given what I've just told you. I don't know if it matters if that's part of the draw, cos I'd probably be drawn if you were just one, or if she was just one. But how can you know for sure, and am I overthinking it, and what the hell does it matter anyway? But, for sure, the way you are with her is part of it, maybe more than part, but that's the package, so what am I worried about? Agh … what the fuck am I saying at all? And I need to stop swearing. I barely swore till I met you – just in my own head, not out loud and definitely not on paper.

Anyway, so we are going to the police. That's a lot of steam blown off to tell you that. S'pose I could have just called, given we have your number even if we don't have the bloody phone any more.

Tell her I miss her. Loads and loads.

———

ÁINE WOKE THREE HOURS LATER. Her sleep had been unusually deep and her head ached as if she'd been drinking. She reached for water that wasn't there, and then remembered the pills Min had given her, that Min was in her apartment, which made her feel immediately at ease, then her sister's letter, which made her feel guilty.

She had known a lot of what was in it. Some of what Sinead had written to Sam had surfaced in the dreadful days and months following Sinead's return from Africa. But there were things she should not know, and for that she felt shame. She had seen inside her sister's heart, and that was not fair.

Áine wondered how she would feel were the roles reversed. Fine, she told herself, grand, no secrets with me. But no lasting damage either. No romantic prospect lurking out of reach, for that matter. And no way she would, or could, ever write a letter like that – so honest and open and gentle. Áine knew that her love would be an ugly love, built on feigned hostility and harsh comments to protect herself from the fear of failure or rejection.

The one good thing about reading the letter was now she had carte blanche to make a call. She got up, pulled on some leggings and walked through to the control room – the screens of which were filled with images of flesh and bed sheets. Min turned as she walked in.

"Let's call the Guards," she said.

"Good morning to you too," Min said, looking at her quizzically.

"And Sinead will be in shit shape, if that's what you needed to know. She will be absolutely terrified and will attack anyone who goes near her."

Min was now completely confused. "Right, ok." He stared at her. "I thought you weren't keen on the cops?"

"Well, I am now. Just ring them."

"I can't. I'm no' supposed to be here, aye? You're no' allowed anybody in other houses, sure."

"I'll ring them, so," she huffed.

"Are you sure Sinead will fight?"

"If they try any of this shit," Áine gestured at the screens, "she'll claw their eyes out."

"That's good," Min said, thinking.

"No," Áine said. "Not good. Not good at all. This could set her back years."

Áine swiped up the phone and dialled the Guards.

———

MIN LOOKED at her as she slumped back into her chair. Her head fell into one hand, the other held the phone she'd just finished talking into. "If they touch her, I'll fucking incinerate them." She broke into a sob.

Min looked at her. "You're exhausted," he tried. "Did you get no sleep at all?"

"I did sleep," she said. "I shouldn't have. I should be looking for her. Fuck's sake, what am I doing sleeping when she's been taken by these bastards?" She pointed at the screen again in anger.

Min reached over and triggered the screen saver, the images weren't helping.

"I think it's time you told me what you mean – set her back how?"

Áine stared at him, desperate to offload, to make her problems his, to share the burden and allow him to apply the solution. She shook her head.

"You can trust me. Whatever it is that's making you so … upset—"

"I'm not upset – I'm bloody angry, and I'm hopeless. I can't find these bastards. They're smarter than they should be and Sinead will be ..." she trailed off, willing Min to press so she could collapse her armour.

"She'll be what?"

Áine allowed her shoulders to fall. "You can never speak of this again – not to Sam, not to me, and certainly not to Sinead."

"Of course."

"Something happened to her. In Africa. Years ago. She was kidnapped, attacked. Repeatedly, horrifically, by a gang, an army, really. Militia, I suppose."

"Where?"

"What?"

"What country?"

"Does it matter?"

"I dunno," he said.

"Uganda."

"LRA?"

"Yes."

"Bloody hell."

"Yes."

"How long did they have her?"

"Five months."

"I see," he said softly. He needed to say no more.

"She's carried all that damage for a long time. That's why she does what she does for work, and why she's so good at it. You know she was top of her year at Trinity in law? She could be coining it at the Four Courts, and instead she's immersed in this salacious shit trying to scrape by on a charity wage."

"Why? Why with all that damage would she surround herself with other damaged folks?"

"Cos she can help them, I guess. It takes one to know one and all that. It's all the stuff she's good at – empathy, sympathy, emotional intelligence. All the things that were confined to her side of the womb."

Min could tell that wasn't the first time Áine had considered their genetic distribution.

"Maybe it helps her too, in a way?"

"Maybe. It's like a vocation or something. It … gives her purpose."

Min's right eyebrow dropped in query. "Purpose?"

"She had none. For a long time after she got back. They broke her will to live." Áine's tears welled again and she looked up at the roof.

"I see," Min said. "I think I understand."

"So Sam bloody Ireland better have something for her when he gets back, cos I don't know how much a person can take, Min. If she gets out of this, she's going to need minding, and I don't know if I'm able for that again. If they lay a finger on her, they might just destroy her."

Chapter Twenty-Three

MIN'S PHONE buzzed on the wide desk and Áine gathered herself before rising.

"I'll put on the breakfast if you're not going to sleep. Empty sack won't stand."

He nodded as he lifted the handset.

She raided the fridge for the stuff she ate that Sinead didn't – the sausages, the pudding, the rashers. The noise of the pan and the smell that rose from it overwhelmed her with a sudden hunger – a desire to get on with the day and get stuck in, and for the first time in ages she realised that her physical pain was abating.

The plates were on the table, the sauces laid out and the coffee mugs steaming by the time Min emerged from her control room. "I've somethin' tae tell ye," he said, in a tone that for him probably passed for urgent.

"What is it?" she said, panicked but eager.

And then the intercom buzzed, and buzzed again. Áine looked at Min. "What is it?" she said again as she moved to the door.

"Get that and I'll explain."

Áine took the phone from its wall cradle. "Yes?"

There was a murmur. She scowled. "You just let them through?"

Min immediately moved towards the door, assuming the worst. Áine held up her hand, and replaced the handset. "It's ok, it's just the cops. Get into my room. That dickhead on the door already let them into the lift. Quick!"

Her bedroom door closed as the front door knocked. She rolled her shoulders, sought composure and opened it a crack.

"Garda McKenna and Garda Kowalczyk," the man said. Áine recognised the voice from last time. "Don't suppose we will be allowed in this time?" She also recognised his sarcasm.

"Have you got ID?" The Polish name had been unexpected.

"Yes, very thorough," the male officer said, handing through his plastic credentials. Áine looked at it closely, although she knew this was the same police officer she'd spoken to previously. "Come in, so," she said, opening the door but standing instinctively behind it. She kept her back to them as she pushed it into its frame.

The two officers entered the wide hallway, evidently taken with the spaciousness of the penthouse. "Eh, what is it you said you do for work, Áine – do you mind if I call you Áine?"

"You can call me what you like so long as you get your bloody finger out this time and find my sister," she replied tersely.

The guard turned to her and his face darkened when he saw the state of hers. "That explains why you wouldn't open the door last time."

"Yeah," she said. The woman Garda cast her eyes over Áine's damaged face in an inscrutable manner.

"Sorry to disturb your breakfast," the impertinent policeman sniffed the air as he invited himself to venture further into the apartment. He stood with the kitchen to his left and gazed over the river to the North Wall Quay. "Some pad," he said absently. "Just the two of you living here, yes?"

"Yeah. Have you turned anything up?" Áine said irritably.

"Your work," Garda McKenna said. "You didn't say—"

"Cos I don't see how that helps, to be honest. You know what Sinead does, that's relevant."

"And I know you either have a large appetite or you've done a breakfast for me," he replied with a sly smile. Áine hadn't even seen him glance at the table, the two plates laid out neatly. The implication was clear: you can't be too worried if you're still on your food and you have someone here who shouldn't be. The lockdown indiscretion hung between them. The female guard said nothing – following the conversation in what was not, presumably, her native tongue.

"Garda McKenna, have you made any progress or not?" she found herself formalising the uncomfortable encounter.

"This isn't even a missing person."

"Five days she's been gone!"

"Four, technically." He smiled. "Your sister is a grown woman who was caught robbing controlled drugs from a convent. Now, that seems to us cause enough to take yourself off for a while, doesn't it, Lena?"

The woman guard nodded. "Yes, perhaps," she agreed, cautiously, with only a light hint of an accent.

Áine suppressed her rising temper. "Robbing? She's

never stolen a thing in her life. Those drugs were for this!" She pointed to her own face.

"Perhaps you should have told me that last time we were here."

"Look, I told you already that I think she's been abducted. I think that the people who attacked me may have taken her."

"Who attacked you?"

"I don't know."

"Are you sure?"

"Yes, I'm sure." Áine struggled to fathom the thinly veiled hostility of this chippy little police officer.

"Maybe whoever was waiting on the drugs being handed over?"

"Excuse me?" Áine's face crumpled in disgust.

"Or are you sure it wasn't your sister, maybe the worse for wear?"

"What!" Áine said. "What are you asking me?"

"She was stealing drugs, maybe she has a dependency problem?"

"Am I going insane here?" was all Áine could manage.

"Look at it from where I'm standing. We have one woman, badly beaten and yet to tell us how. The same woman didn't mention this beating when she failed to open the door when we first called, amid all the pressures of dealing with a global pandemic. We have a missing woman – or not, who was caught stealing drugs from her workplace and has since disappeared. Now we have the badly beaten woman asking us back for help. She apparently lives alone with her missing sister but evidence suggests there's someone else here, which is against current government guidelines. And we have a record of the missing woman being recovered twice from attempts on her own life."

Which was when Áine flipped, despite knowing Min would hear everything. "You are not here to help me, and when this is over I will make sure you pay for this."

The guard spoke over her, looking at his colleague. "Did you hear that, Lena? Threatening a—"

"You came here with one thought in your head!" Áine was shouting now. "You decided drugs and self-harm and you aren't prepared to listen."

"Not just self-harm," the guard said, nodding at Áine and gesturing to her face. "You still haven't explained that."

"Neither will I to a gobshite like you!" she all but screamed.

"Lots of families are struggling with the lockdown," he said. "The number of domestics we've dealt with ..." He shook his head and looked at the nodding Lena.

"How is this a bloody domestic?"

"You were beaten here," he stated, not a question.

"How do you know that?"

"There's blood in the grout of those lovely tiles in the hall. There's the remnants of a smashed plant pot or maybe a vase swept under that table, and there's what is probably blood smeared on the headrest of that sofa. There is someone else here, but I have no warrant to look. And you have told me very little that is true since your first call."

Áine glanced around and her thoughts reeled. How had he seen all of that at a sweep, and why would he not put that intellect to proper use?

"Which makes me wonder," he continued, "who is here with you? Who is squirrelled away waiting for their breakfast?"

"Get out!"

Lena at least had the decency to look awkward. McKenna simply shrugged. "Complainant asked us to leave," he said as he pulled out a small notebook and pencil, jotting down the words he had just uttered.

Áine marched to the door and hauled it open, rage in her eyes.

"You've been wasting our time since you first called," McKenna said just before he left.

"I certainly wasted my own thinking you would help," she snarled.

His colleague moved ahead, out of earshot, and he dropped to a whisper. "Just shows you, money can't buy honesty."

Áine slammed the door behind him and picked up the phone to the front desk. "Joe, unless someone has a search warrant, do not ever let anyone up here again without asking me first." The phone was then thrown at the wall, off which it clattered before dangling down and bouncing on its flex.

Chapter Twenty-Four

MIN EMERGED from Áine's room. Saying nothing, he looked at her and moved to the wall, sweeping up the strangled handset and replacing it on its hook.

"I don't get it," was all Áine could manage at first.

Min just looked at her.

"Why won't they help?" she tried, ashamed of her own reaction.

"We could have done with them," he said quietly.

She felt gently admonished. "You think I lost my temper?"

"There's nothing better than boots on the ground. The plods have plenty of those, and comms, a network and vehicles. All we have is you, me and your control room."

Áine tried hard not to take offence at what he was suggesting. "You think I should have poured the tea and offered him your rashers?"

"Probably," he said, without emotion. Just matter of fact, straightforward. She hated it, and yet she found herself drawn to it. Nobody had ever really taken her to task before – they had all been too afraid.

"Sorry," she muttered.

"We are where we are," he said, shrugging. "We can forget the cops for now. Maybe they'll do more than we think they will, but they left with precious little useful information."

Áine's eyes welled again. She looked for a distraction. "Your breakfast," she said, bustling forward, wiping the corner of her eyes as soon as her back was to him. She poured coffee and they sat. After a while staring at the plate, arms motionless, she looked up, desperate to move on. "You said you had something to tell me?"

"Yeah, but I don't know for sure what it means."

"What is it?"

"You know I've had someone in my team looking into the madam's phone? He's a right techie, this man. Former signals, before he saw the light. Nightmare."

"Why's he a nightmare?"

"No, that's his name. I'll never understand how he managed to get through CTC."

"Through what?"

"The commando training course. He shifted from another unit and went through it all to become a Royal Marine."

"Oh. Why Nightmare?"

"Cos he's tall as a tree and thin as a twig and he eats nothing but dust. Started as 'Sniper's' – 'Sniper's nightmare', but he's smart as a fox and can find ways around firewalls and fencing like I've never seen. Till I met you."

"Thank you, I think. I wouldn't mind being as thin as a twig."

Min looked up suddenly. "Don't be daft," was all he

said, and again something pulsed in her. She waited, struck teenage dumb. "Anyway," he said between shovels of sausage, "this boy says he was hunting the phone around signal masts but had no joy. Then he tries pinging any in-store Wi-Fi – McDonald's cloud bubbles and the like, and the only one he gets, besides when you used it, is on a bus, believe it or not."

"The madam's phone used Wi-Fi on a bus?"

"A coach, I'd say – like one that does airport runs. This one," he said, "was Belfast to Dublin."

"Ok," Áine looked outside, "so their trade is cross-border? What do you think that tells us?"

"I don't think that's important." Min gulped down some coffee.

"So what's the big deal?"

"While he was smashing up the VPN to get the IP pings on the phone, he stumbled across a match."

"A match to what?"

"To his search. You'll know more about all this than me probably, but he says it's all confused by this bloody data matching going on with the contact tracing apps. Basically they're hauling data they're no' supposed to be from these applications."

"Who are?"

"The spooks, I'd guess. They're no gonnae miss a chance like this, to dip into a whole pile of information that people are freely giving the government for other purposes."

"The Covid tracing apps?"

"Aye. If you think about the amount of people who've downloaded those apps all across Europe and are dancing about the place freely giving away their information, it's a pot of gold."

"Would they do that?"

"Download the apps?"

"No – the spooks, would they exploit the information?"

"Sure, that's their job, that's what they're paid to do."

"I know that," Áine bristled. "I'm not naive about what they do."

"Then you'll know what they can achieve better than me – you build these things."

"Not really …" But Áine had built phone apps in the past, and she knew how they offered a window into data that few people understood unless they read every word in the user agreement. "I haven't looked at the Covid apps."

"What do you think, though – could they be useful?"

"Anything that allows location gathering is useful," she said, "but it depends on the app's security functions whether someone hacking would find it beneficial to spend a lot of time using the access for other things."

"These apps were built in a hurry but even locations would help build up an intelligence picture. I'd say that's not what they'll be doing, though."

"Anyone with anything to hide isn't going to download these apps, surely? No terrorist or insurgent is going to take a risk like that."

"Course not," said Min. "Which is what's funny about this."

"What?" Áine said, increasingly ill-tempered at her own inability to grasp what was being suggested.

"Nightmare tells me they're looking for this phone *through* the Covid apps. They know this phone is out there – they're hunting for it, for whatever reason. The way they've chosen to do that is to scan the Covid tracing data to see if they can find a close contact with the madam's phone so they can place it."

"But that's pointless unless the app was downloaded to the madam's phone?"

"Well, they obviously don't think so."

"You reckon they've manipulated the software on the apps?"

"Nightmare reckons they don't need to. A proximity signal can register whether it's collected or not. Only those with the apps will get a notification and all other data is demolished, binned. But it could still be collected, he thinks, by anyone with the know-how."

"And you think the spooks or whatever would do that?"

"Wouldn't you if you were them?"

Áine thought for a moment. "So whoever is looking for the phone, would, in theory, be able to place it here if we hadn't closed down its data?"

"I don't know. I'm not sure if it would need to have Bluetooth or location on to match it to another device, but they'll probably have an easy way around that too. Then again, they're maybe just shooting in the dark. Maybe they've been asked to look for it without a full briefing about why. They might just be going through the usual motions, more in hope than expectation."

"So it's neither here nor there?"

"Well, d'ye no' think it's interesting that somebody, maybe even a government agency, is looking for a phone that's sitting in this apartment?"

"I think it's more worrying than interesting."

"Aye. Maybe. But so long as your kit is up to snuff—"

"It is," she replied immediately.

"Then there's no issue for us. But it's weird that it's suddenly on somebody's radar, aye?"

"So what agency is looking for it?"

"Dunno."

"Can you find out?"

"Naw." Min shook his head. His plate had been cleared completely – she hadn't even noticed him eating.

"How come?"

"Look, my unit is focused on military-type intelligence, not civilian. We are set up tae gather information on an immediate enemy – targets we can sometimes see moving around in front of us. Our comms intercepting stuff is great and everything, but there's other wings that looks in tae all that data hacking and intel mapping. If ye want a picture of a target compound modelled in 3D in advance of an attack, we're your boys. All this other stuff, that's another branch altogether."

"Well, can you ask that branch to find out? Or ask why they're hunting for this phone?"

"Not without raising flags we don't want fluttering, or without giving away my interest in all of this, no. If that's what you want, I can do it, but I'm back to barracks, and the truth is, you might not be any further forward. I'm no' supposed to be here, mind? I canny stay on if they realise I'm moonlighting on something, and whatever happens, I canny be found in a foreign jurisdiction. They'll think I've gone rogue – or mercenary."

Áine sat quietly for a while, trying to find the logic of what she was being told. "You don't think we're wrong, do you?"

"About what?"

"That maybe they *are* looking for Sam after all? That we've been hoodwinked?"

"I wondered that. In all honesty, I can't say for sure. But I don't see how this would be the way to do it. Nightmare seems sure they're trying to locate the device. If they're looking for Sam, they'd want to locate Sam – not the device that contacted him."

"Yeah, but as you say, it's part of an intelligence picture. If they've made that connection—"

"Which is unlikely. It was a phone call to a foreign country and to a man reasonably well removed from Sam. Far as anyone else is concerned, Sam's nowhere near this phone."

"But *if* they've somehow made the connection, and they know Sam has left the Caribbean, then the phone would be an obvious thing to monitor as maybe another call could place and locate him? Or maybe they think he's coming *to* the phone?"

"All of that's possible," Min conceded. "I've been kicking that around a bit too. But it's more credible, I reckon, that whoever owns this phone is on a watch list, or the plods in some UK police force have made a request to trace the phone after a blackmail request. That could happen."

"So a detective investigating, say, the suicide of that kid in England, would ask for information on the phone?"

"I don't think the cops would have the capacity for cracking into this type of tech by themselves. They'd probably hand all the information they have on the blackmail to the National Crime Agency, who might hand it on to GCHQ and hope that it eventually climbs to the top of their in tray."

"And what would happen then?"

"I honestly don't know – it's not my area. I imagine they'll take a look, make an assessment as to whether they want to get evidential, or if there's an intelligence opportunity instead."

"What do you mean?"

"Look, this might be a bit tricky to get your head around, but their job isn't about solving past crimes. Their job is about preventing future crimes. In all honesty, military intelligence and the security services could solve most of the big crimes already committed, but that's no' what they're there for. Their job is about knowing what's coming, building a picture of the networks involved and allowing them to play through their plans so they can get as accurate a picture as possible."

"But that's criminal in itself!" Áine was on the cusp of a rant. "What about that poor suicide kid's family? They deserve justice!"

Min held up his paw. "It's grim, I know, but think it through. If there's an intelligence opportunity in something they find, they'll take it."

"Like what?"

"Like, I dunno – maybe there's a link to some prostitute and some Russian criminal? Maybe the Russian criminal is in the pay of some oligarch with influence on a Kremlin staffer? Who knows what messages or pressure could be sent up the chain and what information could come down it."

"Are you serious? They'd let that kid's family—"

"You're no' being rational. Their job isn't justice for some poor family who has lost a kid, their job is to keep their country safe from cyberattacks and dirty bombs and all sorts of other manipulation. There's bigger fish tae fry for them."

"That's scandalous."

"I'm surprised you're surprised."

"I'm not," Áine said. "Not for one fucking second. But I never thought Sinead would become collateral to this type of shit."

"She might not be. We don't know what's going on here.

It's interesting, though, that someone has asked for this phone to be traced. Chances are, it's got absolutely nothing to do with us at all."

"Apart from the fact it's sitting in the next room."

"Aye, maybe it's just as well you didn't spill the beans to the cops after all. We should have told them about the beating and the abduction, but I'm starting to think that your temper might just have done us a favour."

"Cos nobody official knows we have the phone?"

Min nodded.

"So what do we do next?"

"Two things," he said. "You can keep trying to place that bloody phone – find where it's been, but there's a risk in that."

"You're worried this other interested party might see me looking."

"Exactly. We don't want them turning their attention to you. I dunno what that might mean for any of us."

"But we need to find Sinead, so we deal with all of that later."

"Agreed. We concentrate on the biggest risk – which is to your sister."

"And what will you do?"

"I need to book some leave," he said, looking at her for a moment and almost smiling. "Then I'm gonnae give them what they want."

Chapter Twenty-Five

MIN PEERED out the window of the all but abandoned motor cruiser and stared at a plush, expensive Hallberg-Rassy yacht tied up diagonally opposite on another finger of the pontoon.

It was Áine's idea, but one to which he'd readily agreed. Setting up an OP on board a boat was glamorous compared to the hedges and hides of his younger years, and as the creak of his bones began to mirror the strain on the ropes holding his hide to Dublin Marina, he took comfort that he had what passed for a flushing toilet – no need for plastic doggie bags or cellophane for waste. As observation posts went, it was tolerable.

At first Áine baulked at his plan to set the phone alight again, offering it to the satellites – location, data and all. Her face had dropped, her fear of further attack familiar to Min. Once beaten, forever afraid – the lot of a civilian, and many a new recruit. Some never got beyond their first enemy contact – nerves shredded and instantly useless. Medical discharge was not uncommon among the regulars.

So he'd been surprised at how quickly Áine arrived at a suggested location. "The harbour," she'd rallied, once he'd explained the plan. "It's well covered and I can see everything."

"How do you know?"

Áine hesitated then, looking at him for a while before sighing. "I did it for Sinead, before she was taken. It's where Sam left from when he disappeared. We were trying to see what way his boat turned."

"Out the harbour, ye mean?" Min asked, almost scoffing.

"Yeah, Dún Laoghaire."

"Sure, he could have turned any direction. That doesnae mean that's where he was headed."

Áine bristled. "Well, it did actually. He turned south, which is where we found him next. So, Captain Pugwash, stick that up your smart arse."

Min laughed. "You are some prickly wee bitch," he muttered. "So show me what you can see down there."

They'd bounced around the available cameras. Dublin Harbour was vast, with various yacht clubs and lots of quays and walls, many of which were occupied by large buildings, all overlooking the sea.

"This isn't great," Min murmured. "Everyone seems to be overlooking the boats."

"Ah, but remember," Áine held up a finger, "we're in lockdown. And look at all these fancy yachts that nobody's allowed to go anywhere near."

Min considered for a long minute. "Maybe it makes more sense than I realised," he said absently. "*If* someone is looking for Sam through this phone, a boat will seem logical. He lives on a boat."

"But you're not wanting to attract intelligence types, are

you? You're just trying to hook the people who took Sinead?"

"Aye, I'm wanting the people who beat bells out of you, but whoever turns up is likely to take us one step closer. If it's not the madam or her goons, then we might at least get a sense of who else is looking for that bloody handset."

Áine paused for a moment, alarm swelling in her. "Are you, not, like, worried about that?"

"What?" He turned.

"That some spooky people could come."

Min shrugged. "They'll no' know I'm there."

"They're spooks. Of course they'll know you're there."

"How?"

"I ... I dunno. They just – well, they should, if they're any good."

"No offence taken," he said, smiling.

"I'm not saying you can't keep under the radar—"

"I mean it, no offence taken."

Áine again found herself revelling at Min's self-assuredness, realising that she found it, well, reassuring.

"So what are the requirements?"

"This isnae a tech project but I like your style."

"Tell me what you need and I'll sort it. Brilliantly." She felt the need to assert her own expertise into proceedings.

"Well, whoever comes for the phone will need to be able to physically get to wherever we leave it. And it could take a long time for them to trace it, so it will need power to charge."

"A boat, so," she'd said, dragging the map around the screen. "How about here?" She pointed to an isolated spit of pontoons.

"Aye," he said, reading. "West Pier. Looks more remote than the rest. Less eyes on."

"I can't see how you get down to it, though."

"There's no walkway." He shook his head.

"Surely that's not a barrier to the likes of you," Áine couldn't resist poking.

"But it might be to whoever it is coming for that." He pointed to the case in which the offending phone was still wrapped.

"Point taken. Well, next best option is the main marina. Here." She clicked.

"It's well overlooked," he said. "What's that?"

"Royal Irish Yacht Club," she read off the screen, then did a search.

"Looks more like a town hall or parliament building."

"Welcome to Dublin, Min. Once the most beautiful city in the British Empire, before we got rid of ye."

"I'm Scots, remember."

"Working for the Queen, all the same," she scolded. "It's closed. Members are advised that dining and access is temporarily on hold due to government restrictions."

"Good. And how about that?" He pointed to another large building.

"That's the marina office," she said, typing. "Also closed – as in, access to the marina. So it's all yours."

"And there's power?"

"On every pontoon," she said.

"Right then. Wipe that phone of all of its smut and especially the stuff with the young folks. Then we'll dig in."

And so Min sat, freezing, inside a dilapidated boat while the phone rested snugly inside a beautiful yacht nearby, plugged into its electric supply and sending signals to the moon and back in a kind of cellular honeytrap.

Chapter Twenty-Six

"PICK ME A NICE ONE," he'd said.

She selected an abandoned metal heap lashed to the pontoon by ropes dripping with green weed, rust stains running down its sides. "That one," she announced.

"Why?"

"It's for sale and has been for four years." She was running three screens at once, her hands rattling the keyboards as if she was playing a bodhrán.

"Must be something wrong with it if it's been for sale so long."

"Must be a kip. And nobody wants a kip. And nobody will be looking at an old, abandoned yoke like that, lockdown or no lockdown."

"I can see shore power cables from all the boats around it – but not that one."

"Does that matter?"

"No heating on board."

"Want a hot water bottle?"

"It'll do well," he ignored her wise crack.

"How will you get to it?"

"I'll get spotted if I try to clamber over that fence. I'd better get the togs out."

Áine had stared at him. "You're not going to swim to it, are you?"

"If we want to fly low, it's the best way. Anyway, if this is successful, I canny really just follow whoever comes to collect it by walking up the marina's pontoons behind them, can I? That's no' very ... what de ye call it?"

"Clandestine?"

"Aye. I'll go when it gets dark."

"You're mad. How will you dry your clothes? How will you keep the phone dry?"

"I'll take them with me in a dry bag."

"A wha?"

"Doesnae matter. You stick tae finding any pings that bloody phone made in recent times and try tae map it out. The more information we have, the tighter the net. And then, if someone comes to the marina, you can keep an eye on them using the CCTV cameras in case I lose them, and guide me best ye can."

———

MIN HAD BEEN CONCERNED that his body heat could cause condensation – a giveaway most people overlooked. He needn't have worried. The rust bucket Áine had selected had so many cracks and gaps that the wind whistled through and dispelled any warm air immediately.

He'd boarded the Hallberg-Rassy yacht on the opposite pontoon and switched on the madam's phone with all its attention-grabbing data before plugging it into a twelve-volt socket by a chart table. His eyes fell to a thick sleeping bag on one of its bunks, which he rapidly liberated. Then he'd returned to the rusty, abandoned motor cruiser and sat, knees drawn to his chest, and waited. His own phone had only two full juice packs for recharging, so he switched it off while he was awake and powered it up only when asleep.

He and Áine quickly fell into a routine. Before he dozed, he sent a message via an encrypted app she'd installed to say he was "on the blink". She would then take over monitoring the cameras for any activity. And that's how they operated. For three days.

Min's body began to fossilise, lactic build-up causing pain and weakness, so he used an overhead beam to perform a couple of pull-ups every few hours, and kept a regimen of squats and calf raises. Each time he rewarded himself with half a protein bar and tried to ward off the increasing concern that they may have overestimated their adversaries. They'd made assumptions that whoever was behind the blackmail scam had not only the desire to get the phone back at any cost, but also had the tech to track it. As the days and freezing nights wore on, Min began to doubt everything.

Áine battered away at the data she had taken from the phone, searching for new ways of determining where it had been, and hunting for patterns. Late into the second evening she was lying on the bed when Min sent a message.

On the blink.

As she rose to fire up the monitors to begin her shift, her phone screen reoriented from sideways to vertical. Which made her think.

She almost skipped through to the control room, shaking the mouse but not paying attention to the screens as she, too, had little hope that anyone would breach the security perimeter of the marina. The whole plan seemed like a lost cause.

Her thought, however, about the sensors inbuilt to phone handsets, had intrigued her. She pulled up technical forums and hunted for a thread that might help her understand how to find and analyse the data, and over the course of the hour that Min was asleep she worked out a plan.

But it would take time.

———

MIN HAD BEEN BACK on watch and was nearly ready for another doze by the time Áine had extracted the information she wanted. It wasn't as good as having the real thing in front of her, but she had downloaded most of the data from the madam's device apart from the images – that was not the sort of muck she wanted resting on her drives. The idea was intricate and she felt quietly pleased with herself for having thought of it, but acutely alive to the outlandishness of the notion.

Before her was a maze of numbers relating to the sensors in the phone. She already knew that the normal telltales for any phone – its cellular data and location GPS, had been well managed by its previous owner, but there might just be other ways to map out its history.

She pulled up the data, such as it was, on the phone's non-location sensors; beginning with the accelerometer, which told her how fast the phone had been moving. Then the gyroscope – which had given her the idea in the first place because it tracks what way up the phone was being held and therefore which way to show the display. Finally, she looked at the magnetometer that, while nowhere near as useful as the GPS signal the madam had evidently disabled, was still a digital compass.

There is lots of stuff here, she thought, but how the hell do I make sense of it?

And then she got a message from Min: *On the blink.*

She went back to the cameras.

Chapter Twenty-Seven

BY THE MORNING of day four Áine's increasing hopelessness had brought her close to tears. She reached for her phone, opened the app and typed Min a message.

Know you're sleeping but I think we should ring the Guards again. This has gone on too long and they can't ignore us now.

A reply came back immediately.

Hold fire. Heads-up. Have contact.

Áine's eyes flicked up to the screens and scoured the feeds from the harbour's cameras. It was dark and the imagery was in black and white with an occasional burst of green as an animal triggered a light sensor.

What? Can't see anything?

There was a delay.

Stand by. Need to cover screen. Do not message back.

Áine realised he must be close to someone if he was being forced to conceal the light from a small device. She grabbed a biro and began gnawing its end. With her right hand she continued to scroll around the harbour estate looking at the camera above the marina gate that led down to the pontoons. It appeared undisturbed. She tapped into its drive, scrolled back ten minutes then watched at pace. Again, nothing.

What the hell is he talking about? she wondered, and what does "contact" mean?

The cameras became more widely spaced as she moved down into the marina. She combed every one, taking it back a few minutes to seek any sign of movement, but aside from the sea lapping, there was nothing.

Then her phone lit up.

Just left target boat. Assume they have it. See if it's sending.

Áine's heart began to hammer. At least she knew what that meant. Min had enabled the location to attract the phone's owners to it, and that also allowed Áine to monitor the device if and when it was eventually retrieved. She felt solidly at ease in bringing up the mapping it would send signal to and waited for it to acquire the data.

None appeared.

Not seeing it?

There was silence for a few more minutes and then the app began to blink – a call. She hit green.

"What's happening? Did they not take it?"

"They took it, alright. I'm on the target yacht now and the phone's gone."

"So why am I not seeing it?"

"You know why," Min said. "They were in the boat for fifteen minutes – evidently disabling everything."

"Who were?"

"Two men. Couldn't really see much—"

"But how? They weren't on the cameras and—"

"I know. They came by dinghy, so get looking again, all round the harbour. Tell me what way they're headed and I'll follow."

"How?"

"Just look!" he barked.

Áine jumped a little at the command and tilted her head to hold the phone on her shoulder as she scrolled. "I can't see anything!"

"Keep going. They headed out the mouth of the marina and turned east into the wider harbour."

"There's ... there's nothing. What colour was the dinghy?"

"Dark, I don't know. Just dark."

"And two men?"

"Aye, dressed in darks too. Hats on."

"Shit!" she said as the phone dropped. She set it to speaker when she retrieved it and left it on the desk. "I'm getting nothing – why am I getting nothing, Min?"

"Keep going, lassie, keep going. You'll find them."

"Did they have an engine? Could they be out of the harbour already?"

"Naw," he replied. "They were paddling, not rowing. Like a canoe – but in a dinghy. There should be movement somewhere."

"Nothing east. I'm going west," Áine said decisively.

"They definitely went east." She could sense Min shaking his head.

"I have them!" she yelled, leaning towards her handset.

"Where?"

"West Pier, directly opposite where the fishing boats are tied up." She heard zipping and a flutter. "Min?"

His reply was distant. "Keep an eye on them. I'm going over."

"How?"

But the line went dead.

Chapter Twenty-Eight

ÁINE WATCHED the two men clambering up the pier side. One slipped badly and she noticed that his companion failed to help him in any way, which seemed odd. The first man just stared at the second, as if deliberating whether to leave him dangling down towards the water. Áine got the feeling he was about to turn away when the second managed to catch a grip and began to haul himself upwards again.

The image was grainy but at least she now knew which of the men had the phone. He was the shorter of the two – but height was the only distinguishing feature, because both had hats pulled low and were dressed in what looked like black clothing. The picture offered wouldn't allow her to make out any facial features at all. All she knew was that their builds were similar and when both began down the pier walkway, they moved efficiently.

She stared down at her phone, willing it to light up again, then scoured the water as the men made their way on foot towards the town. There were cars parked alongside what appeared to be yet another yacht club, and she hoped that Min would show himself before they got into one.

Áine found herself rocking back and forth, willing Min's arrival on the scene before the men disappeared into one of the many pools of blackness. She scrambled around, working out which camera would lead onto which – how far she might be able to track them.

Not far, was the answer. The harbour's CCTV coverage ran out at the main road. The two men were less than two hundred metres from that.

She looked desperately for other options – there was a fuel garage to the west, which she imagined would have cameras – but by the time she worked out what, if any, chance there was of finding a way to monitor them, the men could be anywhere. She knew the hack wasn't the difficult bit – it was the working out where to start, and most camera systems remained offline, for internal recording only.

And then she was able to breathe again as she spotted a figure emerging from the water – fully clothed and with a tube slung over his back.

That must be a dry bag, she typed as she saw Min bend over and unroll the top of the tube and withdraw the phone.

What way? she got back.

South. Two men nearly at road. Be quick.

The figure left the bag and began a slow run. He must be frozen stiff, she thought, but was surprised at the pace he quickly managed to gather, and then began to worry that the men ahead of him might hear his heavy footfall. He was built like a barrel and she had no idea what level the ambient sound was down there, but there was a stiff breeze and so she knew the boats would be making clanking noises in the wind.

The men approached the main road and, when they reached it, turned right. That meant left as Áine looked at her Google satellite screen. The men walked casually past the final camera, slowing as they did so, heads lowered.

Boiler suits, she typed, and then swore, realising the ridiculousness of sending messages. She lifted the phone instead and watched Min slow to a jog and the phone rise to his ear.

"They're on the main road," she said.

Silence.

"Can you hear me, Min? They've turned right ahead of you and are walking up the footpath beside the main road."

He was barely panting and still said nothing. Then it dawned on her, he wouldn't speak for fear of attracting attention.

"I see, I think. If you can hear me, get to the main road and turn west – that's right to you, and they're ahead of you in boiler suits and have hats on. The smaller one has the phone – and he might leave the tall fella behind him if things get tight." She stared at the camera and imagined she could see Min nod. His clothing was sticking to his legs – his cargo pants clearly displaying the girth of his legs, even on the gritty camera feed.

Áine turned her attention to the two men but they'd vanished into the night.

"I've lost them. They were about a hundred metres ahead of you, maybe less. They could be in a car by now." She could hear her voice beginning to crack as their last desperate throw to get Sinead slipped away.

Min turned the corner under the final camera and

made his way into the gloom. All went black for Áine – she was blind.

"We've given those bastards the only leverage we had," she said into the phone, her head shaking despondently.

"Easy," he whispered. "I can see them."

And the line went dead.

—————

ÁINE HELD her head in her hands, realising that she should have set Min's phone up for tracking. To set up cellular tracking now would take hours – it would have been so much easier if they'd given the phone permission in the first place.

She kept telling herself that he was just following the men, quietly, and that he had severed the call to allow him to do that.

She forced herself to resist the urge to call him back. To distract herself and feel like she was doing something useful, she got back to the sensors in the madam's phone and tried to make sense of what, if anything, they were telling her.

She began to hunt all the channels she had access to from past employments at Dublin's blue chips and found a stack that discussed user testing with application sensor access. It took her fifteen minutes to scan-read the huge amount of information recorded. The project had come to nothing – it looked like one of the developer lunch-hour challenges. She'd sponsored plenty of those in her time. Devs who were happier sitting at their computer terminal than taking a break and getting some sun would often come up with mad concepts to try and prove while eating sandwiches and pizza.

The information was useful, though. She became fascinated with the gyroscope. Some keen programmer had made assumptions about its use: prolonged horizontal orientation suggested the owner was resting or watching videos, so it was a good time to target advertising for what they termed "wind-down entertainment". Such information would be enormously advantageous to big companies seeking to expand their user base and she followed the thread to find that the only way to collect gyroscope sensor data was through an application on a phone. Her heart sank a little – it was a process that had to be planned in advance – until she found a list of apps that harvested such data – including an off-the-shelf mirror app, a video editing application and, to her excitement, a VPN designed to mask the device from prying eyes. Áine's heart beat a little faster as she scoured the phone's downloaded data for an app she was sure she'd seen stored on it, and sure enough the VPN appeared.

Then the hunt began – more developer channels with information on how to crack into the VPN data. That part didn't take long, and soon she was able to match the rudimentary sensor data she had already obtained to the recent history of the phone through the app.

But the going got tough. She was able to use the accelerometer to tell how fast the phone had travelled – it was generally used for things like fitness steps or running – but Áine was interested in adapting it to a simple physics equation. Speed equals distance over time; distance equals speed multiplied by time. Which was fine, so far as it went.

Then she took the data from the digital compass and was able to twist and turn the phone's movement and match it to the distance and speed travelled, which gave her a twisty line in the middle of nowhere because she had no way of telling where it had started or stopped. She had a route, but no map on which to place it. She used green on her screen to map when the device had moved at anything above walking speed, and red to denote a slower pace. Ok, she thought, I've got a wiggly line.

She stared at the green, which went repeatedly from zero miles per hour, to about sixty for seven miles. Weird. A delivery driver? she wondered, thinking of the main traffic on the roads during lockdown. A postal vehicle?

The stopping and starting seemed strange, but not as strange as the consistency of the speed when moving. She dismissed it for later and instead looked at what she imagined was the walking pace: red. It was higgledy-piggledy, which led her to look again at the green – a series of straight lines.

Then the phone started buzzing.

———

"I'VE LOST THEM."

"Where are ye?"

"I dunno. They began acting up, so I drew back a bit. Then they went down a set of steps and I couldn't follow cos I thought they might have copped me. But I'd be bloody surprised if they had."

"What do you mean acting up?"

"They made a call and then stopped dead. They dithered a bit and changed the direction they'd been heading – like they'd been told something new. That's why I thought maybe there was someone keeping an eye."

"What do you mean?" Áine's frustration burst through her excitement.

"Well, if I was them, I'd have eyes on from above –

cameras or vehicles as well as folks on foot. That's what we used to do, anyway."

"Explain, Min. I don't know any of this shit."

"If you're worried about someone being followed, you keep an eye on them. You double up and watch their back through overt cameras or coverts if you have them."

"Hidden cameras?"

"Assuming you've got some. Anyway, that doesnae apply here, but they could have scouts in houses above. There's loads of big houses round here."

"Where are you? What can you see?"

"Flags, mainly. Foreign ones."

"Street name?"

"Hang on …" She heard him walking.

"What flags?"

"Well, I saw Pakistan and now I can see Poland."

"You're in embassy land. Merrion Road?"

She listened to him walk for a while.

"Nah, Ailsbury … Aye, Ailsbury Road."

"You've covered a good bit of ground there. That could be like, four miles?"

"They're moving fast. Where it's dark they run. Then they walk where they could be seen."

"So where were these steps?" she asked, scrolling around a Google map.

"Fifty yards back."

"What way are you facing?"

"Eh, west, I reckon."

"So the steps are east?"

"Aye."

"You moved away from them?"

"Aye, if one of their people has spotted me, I need to be

able to extract. This way they don't know for definite if I'm following or not."

Áine thought for a moment. "Was there a bridge or anything at the steps?"

"Aye, but no other way down. If I'd followed them down at this time of night, they'd have made me, for sure."

She looked at the green lines on her screen.

This time of night?

Áine turned her gaze slowly to the clock. Three o'clock in the morning. "Min, they're using the rail track – the Dart. It doesn't start running again until six. Nobody will expect people to walk the lines. That's where they are."

"Shit. Ok, I'll have to find another way."

Chapter Twenty-Nine

ÁINE WAS CONFUSED. Min didn't appear willing to walk the train track, and from her view of Google Maps, there was no way he could catch the men by road. No streets ran parallel, and there wasn't a more direct route into Dublin city centre than the Dart line.

She was learning to stop second-guessing what these men – Sam and Min, might do. It was seldom what most people would expect – like following the people he was supposed to be tailing instead of stopping. What the hell was that all about?

She settled on pursuing her own expertise and leaving Min to his.

The spidery line in front of her wasn't really making a great deal of sense. She followed it with the point of a nail file along the screen, imagining what it might represent. Was it Dublin? There was some suggestion the phone had travelled in the north too. It could be any other Irish city.

Áine knew her own city as well as any recluse does – she'd grown up in it, after all. But it was a major European cosmopolitan town, rising from the ground with nude glass cages. It was a place anyone could be held anywhere and not even a neighbour would know. Áine didn't even really know the people who lived on her own landing.

She gave up on the accelerometer and the compass and turned to the gyroscope. The research had suggested its horizontal axis could denote rest. So where do you rest? At home in bed, she reckoned.

The data available was limited, but she was able to determine the time at which the phone tended to be turned on its side – as if it were being watched or, she shuddered to think, used to take pictures or videos.

Then she mapped that with a stylus onto the time and distance line she had created on another screen. What she ended up with was a wiggly red line that ran from the bottom right corner of her wide screen through a series of straight green lines that took her beyond the end of that monitor and onto another, before turning red again and almost doubling back onto the original screen before becoming yellow – which marked the time at which the phone's screen had been turned sideways.

She performed the process three times using dated data from the app, and each time the green and yellow lines stayed broadly consistent, while the red ones varied massively.

Áine sat back and held the nail file to her lips, looking at her work and trying not to conclude that it had been a massive waste of time. What it told her was almost exactly nothing. It was a very bad drawing in three different colours.

———

"RIGHT, so there's good news and there's bad news," Min told her as she opened the door of the apartment to find him standing there.

"Bloody concierge, how did you get up?"

"Never mind."

"You didn't find them?"

"I found them, alright, and I got a wee bit o' luck too." He squelched into the apartment, not quite dripping but not far off it.

"I could really do with the good news, Min."

"Ok, well, there was a taxi passing, so I flagged him down and he agreed to take me – eventually."

"Cos you're soaked?"

"Naw, cos he's only taking frontline workers in and out to hospital. Anyway, I says tae him it's an emergency, so he ran me up tae Lansdowne Road."

"The rugby ground? Why?"

"Cos I remembered it's on the train line – from being over at the matches, and I could see the stadium and it made sense tae get ahead of them. I knew if they'd clocked me before, they wouldnae be expecting me tae be in front of them, aye?"

Áine smiled as her head shook.

"So I did a wee deal with the taxi man, went down into the station and along the line and waited. Sure enough, along they came."

"Ok?"

"And I could hear them, and they were on the phone, and I can't say what they were talking about but they didnae seem one bit concerned that they were being followed, which is good."

"Yeah, I think?"

"So I made a bit o' noise ahead and kinda forced them

to rethink, and up they went to road level. And then my new pal, the taxi man, he asks them do they want a lift cos it's his last run of the night, and in they get!"

"You're feckin' joking me?"

"No, it all just fell together nicely. I couldn't believe it myself."

"So there's bad news?"

"Aye."

"That's why you're back – you didn't find where they were going."

"Naw, I'm back cos I need a few quid to pay the taxi man. He's down the stairs."

"What? How much?"

"A lot, two hundred."

"Where the hell did he take them?"

"A place I'll no' forget."

"Why?"

"Portmarnock," he replied.

"I don't get it?" she said, hunting between books on a shelf for money.

"I grew up just outside the other Portmarnock – in Scotland." He snatched the cash and turned to pay the taxi man.

———

ÁINE WAS AS PERPLEXED as she was annoyed by the time he came back up in the lift.

"So what's the story now, then?"

"They told the taxi driver tae leave them at an industrial estate, then they did a runner."

"A runner. They didn't pay?"

"No."

"So we don't know where they went?" She looked crestfallen.

"I'm sorry, Áine, but we are closer than we were. They're not gonnae go to Portmarnock and then track away to the other side of Dublin, are they?"

"You tell me." Áine was off. "I don't know what the hell we're supposed to do now."

"I think we take it all to the Guards now, and if we absolutely need to, we tell them about me being here, and if it gets messy, we just explain that they weren't doing anything tae help, so we had to press on. Best leave out the bit about breaking into boats and whatnot, though."

"Fine," she said sighing, and reached for the landline phone.

"Hello," she said after a few rings. "I'm calling about a ... How do you know that? Have you found her?" Áine listened for a moment, then her face dropped. "Yes, that's me ... yes. Yes, McKenna was here." She looked up at Min, despondent. "We really need to talk to someone who is prepared to listen ... Yes, I appreciate that but ... ok. But we have information and it is ... eh ..." She held the handset away from her head, her look incredulous. "They fucking hung up on me!"

"What?"

"They knew me by the number, that they've obviously recorded. They probably have me down as some nuisance caller on their database."

"No way?"

"She said they'd send someone if they could, in the morning. *If they fucking could!*"

"What am I no' getting about this? What is it with them?"

"That little shit guard has probably got me blacklisted. I bet you he's told them all that I'm some nutter."

"What time will they come?"

"Said the next shift starts at eight and they'd review it then. That's four hours away. Said they were very busy!"

"Well, maybe we should just go to Portmarnock, see if we can find anything?"

"Like what? Do what? Stare at houses?"

"Well, what's the place like?"

"North of here. I dunno. I was there once, maybe, when I was a youngster. There's a beach, I think. We could have a look online."

They walked through to the control room and sat down.

"What's that?" Min asked, looking at the squiggles on the screens.

"A load of bollocks. I was trying to piece together the woman's phone movements." Min stared at it while Áine pounded "Portmarnock" into Google with a force that could kill most keyboards.

"The madam's phone?"

"Yeah. It was a silly long shot using the compass and other data, doesn't matter. Here, that's Portmarnock. He dropped them at an industrial estate?"

"Yeah."

"There it is, but it's south of Portmarnock, really. I'd say you were diddled on the taxi fare."

"Aye."

"The estate's pretty big. Where would you start?"

Min stared at it. "Maybe you should look for brothels or something. If she is a madam who's blackmailing her clients, maybe they run it from somewhere near there."

"How do you even search for a brothel?"

Min blew out air for a long time. "I don't know. A

sauna? Massage? People must find them handy enough otherwise they'd be out of business." His eyes went back to the squiggles. "What's the colours mean?"

"The green line is when the phone was travelling at speed, and the compass is the direction the phone was travelling, and if you place it over the speed thing, I reckoned it was fast – in a car or a bus or something."

"And the red is slow, so I guess that's when the person's walking?"

"Maybe. Who knows. Doesn't matter."

"As if someone got off a bus and then walked," Min said distractedly. "What's the yellow?"

"That's when the phone was turned sideways."

"This is bloody genius."

"It's a bloody mess," she said, staring up at her sauna search results.

"You've got all that from sensors in a phone?"

"It's a bad kid's drawing, Min."

"It's very possibly exactly what we need."

"How?"

"Well, where have I spent part of the night?"

"In the sea, far as I can see."

Min sighed. "Is there a railway station in Portmarnock?"

Áine blew out her cheeks. "Let's have a look." It took one zoom out and one zoom in. "Who knew? The Dart goes there on the way to Malahide, through Portmarnock."

"Right, then see if your wee drawing fits at all." Áine looked at him with an eyebrow raised.

"Fits the Dart route?"

"Go on, it canny hurt."

Áine grabbed the drawing in its entirety and moved it around the screen aimlessly. "See? It's bollocks."

"Shrink it down. Match the distances to scale, see if you can get it tae fit."

Áine huffed again and reduced the size of the image and blew up the Google map.

"Start with what you thought might be the rail route and lay it against the—"

"Track. I get it. Thank you."

The image was expanded and reduced a few times, then, like an ill-fitting jigsaw piece, it fell in beside the railway line.

Min turned to look at her. "That's bloody genius."

Áine's heart was hammering. "That is, in fact, genius."

They stared at the map. Not only did the green lines fit the Dart line out of Dublin, the red lines almost exactly matched roads leading from the station. Min tapped the screen where red became yellow.

"That's where we need to be. Wish I had time for a quick shower."

Chapter Thirty

MIN DID, in fact, have time for a shower.

"You're kidding me?" he looked at Áine, baffled.

"I never learned."

"How do you get about?"

"I walk or I get the bus, or the Luas."

"The what?"

"The tram. I, I don't really go out all that much, to be honest."

"And your sister?"

"She drives, but she took her car and it's now at the convent."

"I wish I'd brought a bike this time."

"How did you get here?"

"Long story."

"Why not try your extortionate taxi man? I'm sure he'd love to sucker you for another fare – or sucker me, more like."

Min's forehead rose momentarily as if he liked her

suggestion. He took out his phone and hit redial. He stood for a minute, stopped, then repeated the process.

"He's no' answering. He did say he was going off shift. Probably just as well, to be honest."

"Why?"

"Cos if something goes wrong, we don't want some hackney driver placing us there, do we?"

"Something goes wrong?" Áine said quietly.

"I'm sure it'll be fine, but if Sinead is there – and it's a big enough if, Áine, to be honest – and if things get grizzly, then it's best we weren't there at all."

Áine said nothing. Just looked straight at him.

"What about the wee fella? The chatty bastard delivering the letters. Sam seemed to trust him, no?"

"Fran? Eh … well, yeah, Sam trusted him, for sure, but *we* don't know him."

"Well, it's no' like we're teeming wi' options here, are we?"

Áine's lips tightened in resignation. "I took his number." She turned away and made for the kitchen table. Min heard her lift the landline phone. There was a pause. "Is that Fran?" he heard her begin. "Yeah, I know. Yeah, Áine, I'm really sorry. Look it, apologies and everything, but we have a bit of an emergency. We were kinda wondering where you live?" Min heard another silence, then a sigh. "We're needing a lift, like, and we can't really rely on anyone else. And it's important. It really is, and, look, Fran, it needs to be now." Min moved through to the kitchen area. "We think we know where Sinead might be and I'm so worried about her. I think she's been taken." Min saw the tears well in her eyes as she turned away from him. "No, we tried them, three times. They think she's just done a runner. They won't listen to us at all. Can you help, Fran? Please?" Min moved out of the kitchen again, seeking dry clothes, but he heard her finish the call. "Thanks a million. Really, Fran, you might literally be a lifesaver."

———

THE FIRST TIME Min experienced Áine's wrath was in the car park at the apartment block. He had sensed it existed, but to feel its front was a different experience.

"Just what the fuck, exactly, do you mean *I stay here*?" it began.

Min stiffened. He was unaccustomed to people questioning his decisions. "We need someone to man the comms. It just makes sense."

"If you need a man to man the comms, then you better stay here yourself."

Min let out a heavy breath and looked at Fran, who was half asleep and holding open the door of his small car. He turned back to Áine. "I'm gonnae need help – but likely not there. I'm gonnae need you looking at street layouts and the geography – feeding me information. I don't need you getting—"

"In the way. Go on, dickhead. That's what you mean, isn't it?"

"Getting into trouble too," he said, as calmly as he could.

"You can fu—"

"Enough!" he shouted, the command bouncing around the concrete walls and coming back to them again and again. His voice returned to its normal volume but remained resolutely firm. "I've come a long way, in trying times, to help. This is something I have experience of and you don't, so either you give me a hand and do what I ask, or you make a fucking nuisance of yourself where it's not as important to the objective, which – I remind ye, is to get your sister home safe. Is that understood?"

Áine, for the first time in her life, found herself simultaneously admonished, apologetic and pliant. "Yes," she said, her head lowered.

"Right, I'll be on the blower shortly. You," he turned to Fran, "get in the car and let's go."

Fran turned and clambered in. Min stepped forward and took Áine's cheeks in his paws. He tipped her forehead up and kissed it. Then he walked around the car and got in.

"Where to, brother?" Fran asked, as if nothing had happened.

"Portmarnock, please. Fast as ye can but don't be breaking any limits. I canny afford to have some plod asking questions."

The streets were all but empty. The homeless and the hammered from some prohibited house party were the only ones marauding the footpaths. Occasionally a staggering body would wave out an arm as if to flag down a taxi they probably couldn't afford.

"So what's the story, friend?"

"Min's my name, Fran. And the story is that your pal, Sam, and me go back a long way. He dug me out o' a few holes, now it's my turn to do him a wee favour."

"And this is to do with his young one?"

"Young one?"

"Girl, woman, Sinead."

"Ok. Well, aye, we think someone's abducted her."

"Really – why?"

Min wasn't at all sure he should share any information with his new acquaintance, but felt slightly guilty that their last meeting had involved him dangling Fran against a window by his throat. Besides, Fran had come out in the small hours to help two people he didn't know.

"Why did ye come tonight?"

Fran thought for a moment. "Sam's an honourable man. He always stood by the proletariat when I required it of him, so—"

"But this isn't Sam we're helping here."

"It's Sam's love interest, is it not?"

"Aye," Min grunted.

"Well, I am confident that if my good wife or children needed assistance and I was to call Sam, he would come. So in the spirit of being stronger together, I'm returning a favour as yet unrendered."

"You talk some shite, Fran, but I appreciate that, all the same."

"I thought she was just missing."

"It's complicated."

"I suspect I may possess the intellect to process the story."

Min looked at Fran, whose eyes remained on the road, and conceded. "Sinead works at some refuge, right?"

"I'm aware."

"I believe Sam met her when he was doing some work for her charity?"

"Correct, through his company – Charlie, but I suspect Charlie was just him. I know about this part."

"Well, you might know more than me. We kinda lost touch a bit after Shannon was killed."

"Now you have me at a disadvantage, brother."

"His wife – Shannon?"

"I never met her. I didn't know he had a wife."

Min shifted uneasily. "Well, you wouldn't have – she was murdered."

"No way?"

"How well do you actually know Sam?"

"Not as well as I thought, clearly. Who killed her?"

"It was a random. She got into an argument and he stabbed her."

Fran stayed silent.

"Anyway, after that he was kinda freelancing, as I understand it, back here in Ireland."

"He did good work, brother. You'd have been proud of what he achieved."

"And he and Sinead must have got pally, like. Anyway, he took off and she stayed put."

"I'm assuming he was evading the establishment?"

"How do you know that?" Min looked at Fran again.

"It's the twenty-first century," Fran began. "There are more direct means of romantic communication than the letter writing chosen by Sam."

Min grunted. "Well, all of this mess has nothing to do with Sam."

"Really?"

"He's just at sea while Sinead's got herself in a right shit fight."

"I always had an impression she was steady-out."

"Some woman at the refuge did a runner and left a phone behind. Now it seems some right nasty bastards want the phone back."

"Do you mind me asking why you don't just give it to them?"

"It's a wee bit late for that. We think they're involved in all sorts of mucky stuff, including blackmail. And, anyway, long story short, they might have taken Sinead to beat the shit out of her so she'll tell them where the phone is."

"Bloody hell," Fran said. "And how long have they had her?"

"*If* they have her, it's been about …" Min counted on his fingers. "Bloody hell, it's been ten days."

"So she could be …"

"Aye, I'd say that's a real possibility."

"And is this, like, a criminal gang, then? One of the drug cartels?"

"You have drugs cartels in Dublin?" Min was surprised.

"We do, brother. Organised crime is a very real thing in this fine city."

"Well, I don't know. All's I know is that two boys who came looking for the phone ended up at a property in Portmarnock, which is where we're headed. You can drop me there and then get back to your bed."

"Under no circumstances," Fran replied.

"Come again?"

"I will not be turning tail, brother. I am here to help, and I may be wearing pyjamas under my jeans, but I am at your disposal."

Min smiled a little for the first time in days. "Good man, Fran. Good man."

Chapter Thirty-One

"I THINK we drive around in a circle and gradually move in closer." Min was using the inbuilt satnav display between the two men.

"Is time not of the essence here?" Fran seemed confused.

"Rush into a thing like this and you get your arse handed to you," Min replied. "We need to recce a way in and a way out. People always make the mistake of only doing the first bit – but there's no point doing anything if ye can't get away wi' it."

"Sound out." Fran was becoming briefer in his dialogue, Min was grateful to note.

They drove around the edge of the industrial estate, moving further in towards the unit Min had identified.

"This isn't really Portmarnock, strictly speaking," Fran said. "Portmarnock's further north and much more upmarket."

"I don't care, pal. That's where we need to get tae." Min tapped the screen again. "I reckon we go past, you drop me round that corner and then, if you're still game, you wait facing south and ready tae pull into the main road and away. Agreed?"

"And what do I say if the Guards pull up and ask me what I'm doing?"

"You don't seem the sort to be stuck for words, Fran."

"That I am not, brother, that I am not."

"That's it," Min said, staring at the steel shutters of the unit as they drove past. It was a stand-alone and wide, but the outside gave no indication as to its use. "What d'ye reckon it is?"

"Busy," Fran said. "Look at the cars outside at this time of night."

"Maybe it's a mechanic's? They could be waiting for work to be done."

"I hope so, brother, otherwise you're facing at least twelve people inside."

———

MIN MADE his way into the industrial estate, keeping an eye on the format of the units. For the most part the buildings were uniform and boxy with either windows or shutters, depending on whether they wanted to display their wares or protect them from theft. He looked up, but the roofs were uniformly metal and sloping. A flat roof could present a skylight or opportunity but none of the buildings offered a way in from above.

He walked around the back of the building, remaining at a distance, seeking any concealed cameras, but saw only one – covering the entire car park with a poor-quality flood-light on a high pole. That didn't mean there were no other cameras, he reminded himself. There had been a time when he had been expert in using covert imagery – along with Sam. Back then they'd have been directed in by staff who watched endless hours of footage for what often amounted to an intense five-minute window of violent activity.

As satisfied as he was going to be, he crept in closer. He crossed the car park under the eaves of the surrounding terrace of units, stopping short of the corner and staring into the gloom as he waited for his vision to adjust to the lack of light. He panned across the gable of the shuttered building. It was about a hundred feet wide and fifty feet long. There were two shutters and a lot of bare concrete wall. Down the side of it he traced across, searching for what he felt must surely be there. It took a few moments but his eyes came to rest on a darker oblong shape: the door. Shutters, invariably, would be closed from the inside – access and egress was usually achieved elsewhere.

He stood for another few minutes, listening, hunting for any crack of light emitting from the building, but could find none. Perhaps it was empty. Maybe the men had left. Maybe they had never been there at all. He decided that he'd done his appreciation – way in, way out – and should refrain from overthinking it. He walked briskly forward and tugged his jumper cuff over his hand and began pulling the door handles on a few cars. Two alarms started wailing and he walked calmly down the side of the building, beyond the door and into the darkness, where he waited.

The result was telling, but disappointing. Min had hoped the door would open and an inspection of the vehicles would follow. Instead, someone – somewhere, used the remotes to disable the alarms and double lock both cars.

Min's heart rate rose a little as he again hunted around above him and to the sides – worried that he was being watched from within. Most commercial cameras, he knew, gave off a deliberate low light as a preventative measure – a series of red dots or a gentle green glow to tell potential thieves that the property was being monitored. If there was a camera on him, it was higher grade – and hidden – which suggested a more sophisticated reason for the security. Again Min counselled himself against overthinking. Most scenarios were more straightforward than they appeared. Most scenarios.

He nudged around with his boot until he found a stone large enough to achieve what he wanted, and walked quickly back to the parked cars. Selecting a van – which he hoped would be full of tools or equipment worth protecting, he smashed the side window and leaned in, found the door lever and pulled the driver's door open, setting off the alarm. Then he reached back a little and triggered the sliding door, pushing it back hard and loud, hearing it judder on its guide rails as he returned to his station not far from the building's side door.

Within thirty seconds the frame around it lit up and he heard a key insert and turn at a high level, then another lower down. The door opened in, folding out a stream of yellow light, making him edge instinctively further from it. A figure leaned out, hands pressed against the sides of the door frame, and looked both ways before retracting. Then two people emerged quickly from the building. One stepped out and turned to face him directly, the other moved around to the front of the building.

Min stood with his back to the wall, staring at the figure less than twenty feet away, silhouetted but apparently looking straight back at him. He looked about six feet tall, broad at the shoulders, and remained completely motionless. Min knew the man's night vision wouldn't have kicked in – the light inside was too bright, and that meant he remained in the safety of a pool of blackness. It offered little comfort, though, given his exposure.

The van alarm stopped. Min heard the side door draw closed again, the driver's door followed, then footsteps. The second man retraced his steps and appeared at the corner behind the man standing sentry in the door light. "Don't think they got away with anything." Min noted the English accent. "Scally bastards."

The second man turned into the building again, but the silhouette stood for a few more silent seconds, eyes front, before taking a pace backwards and turning firmly to the light. Min stared hard at the figure as he began to move back inside. The man's face turned again in Min's direction, causing his heart to stop for a split second. The man had a wide, long unkempt beard and a tight woollen hat. Then the body vanished into the light and pulled the door behind him, and Min listened as only one of the two locks was rattled home. Then the light went off again, leaving the area in complete darkness, and blurs floating in front of his eyes.

But he knew what he'd seen.

The man who had stood staring was, unmistakably, Sam Ireland.

Chapter Thirty-Two

"WHAT DID YOU JUST SAY?" Áine might have had time to calm down while Min and Fran were away but she was about to re-enter orbit.

"Sam's in there."

"Is this some sort of feckin' joke?"

Fran was standing at Min's side. He knew how to use his mouth, but he also knew when to keep it shut.

"I caused a disturbance outside. I was planning on someone coming out and leaving a chance for me to get in, but he stood there on guard, like, staring over towards me. I dunno. I just don't know."

"Sam's at sea, Min. There's no way he could be back. Come on, like, he couldn't be back. He couldn't be there. He just can't be. You're wrong. You must be."

"Mebbe." Min closed his eyes and shook his head gently.

"Why did you two not stay there? Should you not be finding another way in?"

"Something's not right."

"You think!"

"I need you to work something out."

"You can't—"

"Listen to me. There is nothing I could achieve there that isn't likely to cause more problems. There's a call I need to make and something I need to do – and I need to do it quick cos we either get the police involved or we don't, and I just don't know which it is yet."

"It's get the police involved!" Áine screamed.

"Work out how far it is from Dominica to Ireland – exactly how far."

"What?" Áine shouted. "There's no way it can be Sam. And if it is, and he's tied up in this I'll bloody…"

"You're not seriously thinking he's involved with them?" Min stared at her.

"No, cos he's not there!"

"Just see if there's any flights operating."

"I could just e-mail him and ask," Áine snarked.

"No, there's something…"

"You don't even believe yourself. It's obviously not me who needs to rest."

"Fran, look up AIS and see what ships have made the journey recently. Do all of it now," he ordered. "We need to work out what the hell is happening here."

———

"DOMINICA TO DUBLIN is three and a half thousand nautical miles."

Min's eyes rolled to the ceiling, calculating. "Even if he was doing ten knots, that would take him two weeks, and there's no way he's been doing a steady ten knots."

"Because it's not fucking him! You saw someone else."

Min ignored her and turned to Fran. "What's the fastest cargo ship do?"

"About eighteen knots if they're in a real serious hurry."

"What's that work out at?" He turned to Áine.

"It's still eight or nine days minimum. And that's just to get to the dock. I'm telling you, Min," she softened very slightly, "you're wrong. It can't be him. And it's hurricane season – he's not going to cross the Atlantic with Isla with that hanging over them. It's just not him."

"Isla," Min said absently. "Get Daniel on the phone."

Áine stared at him. "Did you get a bang on the head?"

"Please, just make the call," he said.

Áine stomped into the control room and emerged with the IP phone to her ear. She listened for a moment and then handed it to Min. He listened to the ringtone and, once again, a groggy answer.

"Yeah?"

"Danny, it's Min."

Áine started to pace, staring at him in the reflection of the huge windows against the dawn outside. Fran fell into the sofa, bemused.

"I'm good mate, I'm good. Listen, I need to get to the point, pal. When exactly did Sam leave?"

Áine turned to look straight at him. He held her gaze.

"Right. And Isla – she went with him?"

Min listened and nodded at Áine, who threw up her arms in an *I told you so* gesture.

"And, Danny, did he go on the boat?"

Min listened and nodded again before his expression changed to one of keen interest. "You're on his boat now? What d'ye mean?"

His face was inscrutable for a moment, then he shook

his head repeatedly at Áine. She covered her mouth. Fran leaned forward.

Min listened intently, eyes now on the far wall. He held out his open hand and spoke slowly and deliberately. "So, what boat *did* he leave on?"

He covered the end of the phone and whispered urgently to Áine. "*Caribbean Symphony*, a cruise liner – look up its top speed." He returned to the phone. "Danny, what was his plan? And was he upset or … angry?" Min looked at Áine again. "Naw, man, she's missing – that's the problem. We're trying tae find her. Look, I don't know what's going on here at all, but as soon as I do I'll call you straight back, ok? Honestly, I'll let ye know as soon as I hear anything."

———

"THIRTY KNOTS, top speed. So, even at that, it would have taken most of six days," Áine announced, falling into a chair.

"It's never going to do top speed," Fran said. "The operators will be too miserable to burn extra fuel."

"So it can't be him – it's impossible," Áine repeated.

"It would be impossible," Min said with a grimace, "except that he left three days before we last spoke to Danny."

"What! Why didn't Danny say that before?"

"We didn't ask *when* he'd left – we didn't even ask *how*. And Danny's not the type to give information away for nothing."

"Are you for real?" Áine's face twisted into incomprehension.

"So what's the timeline here?" Min started pacing. "Sinead went missing ten days ago, right?"

"Yeah," Áine replied.

"But we didn't tell Danny she was missing until … when?"

"Seven days ago."

"So Sam left the Caribbean ten days ago?"

"According to tight-lipped Danny," Áine growled.

Fran, quietly, re-entered the fray. "So Sam left before Sinead even went missing."

Min and Áine both looked at him. "That's about the height of it."

"So why did he leave at all?"

Áine stood up. "Maybe he just decided the threat was gone and, with the letter from Sinead – came home?"

"Wait a minute – would he even have received her letter?"

Áine pulled over the Post-it pad and started writing down dates. "Well, he'll have got the first letter, which makes sense cos there was a reply, but, you're right, I don't see how he could have received her second letter unless …" They both looked at Fran.

"The second letter was sent by ship. It was only after that that I was told to use email."

"So, no, he wouldn't have got her second letter – whatever was in it. And he'd have left before she'd have told him that I'd been attacked." Áine confirmed.

"If he was just coming home for Sinead, why not sail home, then?" Min said. "Why get on a cruise liner?"

"He wanted to get back to see her? Maybe he was excited. Maybe has a heart after all."

"I dunno."

"It's hurricane season – you said it yourself. He wouldn't take Isla into a hurricane."

"I reckon he'd just wait."

"How romantic," Áine grunted.

"What about the pandemic – maybe that's why he left?"

Fran raised a hand, as if at school. "If I may," he began, "ships are super spreaders for Covid. I don't see him taking that child on a cruise liner unless he was in a hurry."

"That's a point," Min said, turning to Áine. "He must've been in a rush."

"How is a super spreader ship allowed to travel when every other form of transport is locked down?" Áine remained sceptical. "And how would Sam bloody Ireland manage to get on a ship when nobody's allowed to do shit like that?"

Fran was scrolling on the screen of the iPad. "It was in the news," he said. "Efforts to get British holidaymakers home," he read. "Three thousand passengers on board a luxury cruise liner have made a joint appeal to the Foreign Office to assist in the release of the ship from a Caribbean island. The passengers' request is that a UK port is opened to allow them to return home, amid tightening restrictions on travel and quarantine. The Caribbean Symphony left Southampton and was three weeks into a two-month tour of the Americas when it was detained on the volcanic island of Dominica. There are no reports of infection among the passengers, although the crew and the estimated two thousand Britons on board have been confined to the ship with no permission to disembark. The remainder of the ship's complement is believed to be from Ireland and other parts of Europe."

"See?" said Áine. "There's no way they'd let anyone on

that ship. No bloody way. They're not gonna chance someone taking the virus on board."

"With respect," Fran said, "I have witnessed first-hand that man's ability to get on board sea-going vessels. If he wanted to get onto that ship, he would get on, no questions asked."

"Not with a child," Áine dismissed him. "And where would they even stay? If there are three thousand people on board, there'd hardly be many family cabins left, would there?"

"You make a point," Fran said.

"He'd find a way," Min said, "if he needed tae."

"With Isla in tow?

"It's what we were trained to do. It would be wee buns tae him. Honestly."

"He's not gonna have scaled a rope with his daughter hanging off his back like a chimpanzee."

"Look, it wasnae all guns and grenades. Ye have tae understand that if there was a way tae get on a ship without anyone knowing, that would be the preferred option. No question. He could have got on with cargo, he could be bluffed on as part of the crew. I mind once we were sent to get on board the QE2 cos some gobshite was smuggling guns from the states to the IRA."

"What?"

"We just boarded inside the pallets of grub. None of the crew were to be told. Found a spare cabin, located the weapons, did what we had tae do and sailed across the Atlantic like Lords."

"How?"

"Free beer, great grub."

"No I mean…"

"Just like I said. It really wasnae very hard."

"And Sam was with you?"

"He was team leader."

"Unbelievable."

Fran broke in while staring at his screen. "*Caribbean Symphony* docked in Cork four days ago!"

Min looked up. "I just assumed it would go to England."

"Course you did. You forget there were Irish nationals on board," Áine grunted.

"That's enough time to get someone to look after Isla, then get to Portmarnock, isn't it?"

"S'pose so," Áine conceded. "This is mad, though. It makes no sense. I just don't buy that a ship was sitting pretty and waiting for them."

"It had been there for nearly two weeks remember. It was probably the talk of the island," Fran said.

"Right enough, Danny mentioned it was detained. They'd have to allow it to be provisioned, good business for the island. Then it was probably turned around and sent straight back."

"Exactly," said Áine. "So how did he get a child get on board? He was hardly going to offer them his passport, was he?"

"We all know who we're talking about here," Fran sighed. "Who knows how, but we know he was well able for it."

"This is unbelievable," Áine sat down again and held her hand to her head. "This is completely insane."

"So what's he doing?" Fran asked. "If it *is* him at the lockup, and you've got to admit that it could be, what's he doing there?"

Min looked from Fran to Áine and back again. "I have absolutely no idea."

"Does anyone want to consider the elephant in the room here?" Áine said.

"What?"

"Sam Ireland just might not be the glowing character you both seem to think he is."

"Catch y'erself on."

"Well, I'm just saying we should consider all possibilities, shouldn't we? I mean, if it is Sam, then where's Isla? Who's he palmed her off on this time?"

"Family. Must be."

"In lockdown?" Áine said.

"Come on, Áine, you know how he is with her."

Áine wilted a little. "I just think we need to consider all the alternatives."

"Which are what?" Min's patience with her was exhausting. "What is it you're suggesting?"

Áine failed. She turned away. "Sorry, I don't know. Nothing. Of course, nothing. Stupid, I'm sorry. Ignore me, I didn't mean it."

Min knew she was crying but let her be. "Fran, how long would it take to get from Cork to Dublin?"

"Three hours tops. Less in lockdown traffic."

"Ok, we need to think it out. He came back because of Sinead, yes? He must've, otherwise he wouldn't be at that lock-up."

"Yeah," Fran said in Áine's silence.

"So somehow he knows more than we know. And somehow he's inside that building and that's the only link we have to Sinead."

Áine gradually turned back towards Min, not even trying to mask her distress. "So do we tell all this to the Guards?"

"Maybe," Min said. "But we need to work out the timings – we need to understand how he got there before us. And we're going to have to make a decision."

"On what?"

"Whether one of us is going to read his last letter."

Chapter Thirty-Three

"WE NEED TO EAT," Min broke a solid two minutes of silence. "Without food and rest, we will be at a disadvantage."

Áine stared at him. "Do you seriously just function like a machine?"

Fran decided to get offside. "I am very happy to assist with the preparation of a meal," he said, "if there are no objections?" But he was already making his way across the open living room towards the kitchen area.

"The Guards will be calling soon." Min looked out at the morning light shining off the Liffey.

"I'll not hold my breath," Áine replied.

Min was quiet for a while, facing the windows, mulling. Eventually he sighed and said, "I really don't think we should tell them."

"Why?"

"A, they don't seem likely to do anything. B, worse still, that they *do* do something and make a complete balls of it."

"How?"

"They're called plods for a reason. But, honestly, Áine, there was something about the way he stood, looking towards me."

"Imaginary Sam, you mean?"

"It was Sam, Áine. I think you know that. It fits. The whole thing fits – just about. And I've known that man nearly twenty years. It was him."

"Then he's either a gangster who has somehow been playing us all along, or he's … I dunno what he is."

"The stare, into the blackness, I think, might have been deliberate. He could just have waved me in to give him a hand."

"What – you think he knew you were there?"

"Mebbe. Aye."

"So he could have brought you in to take over whatever's going on in that lock-up?"

"Aye, two's better than one, and we've been against the odds before."

"Unless – and you won't listen to me – he is somehow wrapped up in it all."

"You know that makes no sense." Min turned towards her. "Don't ye, like?"

Áine lay back into her chair, her pain making her wince. "Yeah," she said.

"I think he deliberately came down with the other man to check the car alarms, that he somehow sensed someone was there."

"That's ridiculous."

"He might have seen me – you never know."

"Sure, even if he had, in the black dark, you said it yourself – you and Sam could probably have taken on whoever was inside."

"Aye, but, what if, like, he was somehow working at it –

255

getting the information he needs? He seems to know Sinead's in trouble, right?"

"Well, from emails, he'll know at least that I've been attacked."

"But what I'm thinking is he knew before he left that there was a problem – before you emailed Sinead's last letter. How could he know?"

"Why do you think he knew?"

"Cos he left in a hurry, intae a dangerous environment with his wee lassie. You heard the man," Min nodded to Fran clattering about in the kitchen, "a cruise ship is no place for a kid in a pandemic."

"Ok …"

"And he could have waited it out, instead of presumably stowing away on a liner."

"Yes."

"And he's at the lock-up – I mean, that's the bottom line here. He was there – before we were, so he obviously knows more than we know."

"Well, that I can't argue with." Áine's eyes remained closed, her fingers resting against her temple.

"I think he knew someone was standing in the dark, and, more than that …"

"What?" Áine's eyes fluttered open.

"I can't help it, and I can't say why, but I think he knew it was me."

Áine scoffed. "Unless you glow in the dark—"

"Think about it, though. He very deliberately came to that door and stood guard in a specific way – facing the opposite direction to the car sirens. Anybody else would have expected trouble from the other side – towards the cars."

"I can't picture what you're describing."

"Well, that doesn't matter, but it was weird – the way he stood, like he was … what's the word? Sort of, like … willing me tae stay put."

"Imploring?"

"Aye! Exactly that. Imploring me to no' get involved."

"And you could tell all that without being able to see his face until he turned back into the doorway."

"Ahh, I sensed it, but I know how that sounds. It was a feeling more than anything."

"I reckon he was just standing there to protect the building in case anyone tried to sneak in the way you had planned, and you're making excuses for leaving the place and coming back here."

Min stared at her.

She sat upright and hung her head. "I'm a nasty wee bitch sometimes. I'm really sorry. I didn't mean that."

"Part of ye did," he replied, "otherwise it wouldn't have been said."

"Min, you've been so good to me. I'm sorry."

She heard him move away, and she began to cry yet again.

———

ÁINE LISTENED to Fran and Min in the kitchen. The apartment was open plan but had enough separation for her to remain largely alone. Words between them were few. She knew Fran would have overheard all that had been said and she felt shame and guilt and pain and fear. She wracked her aching head for the words to begin to make amends.

Eventually she rose and, adopting the only tactic she knew, went into the kitchen.

"Min, will you read Sam's letter? Please. I'm so terrified

for her. I'm not able to be rational. I don't mean what I'm saying. I'm just … I don't know what to do or think."

Min looked at her, as if he was able to strip the layers back. For a moment she thought he was done with her.

"Ye need tae understand this," he began, "I don't mind people saying what they're thinkin'. I can manage that – even when they're wrong, but don't pull the soppy shit wi' me. I know you spoke out o' turn there, I know ye said ye were sorry, and once I'm calmed down that'll be the end o' it. But you need tae also understand that this is no' ma first run round the block. You need tae listen tae what I'm tellin' ye, and ye need tae eat, ye need tae sleep, and ye need to be at yer best – cos sure as hell you're rapidly becoming no bloody use to anyone. De ye get that?"

Suitably chastened, she nodded sheepishly, in a manner she was unaccustomed to.

"Now, eat." He pointed a knife at a third plate laid out by Fran, who had continued to eat silently, eyes down, wishing he'd just stayed in bed. "After, I'll read the letter, and then we'll see what's what."

Chapter Thirty-Four

MIN OPENED the envelope and was not one bit surprised by the brevity of the typed message. Fran and Áine were sitting round the table trying to pretend they weren't looking at Min every few seconds to see his reaction to what he read.

"Wait a minute," he paused and looked up at Fran. "How did this arrive?"

Fran drew in a breath. "Well," he began, embarrassed, "that one came in an email on an attachment that got sent to my junk, so it was binned for a few days before I realised it was there."

Áine choked out in incredulity, "You're telling us this *now*?"

Fran turned to her. "It's only in the last few hours that we realised he's in Ireland!"

"Shut up," Min quietened them both. "When did it actually arrive?"

"I think it may have landed eight or nine days back."

"Bloody hell," Áine said, her head shaking painfully.

"Ok, ok," said Min, keeping everyone calm. "So after Sinead disappeared?"

"Seems so," said Fran. "Reason I didn't see it was it came from a weird email with dolphin watching in the address. Course I now know that's this man in Dominica."

"Whales," Áine said.

"What?"

"Whales. Not dolphins."

"Really."

"It's whales," she repeated testily.

"Ok!" Min said again.

"What does the letter say?" Áine held her hands open.

"Gimme a minute." Min finished scanning to decide whether or not it was too private to share, then began reading aloud.

"This is important. More on the other stuff later, I promise, but you need to take this very seriously. Daniel got a call an hour ago from a number we now think might be in Europe. I've got a friend working on that, but he was told by the caller that they know where 'the phone' is, and that if they don't get it back, they're going to do you harm. That's what they said. I know they mean you because they said they would come to the convent and they would hurt you. So I need you to tell Min. I need you to tell him straightaway. I know he has been helping you. I need you to tell Min, and to do whatever he says. WHATEVER he says. You need to stay away from the convent, and you need to stay away from the apartment. And you need to throw away the bloody phone you called Daniel from. And if anything happens, just tell them where it is. Just tell them. No bullshitting around – don't let that other one persuade you otherwise and don't let your conscience kick in. Just tell them, because this is not an idle threat. Just give them what they want and leave the rest to me. You let me worry about everything else.

"This is not a joke and I do not want to scare you but there is no choice here. You must know how important you are to me – to us, so please just do what I ask. Please. I am not going to go through this again. Please, just do what I say. Get out, don't go to work and speak to Min."

Min looked up.

"That's it?" Áine said.

"That's it."

She looked to the window. "That bloody text I sent. It started all of this."

"What?" Min asked.

"When I dumped the madam's phone in the bin in the park and then immediately used my phone to text Sinead. They just joined the dots."

"I don't know—" Min wavered.

"They'll have used location." She found herself keen to convince the men of her guilt. "I texted Daniel from the madam's phone, beside the bin in the park, then I dumped it. Then I texted Sinead, and that must have connected Daniel in Dominica, to me, to Sinead, in a triangle."

"No," Min said. "That would mean they knew where the madam's phone had been. They'd have looked in the park."

Áine was not for having her act of contrition challenged. Her head fell a little. "It's the only way. They'd have had a window – a short one – to see where the phone last was. They had no reason to search the bin – they'd have assumed their phone left with mine. Its location beacon would have failed with the battery."

"However they did it is besides the point. I think we can

agree now that Sam knew before we did that Sinead was in danger."

Áine's face was buried in her hands. Fran flitted his worried stare between the two, but decided to pose a question, quietly, to break the distress.

"That doesn't explain how he knew where to go, though, does it? How he ended up in that lock-up?"

Áine lifted her head again. "No," she nodded, "and who's the friend he mentioned he had working on it?"

"I've an idea who that might be."

"Why didn't he ask you to do it?" Áine snapped her head to Min. "He's asked you for that sort of thing before – and you'd be well placed for it?"

"That, I can't answer," he said. "But at least we know now *how* he knows. He's one step ahead of us, and he's done bloody well to get in there, however the hell he's done it."

The three looked at one another around the table.

"Question is, what do we do now?"

"Trust him, I reckon," Min said. "And I need to make a call."

———

MIN SAT in Áine's bucket seat and debated for a long time whether to dial the number. There were huge potential problems with opening up such a front, yet not doing so would leave Sam on his own – completely isolated – in handling whatever it was he was handling.

The bottom line, he told himself, is there's a missing woman at the hands of dreadful people. She was the sister of someone he very much wanted to help, and she mattered to a man he wouldn't, and couldn't, let down.

There are a small number of occasions, he told himself,

when consequences need to be dealt with later – when his own rules about prior planning ways out of problems need to be ignored. This was one. He needed to get the job done, then he would work out how to clean up the mess.

He held his own phone in his hand and stared at it. His hand hovered over the contact, wavered, and reached for the IP phone. Nightmare had already established that Áine couldn't be easily detected – even by experts, but Nightmare and his team were not GCHQ. Min knew well that there was always some agency out there with greater power, know-how – and in the case of British intelligence, determination to get what they want. So he set the IP phone down as well, pushed back the bucket chair and opened the control room door.

"Fran," he called.

Fran turned from stacking the dishwasher. Min caught sight of the hem of patterned pyjamas sticking out of his waistband as he stood upright. "Yes, brother?"

"Would you mind if I used your phone?"

"Not a bit."

"You should know that it's to make a call to someone who might be on the radar."

"Whose radar?" Fran inquired, but with a glint in his eye.

"British intelligence. It's only a maybe, like, but …"

"Is it important?"

"That I call him? I think so, yeah."

"Then imperial intelligence be damned, my friend. Make the call."

Min looked at Fran with a degree of wonder, smiled at his gleeful roguery, and accepted the proffered phone. He looked at his own as he tapped in the number and returned to his seat. It began to ring.

"Leave a message," a female robotic voice commanded. Min wasn't surprised. This man wasn't going to commit his voice to a line. He did as she directed. "You'll know who this is. Gies a wee call back on this number, please. Urgent, like." Min hung up.

He returned to the kitchen where Áine looked up at him expectantly. "Had tae leave a message. If he's involved in helping Sam, like I suspect he is, then I'm not completely sure he'll return the call."

"Why not? Who is he?"

"He's a man Sam and I worked with way back. I canny say a whole lot about that, but he's the Scouser I mentioned before. Good guy, Rob. He stayed in the unit we were seconded to after we left. Could be fifteen years ago now. He's solid. But him and Sam were kinda reunited not so long ago, and I know they were in touch. Anyway, he got stroked by the folks he was working for—"

"Military?"

"That kind of thing, aye. It's very very complicated, and Sam was in the middle of it. The upshot is, this man will have no love for the powers that be, and if I'm right, I'm guessing that's maybe part of the reason Sam went to him for a hand."

"Part of the reason?" Fran asked.

"He's got top-end surveillance experience. The latest – *the very* latest know-how. He's been using kit we could only dream of. He's the type of boy would be snapped up by private security or tech firms now he's out of the job."

"Oh? So who does he work for now?" Áine's interest was piqued.

"Haven't a clue. He's literally just out, and I mean a few months, that's all, so he's probably no' working for anyone just yet. Except maybe Sam."

The phone in Min's hand began to buzz. Number withheld. "Fran, I'm gonnie take this, ok?"

"No problem."

Min walked back into Áine's control room and hit the green circle.

"Hello?"

"A'right, mate?" The voice was pure Liverpool.

Min smiled, remembering how Rob had often been referred to as Ringo.

"Thanks for coming back to me so quick. How you gettin' on?"

"Eh, mate … whose phone are you calling from? I'm running the number now but it's taking a while cos it's out of jurisdiction."

"An acquaintance of our friend. I'm amazed there are so many people who like him."

"You're not wrong there, mate, for a bloke who does nothing but cause trouble. So you reckon it's safe enough? I'm ok this end, like."

"I think so. He's well removed from it all, this bloke."

"Well, can you use the, eh … the channel?"

"I think so. Why don't you let me try. If you approve this unit, I'll see if I can pick you up. If not, I'll buzz you back here and we'll find another way, aye?"

"Do well, mate, ta-ta."

The line went dead and Min made his way back into the kitchen.

"Fran, I need you to install a new app store on your phone, but first I need to know who pays the bills and who this unit is registered to?"

"I pay the bills," Fran replied.

"So this isnae a work phone? It doesn't belong to your trade union or anything?"

"I have a work phone as well if you want that?"

"No, this is better. It's harder for them tae get permission tae rip private phones. And it's contract, is it?"

"How do you mean?"

"I mean, it's not a pay-as-you-go phone?"

"No. All paid for, direct debit, every month."

"Ok. Well, this is unusual, but I'm gonnie explain to you what you need to do if you're up for that?"

"Whatever you say, brother." Fran smiled.

Min talked him through the settings to allow the installation of a private app store. Fran took obvious pleasure in learning new tricks and watched as the remote management system wormed its way onto his solid-state memory.

"There's only six apps available here?" Fran queried when it had opened up.

"You just need this one." Min stretched over his shoulder and tapped the encrypted messaging application.

Fran watched it begin, supplied his password when prompted, and handed the phone back. The typing began immediately.

We're good.

"Thanks, Fran," Min mumbled as he made his way back again to the privacy of the control room. The phone began to buzz.

"That's us," Min answered. "So how've you been?"

"Ups and downs, mate. Been grim enough, to be honest."

"Hard to find work?"

"No, well, probably – I haven't even started that yet. But I lost someone close, which is gonna be hard for a long long time. You know the drill."

"I'm really sorry. I heard about your pal. Desperate that she got caught up in it all."

"I don't even know if she did, to be honest, mate. It could just have been a road accident."

"It's bloody tough, I know that."

"Course you do, mate. Course you do. Who am I talking to, aye? You know better than anyone."

The statement hung between the two men for a moment, then Min shook it off.

"Look, pal, sorry to cut tae the chase here, but I'm staying with someone. It's hard to explain who but she's a relative of someone close to our friend."

"It's a'right, mate. I know where you are and who you're with."

Min sighed in relief. "I've been hoping you were the helper he was talking about."

"He told you?"

"He wrote a letter – after he left the island. You know that part ok?"

"Yeah. What I know is that he got in touch via some bloke in the Windies."

Min nodded in appreciation at the description. Both men had been trained in the triggers that cause automated intelligence monitoring to be flagged for review by human ears – names, locations, code words. By mashing descriptions, such pitfalls could be more easily avoided.

"After I'd made a few checks, we got talkin'. He was keen to know, obviously, who was after him for his last job, and how much they knew."

"And what did you say?"

"Well, I was in a good position on that question, cos there was talk at one stage of putting me through court martial, so I was given a lawyer."

"Bloody hell, they were gonnie go the whole hog?"

"I think they were trying to scare me more than

267

anything, mate. Anyway, my lawyer had discovery on their evidence – everything they had got handed over in advance so we could prepare our defence. I read a lot of the case against me, and they had nothin', mate, next to nothin'. So when I was released I was able to tell our friend with reasonable confidence that they didn't even have a sniff of him."

"You didn't do any sneaky checks?"

"No, mate. See, they suspected I was passing on intel, but they couldn't say anyone had received it. Without him in the frame, it was clear to them and to me that they didn't have a case at all. They needed someone at the end of their chain to me to prove anything against me, and they had zip. Nada."

"That makes sense. Well, that's good, cos all our back-end file checks came back negative as well."

"He somehow knows that, mate. I reckon that's why he came to me in the first place. Belt and braces, like. He wanted to come back, you see—"

"And when did you realise he was on the way?"

"When he asked me to track some Irish phone, a burner, like. He was really worried for some woman, and he knew her sister had already been beaten shit shaped."

"Did he explain how he knew that?"

"Someone sent him a picture of her lying on the ground bleeding like a slice of liver, mate."

Min closed his eyes. "Ok. Well, all that fills a few gaps. Tell me about what you did with the phone he was looking for."

"Like I say, it's an off-the-shelf burner, but with loads of money in phone credit."

"And you found it?"

"Yes, mate. It took a while cos it was on and it was off

and the settings kept changin', and I had to call in a few old favours in a very gentle way, cos I'm not really that well got as things stand in some quarters of the security establishment after what happened. But I've still some buddies, so I had a bit of a hand."

"We knew someone was looking. It's a relief that it was you."

"Not good for me if you managed to ping me."

"Couldn't tell who it was or why you were looking, but it was a good idea to try those Covid apps to trace it."

"Well, when you're outside the fold you have to find different ways, don't you? If I was back in the – well, you know what – I'd have all the techs I could ask for working away for me. You don't half miss that, I can tell you."

"Look, pal, something weird happened. We also tracked that phone, to a lock-up north of the city."

"Yeah, that's where it spent most time. Took a bit of finding, that."

"I went there."

"Did you?" Rob sounded excited. "How did that go?"

"It's a kind of … I don't know what it is."

"Industrial unit. Actually, inside it seems to be some sort of photo studio."

"Really?" Min asked.

"Looks that way, anyway."

"There were no signs outside saying that."

"I don't really know what's going on in there, but we've been mirroring the searches done via its Wi-Fi and the screens in operation inside. All the usual stuff – watching what they watch on telly, you know."

Min remembered well. Covertly roaming the streets of hostile areas, scanning selected houses to see what they were doing, messing with transmissions and televisions just to keep themselves amused.

"You said *we*? Have you got someone working with you?"

"A nephew. He was medically discharged last year. He's getting there but has a lot to learn."

"Ok. So what did you see inside the lock-up?"

"They're buying video and camera kit, sending imagery – some of it not so nice. Maybe a photo studio is too generous a description."

"Thing is, pal," Min paused for a moment, "I saw our friend there."

"Did you now?" Rob sounded pleased. "He got himself inside, then."

"How?"

"I don't know, mate, I don't know. What I *do* know is that he showed huge interest in an email that was picked up in the place."

"What email?"

"We traced it to a criminal gang in Bristol that said it was sending someone over to help them."

"Help who?"

"Whoever is working from that industrial unit."

"Help them with what?"

"Dunno. We were too late starting to see any email going the other way and we haven't managed to get into the server."

"But our friend seemed interested in it – why?"

"Not sure, mate. What was he doing when you saw him? How did you see him?"

"Just standing, in the dark. He came outside with another person last night. He shouldn't have been able to see me, but I kinda wondered if he had."

"That's a bit weird, mate."

"It was. Tell me more about this man who was being sent to help."

"That's what I'm saying, mate, I don't know. We haven't been able to get into their emails yet, just the traffic that comes and goes."

"So what level of detail did Sam get?"

"It just said that this helper person would be off the Holyhead–Dublin boat and that someone was to collect him at the terminal."

Min thought for a while. "I wonder if the helper was met with a bang on the head?"

"Possibly, mate. But there was no description of him on the email. Our friend would need to have known who he was looking for at the ferry port. Then he'd need to have extracted some information from the helper to be able to take his place if that's what you're thinkin'."

"Mmm, it's a gamble, isn't it – that whoever was collecting this fella didn't know what he looked like?"

"Yeah, I don't know, mate," Rob said, "but the fact he's inside is great."

"Why? How does it move him on?"

"Again, I don't know. All I was told is that wherever the phone he asked me to track was based is likely a link to whoever threatened the girl."

"And are you still in contact with him?"

"I don't message unless he contacts me. He's using this channel. But, to be honest, I think my job is done. He hasn't been in touch in two days now."

"Give us the ping, will ye?"

"Ok. It'll come through shortly."

"Thanks, pal. Is there anything else?"

"Not that I can think of, but if there is, I'll give you a nudge, mate. It's good to hear from you."

"You too, pal, you too."

———

THE PING CAME THROUGH JUST as Min moved back into the apartment's living space. Fran and Áine looked up at him eagerly but he ignored them for a moment as he deliberated what to type. Both he and Rob had reasonable confidence in the app as a channel to scramble messages and voice calls, but they knew only too well that there were watch lists with alerts attached to phrases as well as places and names. Tech moved so quickly that it was an inevitability that encryptions, no matter how good, would eventually be unpicked. Therefore Min chose his words carefully.

Right, pal. Need a hand?

He knew that would be enough to tell Sam who was on the other end.

"Right, then," he looked up at the pair facing him, "let's see if old Sammy boy will allow us to come and play with him."

Chapter Thirty-Five

FRAN AND MIN sat on the sofas and waited. Áine had been ordered to bed with the firm promise that she would be woken if any word came back. The two men looked at RTÉ's News: Six One, stared blankly at the screen through the body count and daily infection rate, and watched the graph of the R number tick upwards. There was no useful comment or reaction to what was happening outside, so as day once more became night, they flicked aimlessly through the channels until it was time to eat again.

"Will we wake her?" Fran asked.

"She hasn't slept well in days. Leave her be, for now."

Fran found a bag of rice and frozen vegetables, then hoked about in the freezer until he produced a bag of prawns. He held them up to Min, who nodded acceptance, and then set about defrosting them.

Min paced along the window a little, looking out into the dark; patient on the outside, while feeling a familiar burn within that something was about to happen. In the same way he'd sensed that Sam had known he was just metres away the previous night, he had that knowledge that they were about to enter the fray. It was something he was well used to – the silence ahead of action, the moments where everyone is ready, just waiting for the go.

They ate at the table and talked a little, Fran explaining the powers he had, which were of genuine interest to Min. They had both amassed significant experience of boarding ships on which they were unwelcome, but Min had to give it to the little man – he usually did it alone and without an automatic rifle.

"So you basically politic your way on board?"

"I use the power of the collective." Fran smiled. "The membership protects me. If I can get the stevedores to refuse to unload a ship before it comes to the dock, the harbour master will refuse to allow the ship to take up space on his quay and block it to other vessels. The harbour master, then having a vested interest in the situation being resolved, might assist me to board the vessel via his pilot boat. Unofficially, of course, but practical."

"Canny," Min said, nodding. "And all this to get a single crewman off?"

"All for one, my friend."

"Dangerous, all the same. Racing up rope ladders in a big sea in the dark isnae fun."

"You're referring to my age." Fran smiled.

"You're no' a duckling, anyway. I'm no' one myself."

"Truth be told, it was getting a bit much. That's why Sam's so useful. We started doing jobs together, which I enjoyed, but gradually he went on his own. I think he preferred it that way. I didn't need to know – I just paid him, and not every time."

"He did it for no money?"

"He sometimes said he'd managed his own compensation. There's a lot of money on some of these ships, so maybe he used that as a sort of punishment for mistreating the poor bastards who worked on them."

"I always knew some shipping companies were shits, but I never realised they'd keep men on board against their will without paying them."

"And worse than that – barely feeding them. Slave labour, brother. Exploitation."

"Sounds up Sam's street, alright. He always did cut his own path, though. I wouldnae take it personally that he went off on his own. He's solitary enough sometimes."

"Took a while to get into his rhythm, yeah," Fran said, lamenting fun times past.

"You know what, we'd better get a bit of shut-eye too. There's no sense in offering tae help him if we're zombified. I'll take the first watch if you wanna get a bit o' kip on the sofa?"

"No way," Fran said. "I made it to my bed last night. You, however, did not, so lie down and I'll wake you if the phone goes."

"Alright, pal. Thank you," Min said, rising from the table. "And, Fran, you're a good man. I'm sorry we got off to a bad start. I got the wrong end of the stick."

"That you did, brother, but no harm done. Sweet dreams."

———

MIN KICKED back in the bucket seat, flicked off the monitors, started the breathing exercises they'd been shown in training and raised his feet slightly. The technique had worked wonders during his younger days. He and his unit could kip on a carrier, a heli or even a rigid raiding craft hammering through a sea if they needed to. Full effectiveness was fifty per cent training, fifty per cent physical fitness, eighty per cent mental strength and twenty per cent rest – or so said their trainer. Over and over. He'd been a brutal man who expected two hundred per cent from any special forces operative, and generally got it, until he died standing up and screaming aged fifty from a massive heart attack.

Min was asleep in minutes.

———

ÁINE, however, was on the prowl. Her rest had morphed into guilt and she emerged from her room with a head full of hellfire and was not amused to find a shift system in operation.

"Where's Min?" was her first salvo.

"Getting some sleep," Fran answered, shaking his phone at her. "But, fear not, I have the comm."

"We're in good hands, so."

Fran wasn't convinced she meant it. "I hope I'm equipped to convey the arrival of a message or alert."

"Didn't manage to tell us about Sam's last email until eight or – wait, was it nine days later?"

"With that I cannot argue, but in all fairness who checks their junk mail – and what system does not bin unsolicited salutations from a dolphin trainer?"

"Whales."

"Mammals from a Caribbean Isle."

"You still didn't tell us everything you knew."

"Had I thought it relevant, I would have. But if you prefer that I take my leave, I am at your command."

Áine just grunted and clattered with the percolator. She

realised that somewhere in the back of her head she was keen to wake Min.

The buzzer sounded at the door, and, startled, she dropped the coffee bowl onto the counter – off which it bounced before spinning to a shatter on the tiled floor.

"You alright?" Fran sprang up from the sofa as the control room door opened, but Áine was already halfway across the room and reaching for the handset.

"What's happened?" Min shouted.

"Someone's at reception." Fran started looking for a dustpan.

"Hello?" Áine said into the intercom. She turned to Min with her hand over the mouthpiece. "The Guards are here."

"I reckoned they'd decided just to drop it." Min's uncertainty was obvious as he looked at Fran, Áine, then the coffee jug and the three places set at the table. Breach, breach, breach. "Look, it's decision time," he said.

Áine spoke into the receiver, "Give me just a minute," then covered it again.

Min held out his hands as if they were scales. "We either tell all and suffer the consequences, which could be advantageous – they might send to the site and they might find her with their resources."

"Or?" Áine asked, bent a little in urgency.

"Or they make a balls of it. Sam went in alone, presumably for a reason, when he could have told the cops."

Fran interjected. "He does everything alone, said it yourself – that's his way."

"Aye," Min accepted. "But we need to explain him," he pointed at Fran while looking at Áine, "explain me, and all the stuff we haven't told them if we want them tae act at all."

Fran's hand suddenly opened flat against his hip and he

withdrew his phone. "It's vibrating!" he said, waltzing towards Min.

"What do I tell them?" Áine was almost pleading.

Min took the phone and read, then he looked up. "Tell them you changed your mind," he said. "Get rid of them."

Chapter Thirty-Six

"FRAN, WE'RE ON," Min said. "And not a word out of you," he said as he turned to Áine. "Sam wants us back and standing by. He even knows where we parked last time."

"How is he—"

"Look, how he knows the half of what he knows is a mystery, but we should just follow his lead and do what he asks." He turned to Áine, looking straight into her eyes. "You need to be on the end of the line. You are probably the most effective tool we have. Force – if force is needed, is far better if it's backed up with intelligence."

Áine knew not to argue again.

"Good to go," Fran said.

"Get a piss or whatever you need. Get some water and let's grab some bars or anything handy. Bananas, ideally."

Fran headed for the heads and Áine moved towards Min, her faced creased with worry. "Is that all he said?"

"That's all he said," Min replied, realising that she was moving to hug him.

"You'll tell me what's happening and what you need?"

"I'll have to. You're the only eyes we'll have. You could well be crucial to whatever it is he wants us to do."

"What's your best guess?"

"I learned a long time ago not to guess what Sam Ireland might do. He's a whole different layer of devious."

Their embrace was broken by the flush of the toilet, and Fran and Min swapped places. Then there was a scramble together of a flask and water and bars from an old selection box, and the men went out the door at speed.

Seconds later, they were slowed right back down.

———

THE LIFT STOPPED, summoned, to reception before it descended to the carpark. The doors opened to a blast of neon yellow. The concierge was standing with both hands raised in a placatory gesture as two cops glared at him – one with impatience, the other with anger.

"I need to speak to her," the male was saying. "This is an offence – wasting time, nuisance calls. Get her on the line again, please."

The female guard was on her mobile, speaking, it seemed, to her station.

"We need you to call her mobile number. She is refusing to let us in."

Min stepped around the woman with Fran at his tail and was making for the door to the stairs down to the car park when he heard the male guard call out to him.

"Excuse me, sir. Where are you going, please?"

"Daily exercise," Min grunted, without turning.

"Odd time of night to be going for a walk?"

"Aye," was all Min said.

"And are you cohabitants?"

"Yeah," Fran started, shuffling past.

"Are they pyjamas?"

Min put his hand to the door and glanced back to catch the guard looking at Fran's ankles. There were, indeed, pyjama patterns peeking around the hem. For the first time he saw Fran stuck for words.

"What apartment are you in?"

Min was through the door and holding it for Fran when he heard the question he didn't want asked being put to the concierge.

"Are these men residents?"

The concierge did his best. "Ah, they ... I don't know every resident, like."

Fran glared back at him. "We are," he clarified. "Apartment 13C."

"Unlucky for some," the guard said turning back to the concierge. "Can you show me the register, please, and details of apartment 13C, please?"

Fran stepped through and the door swung closed. "Wait there, please!" they heard the guard call, but both men forged ahead into the hallway, swung the next door and cantered into the car park. They ran to the car and climbed in.

"He'll hold them for as long as he can," Fran said as he reversed out of the bay, "but he wouldn't be the shiniest button in the sewing box."

"When you get to the barrier, turn right instead of left. Let's see if we can blow a bit o' smoke about the place."

They waited for Áine to trigger the exit barrier lift, which took longer than felt comfortable. Her only hint of their progress was through the CCTV and she was unaware of the contretemps in the foyer. Just as the white bar began to rise, they heard the howling scream of a police siren ignite from within the underground concrete bunker.

"Hold on, brother," Fran shouted, and hit the accelerator, bolting the little car up the ramp and onto the lip of the Liffey.

"This isn't helping," Min shouted.

"How?"

"We're trying not to draw attention to ourselves."

"Fear not, brother," Fran all but laughed, "we're headed for home turf – I grew up in this part of town."

The tiny car hurtled at a speed it ought not to have been capable of through the streets of the inner city, turning hard down short one-ways and bouncing out the other end with a breakneck haul on the wheel.

"Is this absolutely necessary?" Min was gripping the grab rails as Fran played the handbrake. "They're no' gonnie launch a helicopter for a breach of lockdown regulations, are they?" Then the Bluetooth took over with a loud ring.

"Hello," Fran called at the radio.

"Fran, man, I held them off best I could. They were looking for your reg plate and I wouldn't let them look at the cameras without a warrant. Did I do ok?"

"You did grand, my man. You did grand."

"I didn't tell them you weren't residents either. I didn't tell them, Fran."

"Good man, good man!" Fran shouted. "Gotta go!"

Min looked at Fran. "He told them, didn't he?"

"Course he feckin' told them." Fran smiled. "He's got a criminal record and he can't be affording to lose that job."

Min shook his head as the car began to settle. They entered a leafy area before Fran pulled a tight turn and suddenly they were coastal again and headed towards a toll bridge. Min squirmed a little in his seat, but Fran took the right lane and the barrier lifted automatically.

"Do you own the town?"

"It sees me coming!" Fran laughed and tapped a dongle on the dash.

"What sort of car is this?" Min asked as it gripped and turned fast onto a bridge.

"One with a looked-after and carefully remapped engine," Fran said smiling. They passed the Point Depot and within seconds plunged into Dublin Port Tunnel.

"Should we be …?"

"Most direct route," Fran called as the sound in the car changed and they hummed through the yellow illuminated pipe. "So what's the plan?"

"Not tae get arrested would be a start," Min said, "so maybe you should slow down a bit?"

"I mean, when we get there?"

"Just what I said. Park up, wait for instructions."

"Ah, I thought you just weren't saying what he really wanted in front of the young one."

"I'm saying I think we might make a balls of this whole thing if the cops find us and pull us in."

"I have a plan," said Fran.

They fell into silence, Min anxious and fidgeting, glancing through all the windows. There were frighteningly few cars on the motorway and he couldn't help but scan the lanes looking for blue and yellow stripes or a flashing light. He hunted for an excuse for when they, as seemed inevitable, got caught. His mind came up with nothing but tumbleweeds as he considered their predicament: two men, largely unknown to one another and not involved in essential travel, speeding in a car during a lockdown. Not to mention that one was serving military and inexplicably in a different and historically hostile jurisdiction. There was no story that seemed to Min to plausibly fit. For the first time ever he considered posing as a gay lover for the day.

"What's this idea of yours, then?" he eventually asked as they passed the airport.

"I have just the vehicle," Fran announced. He pulled off onto a slip road, opened the engine's throat and kicked fuel down its gullet. Min's back pinned itself to the rear of his seat. They made six or seven turns and within minutes were almost rural. Fran swung the car into a driveway and drew it to a screeching halt in front of an enormous garage.

"You may alight from the vehicle," he said. "We have just the ticket for our next ride."

———

"THAT EXPLAINS THE MENTAL DRIVING," Min said as the garage shutter rolled up to reveal a pristine workshop. Along the edges were steel workbenches, precision drills, grinding discs and presses. On the walls there were what seemed like a hundred spanners and tools of all kinds – shining and oil free. Lit to the rear, Min could just make out road racing motorcycles – he recognised a Honda and a Ducati. But in the middle, staring at them, was a large Mercedes Sprinter van.

"You're a racer?"

"I *was* a racer," Fran said smiling. "Still do a bit but it's the young fellas I look after now."

"How did you know I could ride a bike?"

"I didn't?" Fran said.

"I'm not sure bikes are what Sam's looking for."

"I am *sure* that he is not expecting bikes," Fran said.

"Then what are we …?"

"We'll take the van, man. The van!" Fran called as he moved towards the driver's door.

"Ah, right, ok," Min said, following his lead and making for the other side, his plastic bag of grub swinging at his hip.

"The one vehicle that can travel the roads without suspicion or interrogation!" Fran announced as the doors closed. "They'll think we are agents of Mr Bezos delivering essentials to the needy!"

Min had to hand it to him, it was as flaw free as they could hope for in the circumstances.

"The cops will trace your car, won't they?"

"Eventually," Fran said nodding, "but it's registered to the union office, so it might take them a while. By which time ... job done, hopefully. We'll not be here, anyway."

"Is there naebody in the house?"

"There is, but that woman is well versed in dealing with unsolicited inquiries, brother. I'll text her and give her a nudge when we get to Portmarnock."

Fran turned into the road and took off at an altogether slower pace.

"Have ye lost your mojo?" Min asked.

"This, my friend, is a special vehicle worthy of care and attention. Besides, the back isn't some grimy old wagon. Take a look."

Min arched around in his seat as Fran reached down and pulled a lever, allowing Min to spin backwards. He laughed then pulled back a heavy curtain to reveal a kitchen, raised bunk beds and a small workshop. In the centre, harnessed by cargo straps, was a shining Yamaha XT 1200. Like everything else, it was gleaming.

"Very nice," Min crowed. "Very, very nice."

"Thank you," Fran acknowledged the appreciation.

"Perhaps Sammy boy will need a bit of kip whenever he's done."

———

MIN UNSCREWED the top of a water bottle slowly, trying to soften the snapping plastic cracks to avoid waking Fran in the back. He'd taken to the bunk after an hour's waiting at the rendezvous point.

Min felt exposed – sitting as he was at the side of a road with no evident purpose in mind. He had resolved to plead the need for rest after a ferry journey if questioned, but, still, the lack of a well-rehearsed cover story made him uneasy. Plus, Fran was snoring like a fat dog in the back.

He held the phone low to attract as little attention as possible, checking it every few minutes for further directions. None came. A second hour passed, then he ate. Then he sat. Then he debated what might be going on inside the lock-up.

The knock came into the third hour. A middle-weighted tap on the back barn doors. Min looked in both mirrors and cursed himself for not having seen anyone approach. He glanced down at the armrest console, looking for the central locking and wondering whether it would open the rear doors.

Then he paused – should he just open the door? He swivelled his chair and pulled the curtain back just as the second knock became more vigorous. Fran stirred in the bunk. Better placed to react, Min tensed to pounce if necessary and pressed the unlock button.

One side of the door swung open and a man in a disposable mask with a low-pulled woollen beanie hat lurched inside, falling forward without using his arms to save him. He clipped the exhaust of the motorcycle as he did so, forcing him to roll slightly. Assuming it was Sam – injured and in need of aid, Min sprang up to help the man, but then came a second person, sprightly and alert, who leapt up to the van's floor level and turned to pull the door shut behind him.

"Don't touch him," the second man snapped the command as Min stooped over the injured body. He looked up at the speaker, who was cramped under one of the folding bunk beds. Concealed behind a clinical face mask and hat, Min still knew who he was looking at.

"Took your time," was all he said.

"What's going on?" Fran's head appeared round the edge of the bunk.

"Fuck, Fran," the second man said.

"At your service, brother. Good to see you after all this time. Even if you smell like a bonfire."

One hand reached around to unhook the mask from an ear and Sam stared from one man to the other. "This is hardly Covid compliant," he said smiling.

Min looked down at the man on the floor. "Is that why I'm no' to touch him? Has he got it?"

"Not yet," Sam said, "but he will shortly."

———

MIN HANDED Sam a bottle of water, which he put to his lips and chugged down in one tilt.

"Needed that," he gasped.

Fran slid down from the bunk and flicked up the folding bed, but even still the cabin had suddenly become very cramped. The man lay motionless on the floor, wedged in beside the motorcycle. Sam, remaining crouched, bent over to check his pulse.

"What de ye need, pal?" Min stared at the motionless body.

Sam looked up at them both as if about to deliver bad news. He was thinking hard. "This your van, Fran?"

"It is."

"And your bike?"

"Black Beauty," he said smiling.

"Can you scout for us?"

"How do you mean?"

"We'll be changing location. We need to make sure there's nobody ahead to disturb our progress. You could do it on that." He flicked his head at the bike.

"Yeah," Fran said, "I have a Bluetooth speaker in the lid." He tapped a helmet hanging from a bracket on the van's wall. "Where are we going?"

"Dunno yet. I'll know soon, though. This prick's just pretending to be out so I don't hurt him. Would you be able to get on the road and see who's about?"

The man on the floor stirred, shuffling in discomfort.

"No bother," Fran said. "I'll just leather up."

Sam gave Min a knowing look while Fran was distracted pulling down a set of long-john leathers and a heavy jacket. He retrieved two gloves and a high-vis, then started fiddling with the Bluetooth set-up. "Once for luck," he said, and called his personal phone from his work mobile. The device in Min's pocket began to buzz. Min swiped to answer and Fran held the helmet up to his ear. "Steak and beer, brother. Loud and clear."

They levered off the ratchets, threw open the barn doors and quickly lowered the bike to the ground.

"So just mooch around till you call me?"

"Please, Fran. Thanks a million," Sam said, and pulled the door closed again.

Sam held up his hand until they heard the bike fire up, then Min began.

"Thanks a million for coming Min," Sam started.

"No problem, but are you aware of what's going on?"

"About Sinead?"

"You know she's missing pal?" Min said softly.

"Yeah."

"Well, do d'ye know where she is?"

"That's what we're about to find out." Sam rolled the man on the floor onto his back and pulled off the mask before punching him hard with his palm straight into the lower side of his nose. Min could see the man had already suffered a going-over.

The man choked and gurgled then stared up at Min, pleading for reprieve. Sam produced a phone and prepared a number, then looked up at Min.

"Any more water?"

Min handed him a bottle as Sam looked around the van. He reached out and took a shammy cloth, then noticed something better and unhooked a can of cellulose thinners from a bungee at foot level. He stared down at the man, whose eyes were like frisbees. Min couldn't understand why the captive was so silent.

"I was going to waterboard you," Sam started, "but you see this?" He held up the can. The man gave the tiniest of nods. "This is acetone. If you don't drown, it'll burn its way through your oesophagus and you'll choke to death after a horrible period writhing on the floor of this vehicle."

Min looked at his mate, curious more than concerned that Sam may in fact mean what he said.

"So I'm making a call, and you're going to speak to the

emergency Covid line. You're going to give the address of the lock-up, and this is what you're going to say ... are you ready? Listen carefully, or you'll be drinking thinners, ok?"

The man nodded more enthusiastically than before.

"You're going to describe the lock-up exactly, give its number, and you're going to explain that there are five men in there who all have the virus. Ok?"

The man nodded. Min wondered what shape the five men inside must be in.

"You're going to explain that they all have breathing problems, but if they offer you an ambulance, you say no. You decline. Understand?"

"You can't—" The man croaked in protest and tried to raise his shoulders but Sam rammed an elbow hard into his face again, shuddering him to the floor.

"You're going to say you'll call again later if things get worse. For the moment you just want advice on what to do. Clear?"

The man croaked a little and Min wondered whether he was still capable of speech.

"Then you're going to listen, thank the person and promise to call back in a while. If you mess about, or make any mistakes, it's glug, glug, glug." Sam held the can up again and shook it gently in the man's eyeline.

Min asked, "Will they not send an ambulance anyway?"

Sam hit dial, held the phone to his ear and spoke as he waited. "Bloody hope not. Hospitals are crammed. If we don't ask for an admission, they should be happy to leave it." He held up a hand to pause the conversation, then reached down to rest the phone against the side of the man's head.

Min and Sam watched him intently as the call was answered.

"Yeah, I'm at ..." He stared up at Sam imploringly, who nodded and held up the can once more, "the photo shop on the Baldoyle Industrial Estate and ..."

Sam turned his head very gently in warning while the man listened. "No, I don't want to give any names, I'm just ..."

Min was surprised in a way to hear an English accent out of the man. He realised that he had been expecting either an Irishman or someone from a foreign gang.

"No, it's not an emergency." The man looked pleadingly at Sam, who nodded. "There are five men here who have the virus and we need some ... No, no, we just need advice." Sam nodded at him. "Yeah ... a few days." The man was shrugging again at Sam who just nodded him along, and then began to lurch a little while holding his throat – mimicking a choking motion. "Breathing problems, yeah – hard to breathe." He listened again for a short while. "No, no ambulance, love. Just tell us what to do, yeah?" The man listened again for about a minute and then jumped in as Sam drew his finger across his throat. "Look, thanks, I'll call again in a while if we need more help but you're already busy enough and we're ok for now. Thank you."

Sam drew the phone back and ended the call. Then he reached down and started punching the man hard about the eye sockets, leaving enormous damage. Min retracted to the front of the van as the man yelled in pain. Sam paused and began to explain the next steps to his victim.

"My friend is going to start the van and begin driving, and you're going to tell me in the next twenty seconds where to go to get the woman."

"But I—" Sam set about hitting the man with the buckle of a ratchet he'd ripped off the tool board. "Fuck, right, ok!" the man screamed.

"And keep the noise down," Sam said, whacking him again with a heavy blow.

Min was beginning to get a picture of the scene Sam must have been exposed to inside the lock-up – he had never seen his friend so violently angry.

"Drogheda," the man gargled, pronouncing the place incorrectly – using a K, in the way many outsiders do.

"Where in Drogheda?" Sam shouted.

"I'll show you. I don't know the address. I'll have to show you."

Sam knew it was a bid to stay alive, but he had no intention of killing the man.

Not while he was still of use.

Chapter Thirty-Seven

MIN SETTLED into the driver's seat and waited for Sam to finishing trussing up his hostage in the back. The man was spared no pain and Min kept an eye on the mirrors as he listened to the groans and muffled yells of the lashing process. Sam stepped forward into the cab and whipped the curtain across, falling heavily into the passenger seat.

"Better ring Fran, tell him where we're headed. Remember Drogheda?"

"I remember," Min said.

It had been an illegal foray into the Irish Republic, one year into the peace process. An IRA quartermaster was on the cusp of going rogue and needed some persuasion to stay in line. Min, Sam and another man had been sent to retrieve the man and dump him on the northern side of the border. It had been a messy affair.

"Wasn't expecting a van," Sam said.

"Fran's idea. We had a spot of bother with the plods as we were leaving and had tae ditch the car. Besides, he reckoned it was good cover as a delivery wagon."

"Smart," Sam said nodding. "He's a funny wee fella."

"He is that," Min said smiling. "He's growin' on me."

"He does that—stop!"

Min hit the brakes less than a few hundred yards from where they began. "What is it?" He'd spotted nothing.

Ring Fran and tell him where we're headed and to clear the way ahead. I'm gonna grab some of those boxes." Sam pointed out the window to an upright recycling skip on the edge of the industrial estate. Min dialled and waited for the ringtone through the speakers as he watched Sam grab box after box and stack them against his chest, balancing as he turned towards the van. The phone was answered, muffled and with a din.

"Yeah?"

"Drogheda," Min said.

"Motorway or back roads?"

"Fastest route," Min said. "Motorway."

"On the way," Fran said. "Call me back in five – I'll be on the M1. We'll have to keep the line open from then because it's impossible for me to dial you on the bike."

"Received," Min said and cut the line. Then he leaned over to open the passenger door for Sam, who bundled the boxes into the cab.

"If we get stopped, we're following the plan. Delivery drivers." He pulled the curtain across.

"If they believe that they'll believe anything," Min said as they pulled off, Sam stacking boxes between them.

"They'll want to believe it. No cop's looking for trouble or to make arrests with this virus all over the place."

Job complete, he pointed to a sign for the M1 Northbound, Min nodded and dialled again.

"We're joining the motorway in two," he said.

"I'm two miles ahead, brother. All clear so far."

The growl of the motorbike was a constant in the cab as it droned though the radio speakers. Min knew to be cautious because of the open line, but had questions nonetheless.

"You ok?"

Sam just nodded, reluctant to commit his voice to an external communication.

"Are there others, back there?" Min asked, deciding there was little point in concealing his voice, given he'd already spoken on the same line a number of times that day.

Sam stared ahead and just shook his head slowly. Min took that to mean the five men mentioned on the Covid call had expired.

"Car breakdown on the slip lane. They were trying to flag me over. Be prepared for a responder," Fran's voice was remarkably clear through the speakers.

"Received," Min said.

Sam gestured for Min to hand him the phone. He hit the mute button. "I dunno what this next place will be like, but back there it was six-to-one. You don't need to be involved in the next bit, though. It's best if you're not and can get away and take Sinead with you – if she's there."

"Catch yourself on, pal. I'm here and I'll be at your back."

"I'm the only one tied into this so far. If we can, I really want to keep you from the grubby bits."

Min nodded. "We'll do what it takes. Let's wait and see."

"Blue lights headed south," Fran's voice suddenly rattled through the cab.

Sam took off the mute button.

"Police?" Min asked.

"Yeah."

Min slowed a little, checked his headlights were dipped. The closing speed meant that they saw the lights quickly. Two police cars moving fast in the opposite direction.

"That's good news, aye? Two cars committed to an incident further south. We're close enough to Drogheda. The town canny have that many response vehicles available."

Nobody replied.

Min's and Sam's faces lit up, illuminated by the road lights every few seconds before shuttering into darkness again. Min could sense Sam's cold stare forwards, his shoulders braced and his exposed forearms still pumped from whatever exertion they'd been deployed to.

"Taking the slip into the town," Fran informed them.

Sam spun to the rear, lifted the curtain without pulling it back and Min heard him wrestle with something. Sam's hip pushed through the gap, knocking some boxes onto Min's lap. Sam turned a little, dragging the man's battered face between him and Min, allowing him just enough height to see out of the windscreen.

"Where next?" Sam growled, pulling a rag from the man's mouth.

"Right at the roundabout," the man panted.

Min shouted into the radio, "Can you hear that?"

"No!" Fran replied.

"Right at the roundabout."

"Just as well, I'm beyond it."

"Slow down, we're gettin' directions here."

"Ok!"

"Next?" Sam said.

"Pass a shopping centre," the Englishman said. "Keep going all the way to the river."

Min repeated the instructions to Fran.

"Got all that, what way at the end?"

Sam gave the headlock a tight squeeze and the man yelped out. "Left!"

"Then what?" Sam screamed in his ear.

"Cross the bridge."

"Then?"

"Then stop," the man said.

"Take a left then cross a bridge," Min repeated to Fran. "Then you drive on. We might be stopping." He looked to Sam for confirmation but Sam only shrugged in return.

"All clear," Fran informed them after about twenty seconds. "Turning left along the river ... forking right onto the bridge. I'll go ahead as far as line of sight will allow. Keep an eye ahead for any traffic coming your way. All clear here, though, not a sinner."

Min allowed the van to follow Fran's track, then pulled in at a bus stop and looked at Sam. "Don't wanna be here long, pal."

Sam flattened the fingers on his free hand and sliced it back and forth – *cut the line*.

Min placed the phone on mute again. Sam leaned down.

"Where now?" he rasped into the man's ear.

"Nowhere. You get nothing more from me until I know I'm getting out alive."

Sam looked up at Min. "Tell him we'll call him back. Let's find a spot away from people, this is going to get noisy."

The man began to buck and shout. Min did as requested and pulled into the road while Sam and his charge wrestled and fought their way from the cab into the back of the van. Min could feel motion in the rear as Sam went to work. He looked for a space of wasteland or

297

another industrial unit, then decided to follow the river eastwards. The screaming started and Min could hear the can of thinners being grabbed, garbled conversation, more painful screeching. Silence.

Eventually Sam's head appeared through the curtain. He looked around.

"Tide coming or going?" he asked.

Min looked to out the window. "It's pretty dark, but it's a river – it'll be going, won't it?"

"I don't want this carcass floating back against the flow on a turning tide."

"I thought you needed him?"

"I'm reasonably confident he told me the truth," Sam grunted. "Looks like it's dropping."

"Wha?"

"The tide. Boat hanging seawards – must be flowing out."

"I didnae even see a boat."

"Find a quiet spot and we'll get this thing finished."

Min drove on for a few miles. "I can barely see anything, but all I *can* see is flatlands and marshy shit," Min said, his head shaking.

"Keep going. Closer to the mouth the better."

The phone rang. Min answered, "Quick detour, sorry."

"What are ye doing?"

"Bit of persuasion. Call you back shortly, ok?"

"Grand."

Min pulled a right as the main road ended and they bumped and rolled down a gravel path until they were prevented from going further because of a gate with a bar designed to stop travellers setting up camp.

"Gypsy bars, pal. What d'ye wan tae do?"

"I'll carry him, you turn the van. I'll be quick as I can."

Sam vanished into the back and Min heard the odd clink of the can again. The door opened and Min could feel the van rock on its springs as two bodies alighted.

Min waited a full half hour, tempted to look behind the curtain, but not tempted enough.

Fran rang again. "Fran, I'll get back to you soon as I can?" Min's knuckles tightened around the wheel.

"Sizeable Garda presence now, brother," Fran informed him. "Meat wagon, two cars and a paramedic."

"Where?"

"Town centre."

"Must be attending an incident."

"I'd say so. All blue light. Where are we headed?"

"I dunno. He's no' here just now. I'll let you know."

"He's not there?" Fran sounded baffled. "Oh-kay, so."

Two minutes later Sam rocked the van as he stepped back in. He was holding the can of cellulose and doused his hands and forearms in it.

"Bit extreme way to sanitise," Min remarked.

"It's DNA, not Covid, I'm wanting rid of."

"You didn't make him gargle it, did ye?"

"Didn't need to. But I promise you this," Sam turned to Min, "what those bastards are doing in there … I swear, making him swallow it would have been too good for him."

Min thought back to the suicide of the kid in England. "I might have a sense of it," he replied. "Right, where to?"

"Housing estate. I know how to get there and I know the number. He didn't know the name of it, though. It's not far from where we stopped. We need to go past a burned-out building, and I'll know the rest from that. Fill you in as we go." Sam's head motioned forward.

Chapter Thirty-Eight

"RIGHT, PAL?"

"Freezing my arse off, but, sure."

"Any sign of the cops?"

"No, brother, moved past, but if there's a casualty you'd expect the paramedic to be back at some stage."

"Need ye tae go back to where we pulled in, facing the way you were when you stopped and see if there's a housing estate in red brick off to your right."

"Ok."

They heard Fran's bike start again and the growl of its engine. "It's behind a hospital, apparently." Min looked at Sam for confirmation of what he'd been told. Sam nodded. "Beside a graveyard."

"I know the hospital, alright," Fran replied.

The van moved swiftly but within the speed limit back towards the town as the men listened to Fran's progress. After ten minutes they heard him clear his throat.

"There's any amount of housing estates, but I'm in a

red-brick one. There's a big wall and there could be a graveyard in behind it, alright."

"Ok," said Min. "Standby." He muted the mic and
turned to Sam. "This would be quicker if you guided him
in, you know? He's using the channel. It's as safe as we
know how."

"That's not what I'm worried about, Min. You don't
think I'm happy to have you both fall for this and not me?"

Min turned back to the road. "I dunno – you're no'
saying anything, I just—"

"I haven't spoken because I don't want you linked to *me*.
I'm the only one with a real trail here. Yes, you two have
been in the vicinity, but it's me who's covered in DNA,
prints and whatever else. If they investigate, it's only me
connected to the lock-up, and it will be only me who goes
into this house."

"No way, man."

"No debate – not this time, not with this." Sam's tone
left little room for argument.

"This channel is not something they can track, pal."

"We only think that. You and I both know there's
nothing that can't be cracked, so we can't be sure. We're out
of touch with this stuff."

"But Rob—"

"But Rob nothing. No chances. Enough people have
been fucked about by my decisions. We get her – if she's
here, then we get out. You get back to base, the boy on the
bike goes back to work and she goes home. We'll talk about
the rest after the dust has settled."

"So you're saying nothing on the channel?"

"Correct. Just tell him to go into the estate, see if there's
a burned-out building on the end of a row – it should have

metal shutters on the door and windows. I can find my way from there."

Min shook his head in resigned disagreement, reached forward, took the speaker off mute and conveyed the instructions.

"Moving in now," Fran said. "Red-brick terraces to my left … Bloody hell, it's labyrinthine."

Sam shifted uncomfortably, nervous at the detail being sent down a line – secure or otherwise. Min copped it.

"Maybe keep the comm minimal, aye?" he called to Fran.

"Sorry," Fran came back.

They heard the engine lower in revs. Min held up a finger and circled. *He's turning.*

They entered the warmth of lamp-lit streets once more and took a right past the bus stop, following signs for the hospital.

"I have it," Fran announced. "The building you're looking for."

"Still nae plods about?"

"No, nothing, brother," Fran replied.

"Ok. Standby."

Min hit mute. "What d'ye wanna do?"

"When we're close tell him to come out to the entrance so we're sure it's the right estate, then we drive in and I'll deliver my parcel."

Min opened the line. "Can you drive out and as you see us just point which way."

"Grand."

Within one minute they saw the bike's lights and slowly turned in past Fran. He turned on his saddle and gestured straight, then left. Min could see the tail light of the bike pull off in his wing mirror, and took the left. He could hear

Sam pulling on plastic gloves and looked down for a moment. They were bright orange – he recognised them as gripped protective gloves usually sold in motor factors for mechanics.

Sam leaned forward. Min muted the phone.

"There's the burned-out house," he said. Min's gaze locked on and his head turned as they passed.

"Take a right," Sam said, closing his eyes as he recalled what he'd been told.

They moved deeper into the estate, Sam ticking the directions off on his left hand. Four orange fingers became three as they turned, then two, then one.

"Stop," he said. "Face the van out. Use the horn if Fran sees the cops coming in."

"Understood," Min said. "Are you sure I canny—"

"I'm sure," Sam said. "Thanks again. Really, Min, thank you," he said as he affixed his face mask, pulled down his hat and slipped out with an empty box, moving towards the target house.

Chapter Thirty-Nine

THE ODDITY of a parcel delivery at four o'clock in the morning was not lost on Sam, but he had no option – just as he had no intention of knocking and waiting for a response.

Do it with conviction and nobody will know you're bluffing.

Instead of approaching the front door he moved with the urgency of a parcel delivery man and made straight for the gable wall where he hoped a recycling bin might lurk. That's where parcels were often left, after all. Once shielded from the street light he set the box down and in two seconds clambered, then rolled over the side gate into a small, smelly rectangular yard. Facing him were three big steps up to a door with large glass panels. Five-point lock, he reckoned. It would take several shoulder slams impeded by the steps and too much noise. He possessed neither the time nor patience. Sam knew he could have already been spotted by a neighbour and there was, even more incriminating, a van with a man parked down the street. The best thing to do was achieve his aim without anyone else in the estate knowing he was there, so he took the unconventional option. He knocked the back door quickly and urgently.

A dog a few doors down growled but didn't bark. A light came on and shone down from an upstairs window, went off again, and then a hall light on the ground floor came on. Sam watched shadows appear through the frosted glass of the back door. A figure in white ambled to the door, but moved aside to what two taps at just above Sam's head height betrayed as a kitchen window. The sill was at shoulder level to Sam as he stood in the sunken yard. He decided his next actions in the seconds it took for the window to crack open a fraction. He could try to talk his way in – and had a story loosely prepared – but he'd never been one for conversation.

"Who's that?" a woman's voice rasped with all the guttural phlegm of a heavy smoker.

Sam rocked back, gathering momentum and shoved hard off his left calf, the tread of his right shoe gripping the roughness of the bricks and allowing him to push upwards to grip the windowsill with his right hand and the lip of the open frame with his left, hauling it wide. He scrabbled his feet as hard as he could to get propulsion as the woman yelled and stepped back. Sam flicked his anchor hand onto the other side of the frame and gained enough leverage to haul himself aloft and head first into the sink.

He felt blow after blow of a heavy but dull instrument as he grabbed and pulled, sliding over the sink and head first onto the floor. The woman dropped a large chopping board and he caught sight of her grabbing a knife, but he was easily able to fell her from ground level by using his legs to twist one of hers behind the other and crashing her down. Still she flailed and screamed and Sam stood, pinning her knife hand to the floor while he reached over to close the window. Then he knelt on her chest and tried the name he'd been given.

"Hello, Clodagh."

———

THE WOMAN KICKED and spat and tried to slap Sam as she moved desperately to get her shoulder or back to a wall to assist her upright again. Sam did his best not to, but eventually he was forced to subdue her by grabbing an ankle and twisting it back against itself, precipitating another scream – which he answered with more pain. Her night dress rode to reveal an amateur tattoo.

"Keep quiet or I'll snap this and start on the other one," he hissed, but she was unpersuadable and kept at it to such an extent that it wasn't strictly Sam's punishment that broke her ankle, but her own twisting and writhing. The pain must have been excruciating and Sam was forced to move quickly and stuff her heaving throat full of a balled-up apron he tore from a wall hook. He used its ties to lace it round her head, then tore the neck strap off to secure her wrists. There was little progress she could make on one leg, so he was about to leave it at that and move off when another voice stopped him dead.

"She's not Clodagh," another voice said calmly. "I am."

Something in her self-assured tone made Sam turn slowly, and sure enough, he was treated to the dark circular tubes of what must once have been a fine modern shotgun – had half its barrels not been ground off.

Sam kept his back to the woman with the busted ankle, thinking about the spatter arc a shotgun like that would create when discharged. He'd used enough shotguns in enough dark places to know that the only person or thing in the room that would not be hit in some way by its shot was the woman holding it. He instinctively kept the woman on the floor in the line of fire.

"I don't give a rat's ass if she dies," the real Clodagh said. "She's a tramp and a criminal and I'd be glad to see the back of her."

Sam's heart rate plummeted as he told his body to breathe, to assess, to calculate a way out of this unexpected scenario. He'd expected there to be men in support of this Clodagh – there had been so many at the lock-up. Now he knew there were only women in the house, any man present would have intervened by now.

He looked at Clodagh's face as best he could, the light from the landing shining round her. He reckoned she was a bit older than him, frayed at the edges, of middle weight, average height and unkempt hair, even by the standards of someone just out of bed.

A gunshot would finish everything – not just for Sam, but probably Sinead. Min would run into the building – there was no question, and even if he found her, he'd get caught with a van full of a dead man's DNA and probably blood spatter, and Fran would get drawn in too.

There could be no gunshot – no matter what way it was aimed.

The barrels were angled down towards him, allowing him to see the top of the gun. The safety slide looked to be engaged, but the woman's thumb was dangerously close to it. Her index finger was on the trigger. Sam leaned back a tiny amount, staring into the up-and-over barrels, hoping the sawn-down length might help him work out whether there were cartridges inside. But the light was so low, and even with a torch it would be nigh on impossible to tell if there was definitely nothing in the tubes. He searched the woman's face for a tell. Was she nervous? If she was nervous, could that be because she knew it was unloaded?

All he could detect was anger. She had a snarl and stare that suggested she was willing him to make a move, to give her a reason to rattle off the shot into both of them; a dynamic that in the heat of the moment he struggled to make sense of.

He had only one option.

"I'm really not here to harm anyone," he said, his own anger refusing to allow him to plead. "I've come for someone, and if I get her – I'm gone. That's it. I have no interest beyond that."

"Awh," the woman tilted her head, cooing but mocking. "Here for Sinead, are you?"

Sam's heart stopped for a split second, weighing his next move with extreme care. He decided to say nothing and wait to see why she hadn't shot him already. His silence unnerved her.

"Who are you, anyway?"

He stayed quiet, staring at her.

"You can't be a guard – you're here on your own and, besides, Guards knock the door. And she's not married, and I know she has no boyfriend – I asked around."

Sam placed his hands on the floor as the woman behind began to shout through the cloth in her mouth.

"Shut her the fuck up," Clodagh ordered Sam, and thereby came his opening – a command to move. "Easy, tiger!" Clodagh warned and he placed a palm down and twisted his body over to rest onto his knees. He drew back his right arm in an arc as if to punch the woman on the ground in the back of the head but lifted his heels as he did so to let the toes of his shoes grip the lino.

"You sure?" he asked over his shoulder, measuring her distance and position.

"Do it," she spat. "Hit her hard as ye can, knock the bitch out."

Which explained the dynamic between the women, and also placed Clodagh's thoughts into vitriol and off her focus, so when he pushed back further he didn't wheel his arm downwards but back further to arch his back and grab the barrels, praying that he'd been correct about the safety slide and that his crotch wouldn't take the edge of the buckshot. In the split second he hauled on the gun he saw her finger pump furiously at the trigger as she lurched forward and fell half on top of him and half on the other woman. Sam twisted the gun free and thumbed the action release to open it and spit out two cartridges.

He'd been beyond lucky.

Clodagh twisted round and scrambled to her feet, making for the doorway into the hall. Sam got himself upright and followed her – expecting her to make for the front door and escape. Instead she tore left, slamming a door shut before he heard a lock twist home. A toilet, he assumed. People always head for the toilet because of the lock.

"Clodagh, I just want to get Sinead and get out," he called, struggling for breath.

He was worried that even though the house was an end terrace, the far side bordered another home. If its residents hadn't heard a commotion, they were either in a deep sleep or dead, so he gave up thinking too much and put his shoulder to the door and popped the bathroom lock open with ease.

And there he was exposed to a sight completely unexpected.

———

CLODAGH WAS STANDING by the sink – to his left. She was bent at the hip, slightly twisted with her hand to her mouth, sobbing uncontrollably as she stared not at Sam, but into the bath. In it was the body of a man, partly decomposed but with the stench of some chemical that was causing the flesh to part from the skeleton. Half of the chin had dropped into the gloop, leaving jawbone and teeth exposed. Sam had seen plenty of manky bodies but he fleetingly wondered if this one took the biscuit.

He looked again at Clodagh, his brows creased in query. "What the fu—"

"He'd have killed me! He'd have killed me!" She was gulping air between repeating the excuse. "What did they do to him? What's happening to his face?"

Sam tried hard to set aside the confusion of the situation and get the answer he needed. "Where is she? Where is Sinead?"

"Are they, are they—?"

"Sinead – where is Sinead?" he hissed at her, grabbing her wrist and wheeling her towards him.

"Are they… melting him?"

Sam glanced back at the man. "Looks like it. Now, where is she?"

The woman turned her head in trepidation again, unable not to look at whatever reaction was taking place in the bath. "They only said they'd get rid of him for me," she yelped.

Sam reckoned they'd fulfilled their commitment, whoever *they* were, but that wasn't helping him.

"I thought they'd just scare him away."

"Last chance, Clodagh. Where's Sinead?"

But Clodagh was for the birds, rather like her husband. Sam had to hold her up just to keep some sense to the situation. She placed her fingers into her lower lip and almost ripped at her own gums.

Sam had to move. He dragged her over to the bath and hissed in her ear. "This is acid, smell it – smell it!"

She choked in the vapour and turned her face away as Sam lowered it towards the surface. "Tell me where she is. Tell me or you will burn – just like him."

She began to gag and he worried that she might vomit, thus splashing droplets of the dreadful mixture upwards, but he had to have his answer.

"She's under the steps," Clodagh wailed, and Sam threw her backwards, trepidation rising in him. If they were prepared to kill and melt a man in a bath, what had they done to Sinead?

He tore into the hall and turned around the staircase, looking for a door, but found none. He kicked the plaster-board, punching through holes and tearing at the fabric until the underside of the staircase was exposed, but there was nothing inside beyond waste wood and sawdust. He was about to return to the bathroom when he realised what she'd said.

Steps.

More slowly, he prepared himself for what he was sure must now be an inevitability. The steps were outside. Up to the back door.

He rushed back into the kitchen, walked over the woman with the broken ankle and found the key in the lock. He ripped open the door and made down the steps, turning to peer into the gloom, convinced now that his heart was about to be smashed for a second time, and fully prepared to accept that he deserved it to be so.

Standing at ground level and in slow motion he felt around the steps, following the concrete down to the right, where his hand rested on a different texture – flaking, painted timber. Some sort of coal-hole or space for a dog under the house. He searched for a latch or a bolt, but there was none. He placed his hands against it in frustration only to hear a metallic ping as the door came back towards him when his weight was removed – a spring closing, he realised – like that of a roof-space inspection hatch. The door opened and he fell to his stomach, peering into the black, reaching forward – grappling for her.

He found a foot, then a lower leg and hauled himself inside the hole, feeling his way up the body.

And then a tremble, a tiny shudder, and an almighty kick in the face. Sam recoiled and half rolled.

"Sinead? Sinead!" he shouted.

He got urgent but suppressed grunting in return. He tried to grab the legs and pull but was met with yet more violent moans and a shaking of the feet.

He crawled backwards and ran up the steps looking for anything that would let him see what was going on. By the kitchen sink was an ashtray and on the windowsill was a lighter and cigarettes. He grabbed the lighter and raced back down the steps into the hole again. He flicked the roller twice before it caught fire, exposing a woman tied by the wrists and ankles to two eye hooks. Her eyes were covered and her mouth taped shut.

"Sinead, it's Sam. It's me. It's Sam. It's Sam," he said as he struggled, one-handed, to remove the band from her eyes. The lids remained shut for a moment then slowly cracked – her face twisted and untrusting, as if not believing what she could obviously hear. The lighter went out and he struck it a few times as he used his one free hand to feel around the back of her head to release the gag. Eventually he got it loosened enough to tear it down her face and she spoke clearly but confused.

"I'm dead, aren't I? I'm dead?"

He struck the lighter again, managing to get a flame, and moved to free her hands. The knots were pathetic but plentiful and had been doubled using what looked like a clothes line.

"Are you Sam?"

"Yes, yes, Sam," he tried to assure her.

"I must be dead," she said again. "Sam's in the Caribbean. Bastard."

"Sam's here, Sinead. I came to get you. I'm right here."

He freed her feet then crawled backwards on his belly and grabbed her ankles. "Ready?"

"I'm fucking dead," was all she said, so he hauled her out.

Chapter Forty

SAM KICKED ALL the boxes through the curtain into the back of the van and turned to pull Sinead into the cab.

Min knew to say nothing but leaned forward to give her a nod as he started the engine and pulled away from the kerb. Sam placed his arm around her and whispered in her ear.

"It's ok. You're not dead. We are here. It's Min, and it's Sam. Look." He leaned her forward and she peered again, disbelievingly at Min as he hit the phone to dial, then sat back again.

"How are you here?" she rasped, a million miles distant.

"Long story," Sam said. "Are you injured?"

She jumped in fear as a ringtone burst through the speakers.

"Yes, brother," came the answer.

"Success," Min said, "we're extracting. Anything to worry about?"

"Yep. There's three patrol vehicles now, all on the prowl

around the bridge. You're going to have to go countryside, brother."

"What's happening?" Sinead looked completely dazed as she stared into the hint of light now offered by the sky.

Min hit mute.

"We need to get out of here without the Guards seeing us."

"Get the Guards," she croaked.

"No," Sam said.

She turned to him, baffled, then touched his face as if to make sure he was really beside her.

"No," he said again. "It's complicated. Did they feed you?"

"Yes," he could barely hear her above the din of the van and the noise through the phone.

Min handed a bottle of water over and Sam uncapped it and offered it to her lips, but she took it from him and swigged hard.

"You're away to nothing," he said, his arm round her back, hands on her ribcage.

She leaned into him, touching his jacket, his torso, as if still checking.

"I am here, Sinead. We are here, it's not a trick. It's not a dream."

"The guards," she muttered.

"No," he said. "I'll explain later."

Min had to interrupt. "Which way?"

Sam looked up at where the dawn light was coming from, closed his eyes and tried to orient himself. "We need to cross the river somewhere."

"Cops are at the bridge."

"We'll have to go east. Head towards the sunrise if you can. That should bring us coastal. We'll work north and cross the motorway somewhere up there, then use small roads to get back to Dublin."

Min unmuted then shouted to the radio, "Going coastal, cross motorway further north, then work back down on minor roads."

"Got that. I'll watch for you turning out then overtake and clear the way."

"Good man, good man," Min muttered.

There was silence until they reached the edge of town, turning left and keeping the warm glow to their right.

"Hope you packed your bucket and spade," Fran's voice laughed through the speaker. Sure enough, a minute later they passed a sign to a place called Sandpit.

"Is that Fran?" Sinead's confusion was beginning to upset her. "What is happening?"

Sam gripped her tighter and muted the mic on the phone.

"A lot has happened."

She sat dazed for a moment, the turned to him with a pleading look. "Tell me."

Sam hissed out air between his teeth. "I dunno where to start."

"We're goannie be on the road a while at this rate," Min said. "And I wouldn't mind hearing it meself."

"Tell me," Sinead said again.

"Look, long story short, there was a mobile phone and you seem to have picked it up and used it to call me."

"In the Caribbean," she said vacantly.

"Did they drug you? Give you pills?"

"No," she replied, still distant. "It was hers."

"What?"

"The phone."

"We don't need to get into this now. Just rest."

"It belonged to the woman in the house," she spoke as if in a dream.

"Clodagh?"

"No. There was another woman."

Sam could barely hear what she was saying. Her voice was weak, her will all but shattered.

Min leaned over. "Maybe we should close the comm channel completely?"

"Yes," Sam said.

Min cut the muted line entirely.

Sam turned again to Sinead. "Who was the other woman? Back in that house?"

"She came to the convent. So rude. She ran off but forgot her phone. I took it home. See if Áine could find where to send it."

"To give it back to her?"

"Yeah."

"Why didn't you?"

"Stupid," she muttered.

"What?"

He could feel her shaking slightly and held her a little tighter. "Don't worry, it doesn't matter now."

She was sobbing then, as she spoke, determined. "We thought you were being hunted by the police. In the north. We wanted to contact you, so thought … this phone's not linked to us so it's safe." She snorted in derision with the full benefit of hindsight at the decisions they'd made.

"Look Sinead, that made sense. You couldn't have known. Now rest. Forget about it for now. You're safe."

"Áine!" she said, immediately alarmed.

"She's fine. She's fine."

"What's happened?" she was gripping his jacket now.

"It doesn't matter. Everything's going to be OK."

"Tell me," she growled.

Sam sighed. "Someone was able to work out that you used that woman's phone to call a number in the Caribbean. They got the number you reached me on and then called my friend."

"Daniel."

"Yes. He saw it was an international call and handed the phone to me. But none of this is for you to worry about now. It doesn't matter anymore."

"I wanna know, Sam," she tugged on his lapel.

"They… they threatened to hurt you if they didn't get their phone back."

Sinead stared ahead for a minute. "And you came back," she said softly.

"I knew they weren't joking."

"How?"

"I knew they'd attacked Áine."

"How?"

Sam shifted uncomfortably. "They sent a picture."

"Of what?"

Sam shook his head.

"Tell me," she hissed.

"They took a picture of her – when they beat her."

Sinead's head burrowed into his crooked arm. "You're sure she's OK?"

Sam turned to Min to fill the gaps. "She's fine," he said. "Absolutely fine."

"And you came back as well," Sinead said, her head slightly turned.

"Aye," was all Min had to say.

"You found me," she said again, trying to push herself upright, painfully but with purpose. "We need to call the

Guards. Honestly, Sam, we checked and there's nobody looking for you. Didn't we, Min?" she said desperately.

"Yes," Min conceded, but glanced at his friend.

"What are you not saying," Sinead began to panic again. "Where is Áine?"

"She is safe, I promise. If he says she's fine, then she's fine." Sam held his hand gently against the side of her face. "Listen, what happened before I left isn't the reason we can't call the police. You need to listen to what I'm saying – a lot has happened since then."

"Ok," she said quietly, searching his face, seeking reassurance.

He gave up on any plan of keeping his activities to himself. "I had no way to find you, right? So I had to get inside that gang."

Min cocked his head, curious.

"The people who took you," Sam said, "they were doing really, really dreadful things."

"What things?"

"We can talk about this later, honestly."

"Just bloody tell me."

"They were getting people to …" Sam hunted for a way to explain, "compromise themselves. And those people – young people – were being forced to pay for the gang's silence. Online."

"What?"

"Blackmail," Min said. "But, for what it's worth, your sister has managed to put some of that right."

Sam looked at Min, surprised, then looked at Sinead, who seemed completely lost. There was silence for a few moments as the three of them tried to make sense of the separate strands.

Sinead started to fidget. "If you're here, who's with Áine now?"

"She's at the apartment," Min said.

"Who's minding her?"

Min began to look uneasy.

"Sam?" she turned from Min, the distress choking her. "Who's with Áine?'

"The gang is gone now. They're gone," Sam tried to calm her.

"But she's alone? You left her on her own?"

"There's nobody left to harm her," he tried to lower the pitch.

"So she's safe – she's ok? You're sure?"

"Yes. They're gone, all of them."

"Gone where?"

Sam paused for a second. Min took his eyes off the road seeking the same answer.

"They died of the virus."

Min looked sideways at Sam. "Is it clean?"

"They all suffered asphyxiation."

"Well, how's that gonnie work?" Min asked.

"The Covid emergency line got a call from the man we had in the back of the van."

"Aye."

"Using his own phone."

"I can remember an hour ago, Sam, aye," Min hurried the explanation along.

"Well then you know that he told the emergency line that the people in the lock-up had the virus," Sam struggled to contain his frustration, flicking his head towards Sinead while looking at his mate."

Min didn't get the hint. "So?"

"I researched options on the ship on the way over."

"How?" Min barked, ever suspicious.

"There was a free Google terminal on the ferry."

"Clear as muck."

"Covid cases have no post-mortem. They're body-bagged and burned at the crematorium. It's as clean as I could make it in the time I had."

"Very good," Min said chuckling. "Very good."

———

THEY FELL into a thoughtful silence as the van wound its way east, then north, as unsure of its route as each of the people in the cab were of what, exactly, had happened. Eventually Sinead rose from the crook of Sam's arm.

"What about the women?" she asked.

"At the convent?"

"No. Back there. At the house."

"Well, you'll need to explain that to me," Sam said. "Who was the one with the tattoos?"

"That's the madam. She's the one who left the phone at the convent. We thought she probably ran some sort of brothel. I think she escaped the gang and came to us, but either changed her mind or they came and took her. They must have traced her phone, even back then."

"Well, she's still alive – she's tied up in the house. But there's another woman. When I got inside the gang, they told me you were being kept at Clodagh's house."

"They told you? Why would they just tell you?"

"They thought I was someone else, sent to help them from England."

"She's a dinner lady."

"What?"

"Clodagh. She was in the convent too. I nearly died

when I realised they'd taken me to her house. I can't fucking believe they did that. I can't believe she went back."

"Back where?"

"Back home."

"She's part of this gang?" Sam was confused.

"No, she was escaping her husband. She was in the convent at the same time as the madam one – she seemed to hate her. I threw her out."

"Why?"

"She was doing everyone's nut. I placed her at a hostel in Rathmines, a women's refuge. But she hated that I'd asked her to leave. She was really angry."

"I don't get it."

"It's so fucked up," Sinead placed her head in her hands. "They kept me in the house to begin with. I only got snippets of what had happened."

"It doesn't matter now," Sam said.

Min turned to them. "Wait a minute. There's two women back in that house while we try tae extract?"

"They're not gonna call the police, Min."

"You don't know that?"

"Hundred percent. There's a body in the bath back there."

"What?" Min's hands wavered on the wheel a little.

"A man?" Sinead asked, turning her face up to him.

"Yeah. Did you not see it?"

"No. But I heard him."

"I'm not following this."

"When they took me first, they put me in some photography studio for a few days, then said they'd be moving me. They were worried about something. Some boss was coming to take over, I think. I was put in the back of a car one night and the madam came too. The driver kept me in the car while the madam went up to the door. I couldn't believe it when I saw Clodagh answer it and start talking to the madam."

"Did they know each other?"

"I think years ago, maybe. At school or something, that's what I picked up. Later when I heard them talking in the house. But I thought Clodagh hated her."

"The madam?"

"Yeah. Back at the convent, she said something that made me think she didn't like her. I can't remember what."

"Why did Clodagh let her in?"

"Why was Clodagh not at a refuge in Rathmines, was what I was thinking."

"Well?"

"Sometimes they just give in. Go home. It's pretty common. Bloody maddening. They locked me in the bathroom."

"Downstairs or upstairs?"

"I never went upstairs. Why?"

"Doesn't matter," Sam said.

"I heard Clodagh asking what the hell was it all about and that her husband would be back soon. The madam told her to shut up cos they knew he was away on the rigs."

"Oil rigs?"

"Dunno."

"So they just barged in and commandeered her house?"

"Seemed like it."

"Why her?"

"They'd seen each other at the convent. Then I heard them arguing and the madam told Clodagh that her husband was a dirty bastard."

"Ah, right," Min said.

"What?" Sam asked.

"D'ye no' reckon the madam was telling Clodagh that her husband was a client of hers? That's probably how she knew where to come. They'd have had him by the balls like everyone else."

"OK," Sam said. "Well the husband evidently came home."

"I heard the madam promising Clodagh they'd sort him. All she needed to do was shut up and leave me stay in a room in the house for a few days. Clodagh hated me anyway. She must have agreed."

"So where did they keep you?

"In the bathroom. They had me tied to the sink so I could reach... you know."

Sam and Min stayed silent for a few moments.

"Then something changed," she said.

"How?" Min asked.

"The madam started to panic. I heard her pacing around. She sometimes had her phone on speaker and it just rang and rang."

"Someone was calling her?"

"No, I think she was calling someone else. But they weren't answering. She was getting more and more narky. Clodagh kept saying her husband would be home soon and there would be hell to pay, and the madam kept telling her the men would sort him out."

"And did they?"

"When was this?" Min interrupted, the clock in his head ticking.

"Don't know for sure. A day ago, maybe?"

"They'd have had the phone back by then."

Sam looked over at Min. "But the madam didn't know that."

"Cos you'd got in the way."

"What do you mean?" Sinead looked up.

"Well," Sam started awkwardly. "If all they needed was the phone and they'd got it back, then they didn't need you…"

"Alive," Sinead finished the sentence for him.

Sam said nothing.

"But the madam obviously didn't know the phone was back." Min said.

"So they kept me alive? Is that what you're saying?"

"Maybe," Sam said, staring straight ahead, a dreadful thought brewing.

Min had questions. "So when did the husband come back?"

"Recently," Sinead said. "Like, half a day, I'd say. They put me under the house, I thought then about fighting but I was in bits, and she had a bloody shotgun."

"I saw it," Sam said.

"So, they put me in that bloody coal hole. I heard shouting above a while later, then a fight and I reckoned Clodagh was getting it from the husband."

"Other way round," Sam said, grimly.

"Then it all went quiet. I wasn't sure if the madam was there anymore."

"Ok," Sam said, thinking how quickly the acid had gone to work. "You've probably been in the coal-hole for ten hours or less."

"How can you tell?"

"Well, Clodagh's husband is dead in the bath."

"How?" Min asked.

Sam turned to him and shook his head.

"Did you?"

"No," Sam said, "before I got there."

"They shot him?" Min said.

"No. Don't know. But they were breaking him down."

Min's face creased. "Melting him?"

"What do you mean?" Sinead looked between the two men.

"Doesn't matter," Sam said, rubbing her shoulder.

"Tell me."

"No."

Sinead was quiet for a while, then her distress turned to sobbing. "I thought they were going to leave me there to starve to death. But it was even worse than that, wasn't it?"

"We don't know that."

"You said they were melting him. With, like, chemicals?"

"Just forget about that now, we got away, that's all that matters."

"But they must have had the chemicals before. They must have had them ready."

"We'll need tae ring Fran shortly," Min said.

"They were going to do that to me, weren't they?" Sinead said quietly.

"Must have been for the husband," Sam tried.

"It was for me," Sinead said.

Min tried to shift the talk to the practical. "So we just left two crime scenes with multiple bodies?"

"Yeah," Sam breathed in, irritated at the trail left behind.

"I think Fran's gonnie have to lose his lovely van to the crusher."

Sam closed his eyes. "Yeah."

"And you're gonnie have tae skedaddle, sunshine. This is gonnie be a mess."

"Maybe not," Sam said. "The body at the house won't be there for long."

"And you didn't touch the body?"

"No."

"There's still gonnie be an investigation at some stage, and your DNA is gonnie be all over that house."

"Maybe not. If there's no body," Sam said. He turned to Sinead. "And they didn't hurt you?"

"No," she said, rapidly, then looked up at him. "It wasn't until they put me under the house that I really thought they were going to kill me. I thought they just wanted some muck-filled phone back."

Sam pulled her in tight, closed his eyes and quietly gave thanks for having her back.

"How's Isla?" she asked.

Sam smiled. "She's great. With her granny and grampa. Delighted to see them."

"So," she paused, thinking, "you know now that you're not being chased any more? You're convinced?"

"I had two good friends help me with that."

"Two?"

"This man," he nodded his head sideways, "and the opso – a man we once worked with in the north. Boy called Rob."

"Ok," she said distantly.

"Look, sorry, but we need a plan here," Min interrupted. "There's other problems as well as all the stuff we've left at our arse."

"Other problems?" Sam asked.

"Áine's gone and pissed off a few plods, which would be manageable if it wasn't for everything else. But two people left the apartment in ropey circumstances, and if four people come back, well, that's gonnie be an issue."

"So what do we do?"

"I know this is shit, given the circumstances, but we are gonnie have tae split up – and soon."

"What?" Sinead said, desperation breaking her voice.

"There's two guards convinced Áine's breaking the lock-down rules and is wasting police time. You showing up safe and well is one thing – you showing up with him and me is another whole bag o' hassle. I'm no' supposed to be here, never mind having travelled to a different country with no good excuse. And you," he looked at Sam, "have left your—"

"I know, DNA," Sam said.

"—all over the bloody place. I suggest you let whatever is gonnie happen to that body just take its course, let the dust settle and then just sort the rest out when it's all gone away."

Sam grunted. Sinead began to shake.

"It'll only be for a wee while this time. I promise, Sinead, I promise."

"And that poor wee bugger," Min said nodding at the phone, "needs to be told about his lovely wagon."

"I'll make it good for him," Sam said, as Min leaned over to open the line to Fran. "I have some cash," he said as the speakers shuddered with the ringtone.

"It's some job, no' be cheap," Min warned.

But Fran had other problems. "Lads," he answered, "I'm being pulled over."

Chapter Forty-One

"A CHECKPOINT?" Min's knuckled tightened on the wheel.

"No, a Garda car. It's been tailing me for two minutes. I'll be in the shit, but I had to keep them moving cos you gobshites cut the call."

"Where are you?"

"I sped up a bit. If you can't see the blues and twos, turn off. I'm pulling in now to face the music."

"What will you say?"

"Hang up," Fran commanded.

Sam reached forward and did as they'd been told. "If anyone can talk his way out of it, he can."

Min took a left and they headed west, the tip of the sun occasionally appearing in the wing mirrors.

"Will he be ok?" Min asked.

"I'll find a way to make it right," Sam said. "Mind you, I remember he used to get migrants to take his penalty points."

Min laughed at the roguery of the little Dubliner.

"Can I call Áine?" Sinead said quietly.

The two men were silent for a second before Min answered her query.

"You'd be better not tae, to be honest. She could have those cops with her in the apartment, and until we get him and me clear," he gestured to Sam, "it would be better if you could wait."

Sinead said nothing.

Sam found a road atlas wedged in the passenger door pocket and used what light there was to direct Min south through Duleek and then west again, before following the coast road south through Balbriggan and Malahide.

"We could do with some traffic," Min muttered. "We're a big white van on the road on our own."

As they neared Dublin Min got his wish. It wasn't heavy but even light congestion left them less exposed.

"D'ye know where the bin lorries come to your apartment block?" Min asked.

Sinead stirred, realising the question had been directed at her. "By the car park barrier."

"Sorry, darlin', but I think we leave you there."

She didn't reply. Sam spoke into her ear. "I'll be back soon. I promise."

"Will you?" she turned to him, not pleading, not needy, simply seasoned to his form, gently but self-assuredly unconvinced.

He sat back and looked forward. He couldn't fault her for her scepticism, and he felt even more unable than normal to elaborate with Min at his side.

The phone rang as they crossed the Liffey onto the south side of the city centre.

"You ok?" Min asked Fran.

"Ah, yeah. Told them I was charging the bike's battery with a run while there was no traffic. They nearly did me for speed but they weren't that interested. I think they were looking for someone else."

"Did they ask you for your driving licence or ID?" Min was working through the connections that could lead back to the lock-up.

"Yeah, yeah, but when I reached for it they even didn't bother to look. He was happy enough. Nice lad."

Min swung around the apartment block and saw a police vehicle now parked up at the front door. He wondered whether there might be another in the car park.

"Look, pal," Min told Fran, "we have problems back at the digs. We're gonnie have tae drop the passenger and get offski quick."

"Ok," Fran said. "Well, you could go back to where we got that nice vehicle you're in."

"Aye," Min said gravely, "we'll need tae talk about that."

"Park it up." Fran remained oblivious. "I have just what you need."

Min turned to Sam, who nodded.

"See you there," Min said, as he pulled into the loading bay at the apartment block.

———

SINEAD PUT her hand on the door handle. Min turned his head right to look away into an empty grille window leading onto the block's car park. He wanted to be anywhere but at the side of his best friend at that very moment. He felt movement on the bench seat to his left.

"This is it, then," Sinead said. "Again."

"I'm sorry," Sam didn't know what else to say. "It won't be for long this time."

"You don't know that," she said, then paused, "but you

came for me." She nodded and reached up to lay her palm against his face, a thought occurring to her. "When did you leave?"

"I've lost track," he shrugged. "More than two weeks ago, anyway."

"So … you didn't get my letter?"

"I did get your letter. I replied to it—"

"No," she hushed him, "the one," she dropped to a whisper and looked down, "about Uganda."

"I don't understand?"

She looked up again to search his eyes for a moment. A door slammed on a vehicle behind them and she shook herself. "What will I say? To the guards?"

"Tell them nothing," Sam said firmly. "They have no right to hold you for anything. You just… needed time to yourself."

Sinead thought for a moment. "I know what I need to say," she said, then shimmied over Sam, placing her hand on his shoulder as she passed. She pushed the door and stepped down to the road, closing the door gently and resting her hand against it for a moment. She glanced up at him through the window and walked past the front of the van, around the car park barrier, and didn't turn again before she disappeared into the gloom.

Sam felt like he had just been hit in the stomach and watched the darkness in bafflement.

Min stayed silent and pulled gently into the road, looking above for signs of any cameras at the rear of the building, but he already knew there were none on the internal CCTV system, which triggered two unanswered questions and allowed him to crack the heavy air hanging in the cab.

"How did you know we were at the lock-up?"

"What?" Sam shook himself from his distraction.

"At the lock-up – the first time?"

Sam peered at his friend and took a long breath. "They had three coverts at the perimeter of the estate."

"Must have been good ones – I didn't see them."

Sam felt Min's pain. There was a time when their job had been to help install such hidden cameras, masked by mobile phone masts or TV satellite dishes.

"You know what they were doing in there, don't you?"

"I have a fair idea and don't want to know any more," Min said.

"Well, they wanted to have a heads-up in case the police started sniffing around so they could shift their customers in a hurry. That's why the cameras were so far from the building. None close, though. They didn't want any record of their own team coming and going. They were tricked out," Sam mused. "Great toys in that building, or at least they had."

"I take it you smashed it up?"

"There was a contained fire," Sam replied.

"Who were they?"

"It was run by an English bloke. Small enough team, some Irish, some foreign. They were trying to muscle in on the local organised crime scene. When they lost that bloody phone, the boss got fed up with their constant failure to locate it and came over to read the riot act, but I met him at the ferry terminal and he told me enough to make excuses."

"You took his place?"

"No, they knew the boss. I told them there'd been a last-minute change and he'd sent me instead."

"And they didn't check that with him?"

"That would have been challenging," Sam said. Min took that to mean that the boss had, indeed, been greeted with a bang on the head, or fallen in the dock. Probably both.

"So they just took you back to the lock-up?"

"My story had the unexpected advantage of me not being properly briefed on what was going on because it was all changed last minute. I said I was there to advise and make sure they didn't make a bollocks of it again, and they sucked it up. They didn't have much choice – they were all terrified of this boss bloke."

"So you advised them?"

"When the phone came to life, they located it and I told them to recce it."

"Recce what?"

"The marina. Glad to see your desk job hasn't left you completely unfit."

Min shook his head. "You saw the whole thing?"

"I wasn't expecting you to come out of that wreck of a boat. That made me smile alright." Sam was shaking off Sinead's departure with the recollection.

"And you followed me into the town?"

"Not far. How did you find the lock-up?" Sam asked.

"Mixture of things – taxi the men took and some bizarre idea of Áine's. She's some smart cookie."

"Completely."

"But," Min was confused, "you said there were no cameras on the building itself, so you couldn't have seen me in the dark, then, at the door?"

"No, but when the alarms on the cars outside went off, I knew you'd be there. I needed you to know I was inside and I didn't want you coming in. Sinead wasn't in the building and I still had to work out where she was being held. Besides, I had the Covid cover plan worked out for the gang and I really didn't want a bloodbath – which is what it would have turned into if you'd come inside."

"Ok," Min said. "Bit of a gamble that I wouldn't push in, aye?"

"I was confident enough you'd get it," Sam said, "once I stood in the light from the doorway and you could see my face."

There was peace for a short while as the van made its way north yet again, both men wary of the potential for police interest.

"We looked at the camera recordings from inside the apartment building, from when Áine was attacked," Min said.

"Oh, yeah?"

"Weird thing. The people who beat her up, they went into the car park first."

"Why?"

"That's what I'm wondering."

"Is there no camera in the car park?"

"Not one that could show what they were doing."

Sam thought for a moment. "They had a lump in their kit."

"A tracker?"

"Yeah. They were probably looking for Sinead's car. I don't know if Áine has a car."

"She doesn't drive."

"So we should tell Sinead to look for a lump."

"Her car wasn't there," Min said. "No harm in double-checking, but when they went in tae the car park, she was at the convent. That's where they grabbed her."

Sam nodded grimly.

Min looked over at him. "D'ye think you'll really be able to hang about with all the mess left behind?"

"They'll get next to nothing from the lock-up – all cards and hard drives are destroyed. Far as the authorities are concerned, it's a Covid situation, so there will be a deep clean – probably hefty chemicals – and I'm reasonably happy with that."

"And the house in Drogheda?"

"They were melting a man in a bath. It was fucking disgusting. I just can't see how they'd want to attract any attention there. Two bad bitches live to fight another day, but they're going to have to clean up to save themselves."

"Is there risk for Áine and Sinead from England?"

"There would have been if there was any trail to Áine, but that was done through the boss, and he's all at sea. That's two of them floating around the Irish Sea with no real boating traffic to pick them up."

Min nodded. "They'll likely sink first."

"Hopefully. You're right though. The outstanding problem is this van. I'll need to get Fran to destroy it."

Min shuffled uneasily. "The cops might pay a visit to his house at some stage."

"Why?"

"Speeding, mainly."

"They'll not be searching the place, then?"

"No. But we should drop this into his garage, explain and then clear out ASAP."

"Agreed," Sam said. "Poor fecker, this really is a nice van."

Chapter Forty-Two

SAM LOOKED AT THE ENVELOPE, camouflaged with airmail stickers, and thought about whether to call Sinead before opening it. Their calls were laboured, though, he felt. Something was wrong.

They'd been using the channel, which he had thought was as good a means as any. From his point of view there had been more contact between them than ever before, and he knew she wouldn't blame him that he couldn't travel to see her – or her to him. The cross-border lockdown had seriously begun to grip; new variants and people using the normally lax security to exploit loopholes in the restrictions had resulted in increased patrols on both sides of the invisible line. Plus she knew there was a potential trail from his actions to finding her. A lot of people had died, which could trigger an investigation, and getting picked up for something silly could bring all sorts of unintended consequences – police computer checks, finger printing, maybe even DNA sampling. He couldn't afford questions about why he'd crossed the border and who he was going to see.

So he'd called on the channel. Immediately, in fact, to check how she was. To his surprise he'd found Áine remarkably friendly. Sinead had been sleeping on the first two occasions he'd tapped up the app, and on the third he knew all was not right.

Later he'd tried to inquire of Áine if there was a lingering issue, if the Guards had become difficult, but she'd insisted they had lost all interest after Sinead had turned up safe and well. Sinead had offered nothing of her ordeal to the police, but Áine and she had discussed everything, or so Áine claimed, and Sam could detect no particular concern from Sinead's twin.

Yet the calls had been factual, perfunctory almost. She had inquired after Isla, after him, asked what they had been doing, but there was a coolness, and it disturbed him in a way he couldn't remember having felt before.

He looked again at the letter. It must, he knew, contain something important. The mention of an unanswered letter had changed their parting in the van completely. Even Min had noticed it – he'd asked about it when they got back to Belfast on two of Fran's motorbikes. *Everything ok with you two?* Min's tone had said it all. Sam had just shaken his head gently. *I'm not sure.*

Of course, she had been abducted and held captive for two weeks. It went without saying that life had changed. Yet, and all, there was something else. So Sam looked at the envelope, on which the various journeys of the letter were betrayed: Ireland, Jamaica, Dominica, Barbados, Belfast.

He worked his way through the various redirected incarnations, each envelope larger than the last, like Russian dolls. Finally he tore, gently, along the top of the original, and began to read.

DEAR SINEAD,

That sounds very formal, but it's nice to finally put your name on a letter. A letter, it seems, might be the best way to get some things out, really, because the other channel clearly isn't working. So, I thought, given this was going quite well before, let's try it again. Maybe I'll be able to find the words if they're on paper, because I sure as hell can't seem to find them on the phone.

I got it, at last. Your letter. The one you mentioned in the van, about Uganda. Daniel sent it on. It has taken long enough to find its way back, but then it probably took two moons by camel to find its way there in the first place. But I've got it now and that's what matters. So here it is – my response. I hope, sincerely (how formal), that this comes out the way I mean it.

I'll start by answering your questions. Yes, I've been to Uganda, and, yes, it was with work. I know a little bit about the Lord's Resistance Army. I was briefed, once, but we weren't involved in anything to do with them – we were just there training in the bush and on the rapids from Lake Victoria.

So much for letter writing working better – now I'm stuck for words, but I meant it when I said that if you wanted to go there, I'd go with you.

What do you say to something like that? What you wrote, I mean. Well, in a nutshell, I am so, so sorry that you had to go through that – that they put you through that. I'm gutted you suffered at all. I'm gutted you suffered in that way. I can't honestly say that it came as a complete shock, but what is incredible is the way you have somehow managed to deal with it. That you are so strong, that you are still fighting for people who cannot fight for themselves. It made me so sad and angry to begin with, then it made me so proud, if that makes any sense. It makes me so proud of you. I mean, I was proud of you to begin with – really and truly, I have always completely admired what you do and the way you do it. Asking no thanks, seeking virtually no help, just digging in and getting on with it. Maybe that wasn't clear before. That you've been through all that and survived and came out as strong – well, that's probably one of the most impressive things I've ever heard.

Full disclosure here: it made me completely mad. It made me think the way I used to. I started thinking about what I could do, but gradually I realised that what I was doing was pure selfish, typical of the way I used to be – see a problem, knock it over. So I'm sorry that I immediately reacted like that. But it's fair for you to know that that's a part of me that I haven't managed to shake yet. Who is waffling now?

Few people could have experienced that and come through it. I know you will have suffered terribly at the time. I also know you'll have suffered afterwards. Maybe you still are. Of course you will be, at times. I get that. I understand that. Honestly, Sinead, I really, deeply understand that. Maybe not the violation, that's beyond horrific. I'm … it's, I don't know if you want to talk about that or for me to talk about that. We can work that out.

But I do know about the aftermath of the kind of mayhem you witnessed. The killing. Made worse by the fact that they were children. I'm not going to sit here and say those kids didn't die because you were there. I don't know the details and I hope to never say the worst of platitudes that I hate people saying to me – that things weren't my fault when I know bloody well that they were, but that's not to say it was your fault either.

What I do know is that you were there for good reason. The LRA were killing and abusing children long before you ever arrived. It's crippling that you witnessed it, but unless the world starts to take notice of shit like that, then nobody will ever know and it will keep happening. And unless government agencies, or whoever you were there to make answerable for it, start feeling it in the wallet, they won't bother their holes doing anything about it. What I'm saying, badly, is that it is worthwhile, you and people like you being in these fucking terrible places trying to do your best, because without you this just goes on and on and nobody gives a rat's ass.

I have wrestled with unintended consequences all my adult life. There are times when you just have to trust that there must be some purpose, that there is a sequence of events that would have occurred whether or not you were there to see them. I don't know if this was one of those, I can't say, but I know you and I know you would never have put anyone in danger. You are such a good person, your soul is kind and your heart is huge, and you have suffered for being there, beyond what almost anyone could manage, and I am proud. Of you.

But back to your letter. I'll try to answer everything you asked even though this bit is hard to explain properly as well.

You spoke about Isla and me, and us being one. I accept that this has been a barrier. I'm not sure I had fully reasoned that out in my head, but I knew it all the same – if that makes sense. Just because I hadn't thought it through, doesn't mean I didn't understand it. Do you know?

This is what it is. I am permanently guilty. I have this

pervading and consuming darkness that comes over me, in waves at times, and it scares me, to be honest. I feel like everything I touch or care about has the potential to be damaged by me, as punishment for my behaviour. I can talk more about that later, in a later letter, assuming you want one, of course, because I need to explain and deal with the matters you raise ... and maybe now I'm deflecting the hard bit.

You see, I feel guilty about Shannon. I feel, sometimes, that I'm doing a disservice to her memory to have you forge such a strong, motherly bond with Isla. Perhaps that's stupid. I feel guilty for missing Shannon less, and I feel sad about that. As time passes I learn to live without her, and even writing about her to you seems like a whole other betrayal of her legacy. Because Isla is her legacy, and I sometimes worry and wonder whether it would be fair for her to be raised by another mother. And I know how many assumptions are involved in that statement – me assuming that you would even want that – and I fear that she was so young that she might not remember her mam. I would hate that for Shannon. Yes, I know she's gone, but I would hate for Isla to not remember me, and so I would hate for her memory of her mam to wither. Wither is the wrong word. It's ... it's like a scent that gradually disappears. I want her to keep the scent.

I know this is confusing. I know this is probably hard to hear, but I need to be honest and explain. If I can explain it, perhaps you can understand and we can find a way. I'm afraid of Isla thinking ... I don't know. I see Shannon in her all the time, and I wonder if that will become a problem, you know, that she's so like my dead wife. That's the first time I've ever said that. My dead wife. I don't know what that means. That I finally said it.

I'm scared that Isla is my everything, and I'm constantly terrified that I will lose her, and I worry that if I let myself care about someone else, that's just someone else to lose too, as punishment, for all the shit I've done. When that bomb went off, you can't imagine. Actually, maybe you can imagine. Maybe, of all people, you can. I just thought, that's it – it's happened. Knew it would happen and now it's happened. You've finally got what was coming to you. And then you found her for me and she was ok, and the relief, and then what did I do? I did what I always do. I went and created a whole new batch of consequences that some day I will have to answer for. And the bottom line is, I don't want to add you to my list of collateral. In my darker hours I think that if I allow it all to go the way I want it to, you will fall foul of me as well.

There are so many things, Sinead, that I've done. So many. You can't do all that and not answer for it. I did wonder for a long time whether Shannon was my punishment. But as time passes and the pain of that lessens, I wonder if I am due some fresh hell, and I wonder if you are going to be that.

So when they took you, I was sure – again – that this was it. And when they said you were under the house, I was again sure, and then I somehow got to wondering whether you were like my sacrifice to protect Isla – that if they took you, they might spare Isla. I appreciate how completely mad that is, I know that, I do know that. It's horrendous as a thought, but I thought it and I can't deny that. I worried that maybe that's what I was subconsciously doing.

Since I've learned about Uganda, and now that you've been taken for a second time, I can't imagine what you must have been thinking. Two weeks they had you – how can that not bring back all that damage? And me talking about it like this, I mean – is that making it worse?

I've learned that it is better to talk about this stuff, but it's impossible for me to find the words with my mouth. Putting it down like this is easier, but that's not to say that it's easy. I know what you mean about persuading yourself that you might not send the letter, and then you go ahead and send it anyway. That helps, I think. So now that I know about Uganda, about what happened to you before, I want you to know that you can talk to me about that if you want to and if it doesn't make things worse. I might understand.

That's assuming that you want anything to do with me. Maybe what happened these last few months has changed everything again. Maybe that will be my punishment for the past, but also for not being sensible about us. About us.

You mentioned children. Of course that's not an issue. That sounds so stupid I'd cross it out but, sure, we're being honest here and I can be so rough. I know that for you that must be an enormous issue. You would be such a fantastic mother, you really, really would, but for me, that's not, as you asked, a deal-breaker at all. Not one bit.

Maybe we can find a way that you can be? If you want. If you'd still like that.

I think the best thing is for me to stop now. I'm worried I might be making things worse. I know you were sort of, maybe, crestfallen – is that anywhere close to the correct word? – when you got out of the van and left me and Min to clear off away again. I think, maybe I'm wrong, that you thought I'd got the Uganda letter by then, and that when you realised I hadn't there was still stuff to be said. But what matters, to me anyway, is that I have it now. And that I am so proud of you.

Sam

He folded the paper, wrote Fran's address on it, placed it in another envelope with instructions, opened the channel and typed.

In a couple of days, get her to check the recycling.

————

SAM, Hi Sam, Dear Sam,

How do you start a letter like this?

You've made me happy and sad. In the interests of being honest – brace yourself here, Sammy boy, we are in for a rough ride.

That's more than you've said in all the time I've known you. Four years it is now – did you even know that? I'm grateful, I'm grateful for your honesty, and I know this stuff doesn't come easy to you. If I'm being honest, as we are, then it's not entirely a walk in the park for me either.

It means so much to hear that you're proud of me – and, no, it wasn't clear before. It wasn't very clear what you thought of me, really, other than I assumed you liked having me around because you asked me to be around. But, and here's the hard bit – Sam, you didn't say what I am to you. You hinted and you hinted at it and you seemed to suggest a future but I bloody need you to say it, Sam. I need to hear it – read it, whatever. I need you to remove any ambiguity at this stage and just say what you want.

And now I feel bad because you've explained all that about Shannon. I had to read that, like, a dozen times and then go for my daily allowance of a walk to think it all through, again and again, but it does make sense. It does. I get it.

But then I get selfish and start to think, well, what room does that leave for me? Cos I can't have children, Sam, so, what, if there is to be a role (see earlier note about clarification required), does that mean someone like me would have?

I love that you've been so open with me, I do, and that's making me feel like a spoilt little bitch by demanding more, but I'm in it now and I might as well give you the whole shebang.

You didn't say if it matters, what happened to me. I'm really terrified of that. That you will, somehow, think I'm … The stuff that happened in Uganda – not that I can't have children, although that was a huge relief, thank you – the other bit. The fact that I was – you said it – violated. Ugh. This is so hard to ask, but does that matter to you? Cos we can't walk on eggshells for the rest of our lives, and I don't ever want you to treat me like I'm broken.

You mentioned sacrifice. On some level I understand that. It's funny how two people can think the same thing, dark as such thoughts may be, and that they can follow that twisted, mangled logic. I don't have a great deal more to say about that other than we both suffer from dark thoughts. That's just the way it seems to be.

Finally. I'm in a panic writing this, so I'll write it really quick, and maybe tear the end off the page before I send it but maybe I'm kidding myself.

You didn't say it. I need you to tell me one way or another. Do you love me?

And you never said explicitly that you WANT me to be Isla's stepmother – that you WANT me to be your, I dunno, your partner, or whatever.

Shit. Wow. Stopping now.

Sinead

———

DEAR SINEAD,
I'll be brief.
Of course it doesn't matter.
And I love you. I've loved you for a very long time.
Sam